REUNITE

DRAGONBORN, BOOK THREE

BRETT HUMPHREY

BRETT HUMPHREY AUTHOR, LLC

Print ISBN13: 978-1-73411-765-3
eBook ISBN13: 978-1-73411-764-6

Published by Brett Humphrey
2487 S. Gilbert Rd.
Ste. 106-105
Gilbert, AZ 85295

To Jennifer, my biggest fan and supporter.
Thank you for being on the adventure with me.

To those who love to read, we can change the world if we choose to
positively impact people we come into
contact with each day.

ACKNOWLEDGMENTS

I wouldn't have made it this far in my life and my new endeavor as an author without the following influences:

Jennifer, Kenny, Sarah, Josh, Chelsea, Sofie and Avery, you are an awesome family and have never complained when I headed to my desk to write.

Dana, Kira, Anthony, Jenesis, Grace, Michelle, Jessa, Rachel, Jacob, Griffin and the rest of my peeps at Starbucks #9413, your encouragement, and the gallons of coffee, you've given me when I sit and write in my community Starbucks have helped tremendously.

Amazing Beta Readers: Brian, Dianne, Hans, Joe, Joshua, Kelly, Kim and Mark.

Steve Zalewski — For your input on the Gulfstream G500 and the best way to make it crash.

Emily with Fantasynamegenerators.com — For your amazing website, you helped create many of the names I used in Reunite.

C.S. Lewis & J.R.R. Tolkien — The worlds you built continue to inspire me and I enjoy re-reading your books and connecting with old friends when I do.

Brian Tedeschi — I love you brother and couldn't imagine a better friend.

Every fan who bought my earlier books, *Awakening* and *Return*. Your feedback on how much you enjoy my stories keep me writing; thank you.

And finally, my editor, Joe Scholes, who has helped me become a better storyteller.

A heartfelt ***thank you*** to everyone. Your support, inspiration and participation have all contributed to my happiness and success.

Brett Humphrey
April 2020

ABOUT THE AUTHOR

Brett Humphrey is the author of the Dragonborn Series as well as various comedic sketches, plays and many other stories he hasn't written—yet.

He has worked with children and families for thirty years and has taught in the United States and countries around the world. His passion for reading started when he was a young child and he is still an avid reader of both fiction and non-fiction. His greatest desire as an author is to create books parents will want to read to their children, hopefully using different voices for the characters.

Brett lives in Arizona with his patient and supportive wife, who encouraged him to finally sit down and write one of the stories that lives in his head.

ALSO BY BRETT HUMPHREY

Dragonborn Series:

Awakening

Return

Reunite

Rebellion *

** Forthcoming*

PROLOGUE

The stench of death assaulted my nostrils as I climbed the hill. Something was wrong, and I was desperate to get to the top to find out what. Even though I was running, it was impossible for me to climb any higher. The sounds of battle from the other side assailed my senses. My heart beat faster as I panicked and redoubled my efforts. I looked up at the sound of a roar and saw Aileene and me fly overhead in our dragon forms. This calmed me, so I stopped running because I knew Alister and Aileene would take care of the problem I couldn't reach. But since I'm Alister, it looked like my dragon would take care of one problem while I had to deal with another. "Dreams are so weird," I muttered and started down the trail. The landscape changed, and I was standing in a clearing surrounded by trees. I heard voices calling out to me from the forest but couldn't understand the words being said. Even though each of the voices was distinct, I felt like they were part of me and it was wrong we had been separated.. The babel of voices became more frantic but I still could not distinguish understandable words. I tried to enter the forest but slammed into an invisible barrier and bounced back. As I stood looking into the forest a sense of terror washed over me and the voices once again rose in volume. I wasn't afraid for myself but felt fear carried in those voices.

As I closed my eyes in concentration I noticed there were fewer voices calling out than before. One by one, the voices quieted but the sense of terror grew each time another voice disappeared. This continued until there was only one voice left. As the last voice faded I finally understood what they had all been crying out—"Help me!"

CHAPTER ONE

Images from the dream ran through my mind as I lay in the darkness. Even though dreams had been important to me in the past, I hadn't had one like this for months. It had something to do with the battle for Theria, but the additional elements of the crying voices puzzled me. There wasn't a sense of urgency, as though I had to do something about the battle today, but I couldn't ignore the warning. If I didn't reunite the seven kingdoms of Theria under my banner as High King, we could face war. I wouldn't let that happen.

I opened my senses and called out to An'Ceann to see if he would answer my questions, but he was silent. It was pleasant to lie there and meditate on the things I had been learning since taking the throne in Theria, but when I realized An'Ceann would not answer me, I decided it was time to get up. If I've learned one thing, An'Ceann would answer me in his own time. I pushed aside the covers and got out of bed. Even though it was an hour before dawn, it was time I started my day.

I'm going on a flight, I sent to Bernie, Shelley and Aileene.

Good for you—why wake us up? Shelley grouched.

Because, Grumpy, we don't like it when Alister goes off on his own without telling us, Bernie sent.

Yeah, but just because he can't sleep doesn't mean the rest of us have to get up, Shelley grumbled.

Actually, it does, Sir Arktos, or did you forget what it means to be a Knight in the King's service? Bernie admonished.

I'd like to come, Aileene answered, ignoring my two best friends as they bickered.

Sounds great, I grinned, *anyone else?*

Can't, Bernie answered, *Mkali will be here soon to have breakfast with my parents and me and then we will train for a while before attending the council meeting.*

Oh, yeah, that's today, I sighed. *Aileene and I will grab breakfast while we're out so we can take our time eating. What about you, Shelley?*

Fine, if I can't sleep in, then I might as well come with you, Shelley answered.

If it makes you feel any better, we'll be hunting gambon, I sent.

What are we waiting for? Aileene enthused, *let's get going.*

Shelley and I will meet you in the courtyard, I sent as I dressed. While I had gotten more used to the common attitude by most shifters about nudity, I was still more comfortable getting dressed before shifting. The magic in the thought-medallion held my clothes in a dimensional pocket when I shifted but reappeared when I transformed back to my human form, so I'm always clothed.

My stomach rumbled as I thought about the gambon we would soon be hunting. These beasts were native to the Kingdom of Theria, looked a lot like moose without the antlers, and tasted like the spicy animals we'd hunted in Eutheria.

Hurry, you two, I'm hungry, Aileene sent.

Aileene loved to hunt, and I smiled at her enthusiasm, taking the quickest route to the courtyard.

Shelley, I'm not waiting for you, meet us in the courtyard, I sent and dove out the large opening in the wall. This opening was large enough to accommodate my dragon form and I could use it to enter and exit my bedroom, which was larger than my entire house on Earth. As I fell, I transformed into my dragon and roared with joy, fire shooting from my mouth. My massive wings beat once and I shot into the predawn sky. The stars were shining above me and I flew towards them using the momentum from the first sweep of my wings. After reaching the apex of my first thrust, I fell to the earth. Arching my back, I flipped over, facing the ground, and rushed towards it. I snapped open my wings to slow my descent, and began a lazy spiral towards the palace.

Aileene was already in the courtyard, illuminated by the light spilling into it from the wide windows. Enthralled by her beautiful, green dragon, I watched her the entire time I was gliding down. She preened for me and kept her eyes trained on me. Landing in front of her, I stretched my neck and we rubbed muzzles in greeting. The dragon version of a morning kiss.

Good morning, I'm hungry, Aileene growled.

I laughed, *it's good to see you too, my love. The moment Shelley gets here, we'll go hunting.*

He'd better hurry, he knows I get cranky before breakfast, Aileene sent and with that, she let out a roar that sounded like the T-Rex from the first *Jurassic Park* movie. She loved those movies, and we watched them many times in the months since we'd liberated Theria. She loved the T-Rex parents and would cheer for them whenever they killed the villains who kidnapped their baby.

Wow, I sent, *you sound amazing. You've been practicing.*

Aileene chuffed with laughter and proudly exclaimed. *Thanks, I knew you'd like it. Our enemies will quake in fear when they hear me roar.*

What enemies? I asked.

Anyone who is foolish enough to try to harm my mate is my enemy, Aileene explained.

I looked at her in wonder, filled with gratitude that she was in my life. Aileene was teaching me more about how to be a dragon and I was teaching her how to be more human. For me, her views tended to be more dragonish and she divided the world into friends and potential enemies. So far, she had roasted no one she decided didn't give me enough deference, and it was my plan to keep it that way. Shelley came running into the courtyard and skidded to a stop in front of Aileene, with an enormous grin on his face.

"You nailed it," he exclaimed. "You sounded just like Rexie, way to go."

Thank you, now let's go, she said primly then launched herself into the air.

Shelley clambered up my back and we took off after Aileene.

Why are you up so early? Shelley asked as we flew through the inky sky.

Because I had a dream about the shifter kingdoms going to war with some extra weirdness thrown in for good measure. I haven't had a dream like it in a while and was thinking about what it could mean. After that, I couldn't get back to sleep and started my day.

Well, if you start your day, I start my day, Shelley grumbled, *I just wish you started your day a couple of hours later. We were up late watching the second Hobbit movie.*

Laughing, I thought about our nightly ritual of watching some of our favorite movies. Not only had Shelley, Bernie and I been best friends since we were kids, we also loved the same books, movies and stories about adventure and heroes. We were tremendous fans of C. S. Lewis and his *Chronicles of Narnia* series, and all *The Hobbit* and *The Lord of the Rings* books by J. R. R. Tolkien; and all the movies based on them. However, we were equal-opportunity geeks and enjoyed sci-fi, fantasy, adventure, superheroes and movies about dinosaurs. My mom and dad thought to bring a small flat-screen TV, Blu-Ray player and many of the movies we loved when they left Earth.

Aileene had grown up in Theria and had never seen a movie before meeting us. We showed her our favorites. We were working our way through *The Hobbit* trilogy. The night before we had watched *The Hobbit: The Desolation of Smaug*. Aileene's favorite character was Smaug the dragon. We ended up watching any movie with a dragon or T-Rex multiple times because Aileene liked those.

It was fun to watch the movies with my friends, but it was even better to spend that time together each night. Bernie and Shelley would be snuggled up on one end of the couch and Aileene and I on the other.

We took turns choosing the movies, the girls picking one night, and Shelley and I picking the next unless we watched a series of movies; then we would watch them in order. I was looking forward to tonight when we finished the last Hobbit movie; I would need it after an endless day of council meetings.

Shelley and I caught up to Aileene and were flying off her right when she arrowed toward the herd of gambon in the meadow. It amazed me how an enormous dragon could be so silent as I watched Aileene streak toward two stragglers that had wandered away from the bulk of the herd. She glided behind the grazing beasts and dispatched the two animals she hunted by breaking their necks with her outstretched front claws. She beat her wings once and carried them farther down the meadow where she landed to enjoy her breakfast.

I take it Aileene's already eating her breakfast, Shelley sent.

Yep, she said she was hungry. Where do you want me to set you down? I asked.

How about the opposite end from Aileene? Shelley suggested.

With one last look at Aileene, I turned until we were facing the correct way and began my descent. Shelley and I had been doing a lot of training over the months we had been in Theria and we had developed a few techniques for fighting from dragon-back, which we used while hunting.

Let's use The Gimli, Shelley sent.

We had named our techniques after some of our favorite characters in books and movies. Since Gimli, the dwarf, was always the first to jump into battle, we named this maneuver after him. Shelley would stand, run along my neck up to my head and then dive off. It was my job to grab him with my forelegs as he fell, maneuver him below my chest downward and then release him about five feet from the ground. He would shift into his bear before he hit and would use his speed combined with our forward momentum to engage the enemy in combat so he could take them out. At least that was the theory. We had tried this many times and only had about a fifty-percent success rate. It's a good thing shifters heal fast.

Are you sure? I asked.

We've got to perfect this eventually. The ground looks soft here so let's do it, he answered with enthusiasm.

Okay, here goes, I agreed.

I turned back toward the herd and leveled, slowing down as I did so. When we were level, I sent, *Now...five, four, three, two, one, jump.*

Shelley came into view a half-second after the 'jump' and he shot ahead of me and plummeted towards the ground. As he fell past me, I reached out with my claws and grabbed the back of the heavy leather jerkin he was wearing. Extending my forelegs below my body, as far as they would go, I dropped him as planned and he transformed into his grizzly bear and ran towards a large male that was startled by his sudden appearance. *The Gimli* worked flawlessly, and Shelley settled down to enjoy his breakfast. Now it was my turn.

The danger calls from the scouts in the herd were rising in the predawn air and the rest of the herd was on high alert. The gambon ran for the woods but I was too quick for three who were so startled by my appearance they hesitated. Never wanting my prey to suffer, I killed them at once then landed to enjoy my meal.

No matter how hard I try, eating as a dragon is a messy business. It didn't take me long to finish my breakfast, so I curled up to take a quick nap while enjoying my full belly. Aileene landed next to me and I smiled to myself as she settled against my back, draping her head and neck over my shoulder.

Happy? I asked.

Yes, she purred, *I've got a full belly and I'm with you. Life is wonderful.* After enjoying the silence and each other's company for a few minutes, Aileene broke into my thoughts. *Something's troubling you, my mate, what is it?*

I had a dream about the shifter battle last night but it was different than any dream I've had about it before.

How was it different? Aileene asked.

I told Aileene about my dream and we talked about how it had changed since the last time I had it.

Is that why you woke up so early?

I hummed in agreement.

What do you think it means? Aileene asked.

I'm not sure, but don't feel like we have to do something about it today.

Good, she sent, *because I want to take a nap.*

I laughed at her response, agreed that it sounded like a superb idea, and dropped into cozy slumber with her.

Only an hour had passed since we fell asleep, but I knew it was time to return to the palace. I opened my eyes and took a few moments to appreciate the streaks of yellow, pink, orange and blue in the sky as the sun rose. On Earth, I hadn't been an early riser but now could appreciate the simple beauty of a sunrise. Maybe it was the way I perceived colors as a dragon, but the streaks of sunlight seemed to shimmer and weave like ballroom dancers as they chased the darkness from the sky.

Contentment settled over me like a warm blanket as I heard Aileene's deep breathing behind me and Shelley's raucous snoring as he leaned against my side.

Okay, sleeping beauties, I sent, *it's time to head back.*

I"m not sure if it was my sending or his own loud snore that woke Shelley up, but he jumped to his feet, transformed into his bear, and bellowed a challenging roar.

Woah there, settle down Pooh, there's no danger, I laughed.

Shelley wheeled on me with a wild look in his eyes.

Did you just call Shelley, poop? Aileene snickered.

No, Shelley exclaimed as I burst out laughing in the chuffing way I did while in dragon form. *He called me, Pooh, as in Winnie the Pooh, who was a character in a book and a bunch of cartoons.*

Yeah, I continued to chuckle, *I would never call him poop, that's just undignified for a Knight of the Realm.*

So is calling me Pooh, Shelley grumped. *Since Aileene is our witness, I challenge you to a royal butt-kicking this afternoon when we get a break from the council meeting.*

I accept, what are the stakes? I queried.

The loser must do the winner's laundry for a week, Shelley countered.

But, don't the maids already take care of the laundry? Aileene asked.

Yes, but they're willing to make exceptions whenever we make one of our bets, I explained. *Sir Arktos, I accept your invitation to the royal butt-kicking this afternoon and will have my laundry piled outside the door of my bedroom for you to pick up before dinner. Now that we've got that settled, let's head to the palace, we've got an exhausting day of meetings ahead of us.*

Shelley transformed and climbed onto my back for the journey home. We kept talking smack to one another on the return journey and Aileene would join in, so she could take part in the fun. It had taken me a while to convince her that Shelley and I never fought each other in anger, we just did it to let off steam. We'd been wrestling with each other since we were little and that hadn't changed just because we were technically adults. Once she realized this was another form of play for us, she relaxed and no longer wanted to rip Shelley apart for hurting me. Aileene could be protective; I loved it.

There was a surprise waiting when we landed at the palace; my royal parents had returned from their vacation after half a year away. Shelley slid from my back as soon as I landed so I could transform into my human self. It may not have been proper, but I ran to my parents and hugged them. It was important for them to spend time with each other after being imprisoned for so many years, but it was hard to have them gone so long.

"I missed you both," I said and stepped back to look at them.

Even though they had mostly healed before they began their vacation, they now glowed with happiness and renewed life. My father stood tall and proud and even though I was taller than him by a few inches, he was still broader than me at the shoulders and chest. His life force was powerful, and he could have cradled me to his chest like a small child if he wanted to. My mother was six inches shorter than my father, around six feet four inches tall, and was all smiles as she looked at me. Her fiery red hair curled down her back and her eyes shone with a joy I had only seen in my memories. She waved Aileene over to us then wrapped her in a loving embrace.

"And how are you, daughter of my heart?" Mother asked.

"I am well, Mother, but I missed you and Father terribly," Aileene answered.

It was still strange for me to hear Aileene call my parents Mother and Father but since we were destined to be mates, it's what they should have been to her all along. Royal Dragon mates are hatched on the same day. When they are six years old, the Royal Dragon hatched in another kingdom comes to live with the ruling King and Queen, along with the heir, so they can experience life together while being trained to rule at the same time.

Because my parents were prisoners for thirteen years, and I had been on Earth for most of that time, Aileene and I hadn't met until eight months ago. The four of us were still exploring what our new relationship should be like. Aileene and I had grown to love one another and knew we were true-mates but weren't ready to get married —yet.

"My dear," Mother said as she gently lay her hand on Aileene's cheek, "we missed you, too."

Father held his arms open and Aileene threw herself into his embrace and I turned to my mother and gave her another hug.

"When did you return?" I asked.

"About ten minutes ago," she answered as she gave me one last squeeze then stepped back again.

I looked around the courtyard and noticed Bernie and Mkali standing guard in front of the entrance to the palace. Fritz was standing a scant distance away watching our family reunion, so I waved him over.

"Fritz, please inform the Council that we will postpone the meeting until tomorrow so Aileene and I can spend the day catching up with my parents," I asked.

"Very good, Sire," Fritz said as he bowed, "it will be as you say."

"We missed you too, you stuffy unicorn," my father snickered.

"Also, please ask all the members of my parents' Inner Circle to join us for lunch. Aileene and I will spend the morning with them first and then we can all catch up later," I continued.

Fritz was about to bow again but he saw my father's face and stopped himself. "It would be my pleasure, Sire," Fritz grinned and stuck his tongue out at his old friend.

"Alister, I don't know what you've done to Fritz," Father laughed, "but I like it."

The four of us had a splendid morning talking, laughing and just hanging out together; it was as if we'd never been apart. We spent two months together before they took their vacation and both Aileene and I bonded quickly with my parents. While we couldn't get back the thirteen years that Dimitri stole from us, we were forging new relationships with each other. Bernie once asked if I was angry that my parents left for their vacation only two months after we rescued them.

It took me a couple of days to answer her. After much thought, I explained that all of us were broken by what Dimitri did to us and we all needed to heal in our own way, so I felt more sadness than anger for those years we lost. Now that we were together again, I understood it was important they left when they did for their continued healing.

We were sitting in their suite of rooms, enjoying a mid-morning snack and talking about the latest things we'd been doing.

"So, Aileene, how are things going with Alister? Is he treating you right?" Mother asked with a wicked smile.

Choking on the juice I was drinking, I started coughing and my face turned red. Everyone laughed at my misfortune while my father pounded me on the back.

After a minute I gasped out, "Well, it's been fun seeing you again. Don't you have somewhere else to go now?"

"You're hilarious, Son," Father smirked, "you'll have to get used to parents embarrassing you."

"We're already used to that," Aileene laughed, "the Drakes tease us every chance they get."

Mother's face froze at that comment, and it appeared she disengaged from the conversation. Aileene didn't notice the change, but I wanted to address the issue before it could turn into a problem for all of us.

"Aileene and I are fortunate to have two sets of parents who love us and will guide us in our relationship." Pointing at my mother I continued. "Mother, I know that face, it's the same one I see in the mirror when I feel like I haven't done enough to solve a problem. There's nothing to feel guilty about."

Mother surreptitiously wiped a tear from her eye and turned her head.

"Did I say something wrong?" Aileene asked nervously. "I'm still learning how to communicate more like a human and sometimes say the wrong thing."

Mother turned back to her and took her hands in her own. "No, honey, you said nothing wrong, it's just that, all of us have suffered because Dimitri betrayed us, and we lost so much time together. When I think about how Albert and Fiona raised Alister so well, I'm overwhelmed with gratitude. They've been loving and caring parents for both of you, but I just wish Phillip and I could have been here the whole time."

"Me too but we can't change the past, so we have to move forward," Aileene answered.

"That's a wise way of looking at it, but it's not always easy to do," my father added.

"An'Ceann taught me the most important things in life aren't easy but they're worth the effort you have to put in to obtain them," Aileene said matter-of-factly.

"You've spoken to An'Ceann?" Mother asked in shock.

Aileene nodded. "At least once a week, in my dreams. Although, I'm sure he was here in person one time when I was sitting in the garden."

"What happened?" Mother asked.

"Bernie and I had been talking about our future hopes and dreams. I got frustrated and angry because I have to wait so long to marry Alister, even though we both know we're true-mates." Aileene laughed at herself, "I'm not the most patient dragon when I see something I want."

Feeling a pang of guilt because I hadn't known Aileene had been hurting, I turned to her and put my hand on her shoulder. "I'm so sorry, Aileene, I didn't know you felt that way."

"I didn't tell you because I knew you'd feel guilty," she smiled and patted my hand with her own. "An'Ceann sat beside me on the bench, put his arm around me and talked to me about our future and how it would be worth waiting for. I still want to start our life together as a married couple, but I'm feeling better now about waiting for the right time."

"Beatrice and I met when we were almost six years old," Father spoke up. "She came from the Kingdom of Marsupia and at first, I was less than thrilled she came to live with us."

"Let's be honest dear," Mother interrupted with a smile. "The first time we met, you told me I was stinky, and you would not share your parents with me. It only continued downhill from there."

Father grimaced at the memories while we laughed. He cleared his throat and started again. "Yes, well—I'd never met any of the fair-folk before and had a hard time recognizing your scent."

"Wait," I interrupted, "what do you mean by fair-folk?"

Mother smiled as she answered. "Since I've watched some of the movies you love, I guess you could say elves raised me." She continued as I gaped at her answer. "My foster parents were kind to me when I was young and they taught me how to be one with the forest, interact with nature and everything else you can think of that elves do. Unfortunately, the one thing they couldn't teach me was how to be a dragon. I was very unprepared to live in a dragon household when I moved here to live in the palace. Even though Phillip was harsh to me that first day, I didn't make things easy on him either. It took us years to get to the place where we cared for each other the way you two do. In fact, we had been married a year before we fell in love." Mother stood and sat next to her husband so she could lean against his chest.

"I respected your mother and married her out of duty, but life was so much better once we learned to love each other as husband and wife," Father said as he kissed the top of Mother's head.

"An'Ceann told me it's better to take the time to get to know one another so we can learn how to love each other now. Another thing he told me was that for most of my life I only learned how to be a dragon and if we're going to have a good life together, I have to learn to be more human while Alister needs to learn how to be more dragonish. That's why I'm willing to wait until the right time to marry him," Aileene finished.

My head was spinning from all the information I'd just heard. It was interesting that Aileene and I had so much to learn from one another, and my parents didn't even like each other when they first met. There were so many things to take in, but my mind kept sticking to one point.

"Elves raised you?" I blurted out then felt my cheeks flush when I realized there were other questions that I should have asked first. My mother didn't seem to mind but my father laughed at my expression and Aileene elbowed me in the side.

"I used to tell you bedtime stories about my life with my foster parents when you were young. You loved hearing about the special magics they could use to communicate with the trees and woodland creatures. Your subconscious remembered these stories and kept searching for ways to connect back to them while you were trapped in your human form on Earth. That must be why you love books and movies about those things," she mused. "Anyway, the point is, you and Aileene seem to be better connected than your father and I were at your age. I'm happy for both of you."

"Mother, I have been living with the Drakes while you've been away. Should I move in here with you and Father, now that you're back?" Aileene asked.

"What would you like to do?" Father asked with hope in his voice.

"I would like to move in here so I can get to know you better, but don't want to hurt the Drakes," Aileene answered. We sat in silence while we thought about the complications that could arise from this change.

"Why don't you all move in together?" I ventured. "The Drakes have plenty of space in their suite for everyone but then again, you do, too. Everyone wants the same thing, so it should be easy to make it happen."

Everyone must have seen the hopeful look on my face because they nodded in agreement. There was a knock at the door. "We can talk about it over lunch." I smiled but I knew this would work out.

The rest of the day passed rapidly, and I was glad to be hanging out with my friends in the entertainment room that evening. Shelley wanted to name the room "man-cave" but since Aileene and Bernie always joined us when we were in here, the girls vetoed that idea. The time we spent together was always the best part of my day. Sometimes it would just be the four of us, and sometimes Mkali would join us. Bernie said it was part of her training, but we all liked Mkali, so we enjoyed hanging out with her. But tonight, it was just the four of us and we were watching *The Hobbit: The Battle of Five Armies.*

As the movie started, I was thinking about the lunch meeting with my royal parents and their friends. It was great to see them laugh together as they told more stories about the years they spent together when they were younger. Everyone quickly decided that Phillip and Beatrice would move in with Albert and Fiona, so Aileene didn't have to move again. I was glad she would get a double dose of love from both sets of parents. Shelley and I had moved into the Royal Suite when we moved into the palace, so I didn't have to go anywhere.

In fact, since I was High King, I would stay in the Royal Suite and Aileene would join me once we were married. We would only move out when our child became the High King or Queen. It was strange to think about getting married so young, but I was warming to the idea because Aileene was such an amazing person. A shout from Aileene startled me out of my reverie in time for me to see an amazing sight.

"Noooo!" She roared and a gout of flame shot from her mouth hitting the TV, Blu-Ray player and cabinet they sat on; turning everything instantly to ash.

Jumping to my feet, I looked around for an enemy but only saw my three friends sitting on the couch. Shelley and Bernie were snuggled together but were frozen in place, mouths agape. Aileene's eyes were the color of molten gold and were still blazing. She radiated heat and her body was rigid as she leaned forward, scales had formed on her face, arms and hands. There wasn't any danger in the room, so I sat on the couch again and turned to gather Aileene in my arms. She was vibrating with anger but as I spoke soothing words to her, she gradually relaxed and pressed her face to my chest.

"What happened?" I asked her.

Aileene's voice was muffled against my chest as she answered. "They killed him, they killed Smaug."

It puzzled me for a few seconds until I realized she was talking about the movie. I weighed my words before speaking again. Shelley opened his mouth to say something, but I looked at him meaningfully until he shut it.

"I'm sorry, I should have warned you that was part of the story. They didn't kill an actual dragon; he was just a make-believe character in the movie," I whispered.

"I know, but couldn't help my reaction," Aileene answered as she sat up and surveyed the damage she'd done. She suddenly burst into tears and pressed her face into my chest again. "I've ruined our movie nights," she sobbed, "that was the only TV you brought from Earth."

My face must have shown the panic I was feeling but since he didn't know what to do either, Shelley just shrugged at me. Thankfully, Bernie was there, and she sat up and hugged Aileene from behind.

"Don't worry about it," Bernie soothed, "movie nights are more about hanging out together than watching the movie."

"Yeah, no problem. We can change the name from 'movie night' to 'stare at the wall' night; it'll be fun," Shelley added.

Even though I was worried about how Aileene would react, once she started giggling, I knew she would be okay.

Thanks, I sent to Shelley.

No problem, he answered, *you, Bernie and I must've seen this movie ten times already and I always get emotional at the end of the big battle. Aileene saved me from making a fool of myself.*

Again, I sent dryly.
Again, he agreed with a chuckle.

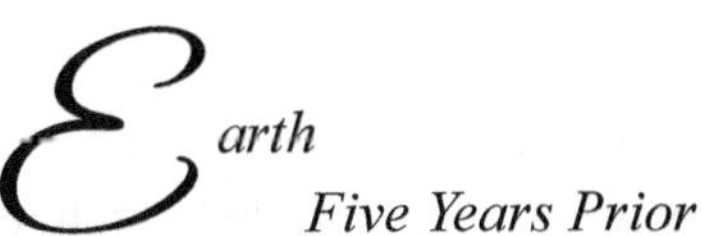

arth
Five Years Prior

He stood behind a tree next to the road. The conditions were perfect for his plan, but the rain irritated him as it dripped down the back of his jacket. "It's your fault I'm standing out in the rain rather than at home in bed; one more reason for you to die," he muttered to himself.

The storm clouds obscured the moon, so the only light available to drivers on the road came from the headlights of their vehicles. Not that there had been any other cars on the road for the past hour. Most people would refuse to drive under these stormy conditions. It was fortunate for him that his father wasn't most people.

As the head of Paterson Munitions, Edward Paterson was used to everyone either getting out of his way or getting crushed by him. When he made a decision, he stuck to it even if presented with information he'd made a poor choice. He'd decided he and his wife would spend this weekend at their home in the mountains, and the weather wouldn't deter him.

Victoria Paterson was even worse than her husband and faced the world with belligerence and a sense of entitlement that shaped every decision in her life. She would not let a storm interfere with her plans to relax this weekend; she had added this weekend to her planner.

Neil forced himself to relax when he noticed he was clenching his hands into fists and his jaw ached from grinding his teeth. It didn't matter who his parents were; their personal foibles suited his plans, and for that he was grateful. He laughed bitterly as he realized he was grateful for things that would hasten his parents to their deaths.

He looked at his watch and smiled. If there was anything else he could rely on about Edward and Victoria, they were punctual. They would have finished dining at their restaurant of choice at the bottom of the mountain thirty minutes ago. His father would have ordered his usual Porterhouse Steak, baked potato, steamed French cut green beans and three martinis while his mother would have her usual salad and four glasses of Merlot.

Their car would appear within the next five minutes and he prepared himself to act when it did. The plan was simple. He had positioned himself at the bottom of a steep grade with a sharp left-hand turn. The posted signs cautioned drivers to slow down to make the tight turn because there was a sheer drop on the other side of the guardrail.

When his parents' car got close, he would shine the hundred thousand lumens flashlight into his father's face to blind him. In his inebriated state he would shy away from the light and turn towards the drop off.

Neil looked at his watch again and decided it was time to add his last piece of insurance. He dashed across the road and dumped the gallon of liquid detergent on the road to further decrease the effectiveness of the car's brakes. He finished pouring the detergent as headlights appeared at the top of the grade. Neil ran back to his original position near the tree to await his prey. Hopefully, it was his parents, if not the person in the car was in for a rough landing.

It relieved Neil when the car got close enough that he could tell it was his parents' vehicle. He was tired of standing in the rain. When the approaching car was four hundred feet from his position, he shined the light into the driver's face. Since Edward had been drinking, it took an extra moment for him to respond to the light shining in his eyes, but he did what Neil thought he would and swerved to the right to avoid the bright light shining in his face. Since the flashlight illuminated the interior of the car as passed by he could see Victoria's startled face. Neil waved and smiled at her, even though she couldn't see him.

Edward slammed on his brakes but the slick surface didn't allow the tires to get a grip on the road and the car headed straight for the drop-off; the only thing between his parents' car and their sudden death was the guardrail on the side of the road. Their car hit the guardrail at almost forty miles per hour and crashed through it, which was as effective as aluminum foil. The car flew over the abyss and seemed to hang there for a moment before gravity took over and then plunged down to the rocks below.

Neil whistled to himself as he stuffed the flashlight and empty soap bottle into his backpack and prepared to hike back to his camping spot about ten miles away where he would finish his vacation. When he returned from his time in the wilderness, it would devastate him to learn of his parents' deaths. He watched the rain wash away the soap from the road, then turned and headed back into the forest and his future as the head of Paterson Munitions.

Alister

 Theria

 Present Day

We gathered in the Council Chambers next to the Throne Room. The oval table surrounded by twenty chairs dominated the chamber. They had carved the table and chairs from a single, massive tree. The wood looked like mahogany, but with streaks of burnt orange running through the wood grain. Eighteen of the chairs were identical to each other but two resembled the thrones from the other room. That's where my Queen and I would sit during council meetings. For now, Aileene sat on my right in a normal chair but would make the change once we were married. Mom sat next to Aileene, then my dad, Fritz, Frieda, Wu, Gustav, Stavros, Miriam, my father and mother.

Even though Shelley and Bernie are my Knights, they're also part of my Inner Circle, so they also sat at the table. Shelley used to sit right next to me but since he made it his life goal to make me laugh at least once each meeting, Fritz made him sit as far away from me as possible. Unfortunately, that meant he could sit in my line of sight and make faces at me when no one else was looking.

Mkali stood just inside the chamber on one side of the door and another guard stood on the other. There were also guards stationed outside the chamber on either side of the door to keep out uninvited guests. Mkali took her duties as squire seriously and always looked fierce as she stood guard. She was mature even though she was only a little over nine years old.

Mkali is doing well Bernie, you're doing a superb job with her, I sent.

I'm proud of her, but sometimes I want to gather her in an enormous hug because she looks so cute, Bernie responded.

Hmmming in agreement, I looked around the room as people continued to settle in their seats. My Council Chambers reminded me of the ones the House of Representatives used in the Capitol Building in Washington, DC. Mr. Schliebe had taken our sixth-grade class on a tour of the monuments and government buildings and we had the chance to see our government in action. Three of the four walls had rows of chairs for those spectators and guests we invited to the proceedings. Usually, the chairs were full but because we were holding a closed-door meeting today, they were empty.

These chambers were a hybrid of technology and tradition like the rest of the palace. Technology on Theria was far superior to anything we had on Earth, but the architecture of the palace reminded me of that castle in Germany; the one that looks like it came right from a Disney movie. They built screens into the table in front of each seat so we could take notes or review the material being presented.

"Sire, would you report on your findings?" Fritz asked, interrupting my thoughts.

"Excuse me? Was I supposed to have something prepared for today's meeting?" I asked in confusion.

"Pardon me, Sire, a force of habit." Fritz responded, "I was speaking to your father."

"That makes more sense then, please continue." I smiled and nodded at my father.

He caught my eye and smirked. "Darn it, Fritz, I was looking forward to seeing what Alister would come up with." Everyone laughed, and he continued.

"One thing Beatrice and I did on our vacation was attempt to locate our people who fled to other parts of the Kingdom of Theria when Dimitri usurped the throne. We wanted to let them know it was safe to return home if they wanted to, but we mostly wanted to make sure everyone was okay. Since the shield around the kingdom prevented anyone from entering or leaving for thirteen years, we figured we could track everyone down."

"To be fair, we overestimated our ability to locate everyone. Our plan was to spend three months searching and three months lounging on a warm beach down south. It took us the full six months to locate everyone we could," Mother added.

"We'll head down to the beach as soon as we can," Father promised and smiled at Mother.

"I'll hold you to that, Phillip," she purred.

"Oh brother, you two are as bad as they are," I said and jerked my thumb in the direction where my other parents were sitting. "Before we get too far off topic, were you able to locate the missing shifters?"

"Yes and no," he responded. "We could locate almost everyone who fled from this part of the kingdom but there are still some who are unaccounted for. As you can see from the report I'm sending to your screen, there are many shifters missing. Everyone we spoke with remembered seeing them around the palace before the big day, but no one can recall seeing them after that."

Shelley raised his hand. "Can't you just connect to all the shifters using that connecting tendril thingy Alister does?"

I'd explained to everyone in the room about my powers as High King and about my ability to connect with other shifters across the planet. Even though Shelley asked in his usual way, I was also curious about the answer.

"No," my father replied. "Once Alister accepted the role of High King, many of the abilities I possessed when I was High King transferred to him. I'm no longer able to connect to other shifters with power, just like I'm no longer able to open any dimensional gates, either on Theria or other dimensions."

"And we couldn't be happier about that," my mother added seeing the discomfort on my face. "We ruled Theria for centuries. It's a relief to act as advisors for the High King rather than still be in charge."

Thank you, I sent to her.

You're welcome Son, your father and I love you and we are pleased you're King now. It'll give us more time to play, she smiled through our mental connection.

Returning to the topic at hand I looked down at the screen in front of me. As I scrolled through the list, one name stood out to me.

"Cyndi—that name's familiar, isn't she the mermaid who lives in the lake behind the palace?" I asked.

"Yes, she taught you kids how to swim," Mother answered.

We spent the next thirty minutes discussing the missing shifters before Wu came up with an idea.

"What if we ask Jeffrey if he knows anything about these missing people? It's possible they never made it to Middle Earth, and Dimitri captured them instead. If that happened, he could have killed them and we wouldn't know about it," Wu explained.

I looked around the table and received nods of agreement from everyone sitting there. "Very well. Frieda, please speak with Jeffrey about this. He's still working in the medical ward to help the shifters from Dimitri's fortress who need the most care, correct?"

"Yes, Sire, he's striving to serve those Dimitri forced him to oppress. I will happily ask him about the people on this list," Frieda answered and gestured towards the names on the screen in front of her.

She tilted her head to the side and it was clear she was communicating with Jeffrey through thought-speech. After a few minutes of mental conversation, she focused on the people around the table who were staring at her.

"Sorry about that," she said as she tapped her screen. "I figured it would be best to get Jeffrey working on this immediately. He asked for the list of names and told me he would get back to me soon."

Shelley clapped his hands and rubbed them together. "Well, since we could wait awhile for him to get back to us, I move that we take a short recess and have some food and drinks brought in."

"Seconded," Aileene added, her stomach growling at the thought of food.

"All in favor, say 'aye'." I concluded. Every person in the room raised a hand amid a chorus of chuckles.

"And that's why these meetings always take so long," I muttered.

While we were waiting for the food and drinks to arrive Bernie asked me, "How have your magic lessons been going?"

Ever since I'd opened myself up to the enormous amount of magical energy I needed to heal my parents; I'd developed a second reservoir to hold it. At least, that's how I described it. The first reservoir held the tremendous amount of power I received from other shifters when I connected to them. This was the power I used to create dimensional gates. I also used it to connect with shifters over great distances.

The second reservoir developed and expanded when I opened a gate from Middle Earth to gather magical energy when I was healing my parents. Just as Theria is more technologically advanced than other dimensions, Middle Earth has more natural magic than others. One time I asked An'Ceann where the magic came from, and he told me it was residual energy from when he created the universes. He explained the physics to me, but I just smiled and nodded as though I understood what he was talking about.

All I knew was when I opened myself up to the magic on Middle Earth, I felt like the magic was an ocean and my body was the garden hose the magic passed through. Ever since that day, I could hold magical energy in my second reservoir and could use it whenever I needed. Both my magic and personal reservoirs were about the same size and I had been training with both.

My father and mother could help Aileene and me with our personal reservoirs because that was something that all Royal Dragons shared. However, they couldn't help me with the magical one since no one else in our recorded history had developed the capacity for magic the way I had.

Gustav contacted his friend Garket from Middle Earth to find someone who could teach me more about magic. Garket and his family came to visit four months ago and have been staying at the palace ever since. Garket brought his sister, Hillaes, who turned out to be one of the most powerful sorceresses on Middle Earth. I'd worked with Hillaes every day and had learned many spells to siphon magic from the environment of Theria, which has less natural magic than Middle Earth.

Bernie was looking at me and I noticed the others in the room had quit talking and waited for me to respond. "The lessons have been going well. I'm able to refill my magical reservoir in a fraction of the time than before we started training together. I've also learned dozens more spells and have become proficient in all of them. Hillaes has a tough time generating enough magic on Theria but we've figured out a way for me to pass some of my magical energy to her; this has improved our lessons significantly."

For the next twenty minutes we enjoyed the snacks prepared by the palace chef as we chatted about how much our lives have changed in the last eleven months.

"I've just heard from Jeffrey," Frieda interrupted our small talk, "he looked over the list and checked with every person in the medical ward and no one remembers any of those names or types of shifters ever being taken by Dimitri."

"Is it possible that any of them made their way to Earth?" Mkali asked from her post by the door.

"That's a good question Mkali. Reason it out," Bernie encouraged her squire.

"Well—" Mkali paused, "If they couldn't have left Theria with the shield in place, and if Dimitri didn't capture them and they're not here at the palace, then that only leaves the possibility that they fled when everyone else did and they weren't noticed in the confusion of the move," Mkali responded.

"You've been paying attention to your lessons on tactics and logic, very good young centaur," Stavros said proudly.

Mkali blushed and I considered her suggestion. If I opened a small gateway to Middle Earth it should be easy for me to find out if there are any shifters there. I explained what I would try, and everyone watched me expectantly as I created the small gate. I felt a rush of magic when the gate opened, but I ignored it while I searched for shifters with my mind. It took a bit of concentration to block out everyone on Theria, but I could focus on the planet of Middle Earth. I couldn't find any shifters across that planet.

"They're not on Middle Earth," I said after closing the gate, "but I will make a small gate to Earth to check there."

The gate to Earth opened in the middle of a national forest in Maine. There weren't any people around to see the opening, but I startled a squirrel as the gate opened next to the branch it was resting on. With a squeak of alarm, it shot down the trunk of the tree and I opened my senses to find any shifters on Earth. There was an immediate response as I connected to the shifters who were closest to the gate. The distance from where I was sitting was too great for me to determine where they were, but I could tell they were on Earth. I sent a pulse of my energy along with hope and comfort through each connection before I closed the gate.

"They're on Earth," I announced to the people gathered around the council table. Father and Mother had been leaning forward waiting for my response and they sat back in relief at my announcement.

"Why didn't they come back with everyone else when you left?" Shelley asked.

"Since we didn't know they had come with us, I didn't have a way to contact them. I feel terrible that we left them on Earth," Dad answered.

"The outstanding thing is we know they're on Earth, we'll figure out a way to bring them home," Mom said as she patted Dad's hand.

"I wasn't able to connect with everyone on this list because of the distance across dimensions," I said, "but let's assume every missing shifter is there. Father, will you and Mother work on a rescue plan? Let's bring them home soon."

At their nods of agreement, I continued. "What's the next order of business?"

Before anyone else could respond, Aileene spoke up. "The next order of business is the dream you had the night before last."

"What dream, honey?" Mom asked me from her seat next to Aileene.

I described the dream to everyone in the room but also let them know I wasn't feeling the same sense of urgency I had from other repeating dreams in the past.

Thank you for bringing this up, I sent to Aileene, *although I was going to after we got more important items on the agenda out of the way first.*

You are the most important item on my agenda and if something bothers you in one of your dreams, my mate, we should take this seriously.

Before I could add anything else, Fritz spoke up.

"Sire, your dream relates to my item on the agenda. As you know, I've made official visits to the other shifter kingdoms across Theria over the past six months to explain why the Kingdom of Theria had been closed off from everyone else."

Even though the planet of Theria was advanced technologically, in matters of diplomacy, the ruler of every kingdom insisted on face-to-face meetings rather than through technology. And while they would accept an envoy from the Kingdom of Theria, unless they invited the High King and Queen it made everyone nervous if they just showed up. Fritz had gone on our behalf to explain things to the other rulers.

"How did things go, Dad?" Bernie asked Fritz.

"First, most of the rulers refused to accept the abdication of Phillip and Beatrice without first meeting Alister and Aileene," Fritz answered. "However, Lord Moss of Eutheria and Lord Elandorr of Marsupia will accept the written decree as presented."

"What does this mean?" I asked.

"Unfortunately, it means that you and Lady Aileene will need to travel to each kingdom and present yourselves as the succeeding King and Queen. This is how we have traditionally done things for millennia and many rulers are sticklers for tradition, especially Lady Baolong of Sirenea. I am concerned that she has influenced Lord Carmanor of Carnivoria and Lady Lynx of Metatheria, to stand by her in these demands. It is my belief they have enjoyed their freedom from oversight the past fourteen years and want to test your mettle as King."

The growls from my royal parents matched the growl from Aileene and the tension in the room thickened.

"None of those kingdoms has produced a Royal Dragon since Síocháin married Milleadh in the Dark Times," Father ground out. "It seems like they're still angry about this. You only mentioned three rulers who insisted on a visit from Alister and Aileene. Where does Lady Zhaleh from Cetacea stand on this?"

Fritz answered. "As usual, she wishes to stay neutral but asks for a visit. She doesn't oppose your abdication, but she still wants to meet King Alister and Lady Aileene before she commits."

"I'm not sure I understand what all this means. Alister is High King. Why must we have the other rulers agree to this when An'Ceann has already declared it to be true?" Aileene asked in confusion.

"Daughter of my heart," Mother began. "Alister is High King and could command their obedience but if he did that, those foolish rulers could declare war on the High Kingdom and many of our people would die. Even though Lady Baolong seems to play a political game, her expectations aren't unreasonable. Before Phillip's coronation as High King, we traveled to every Kingdom on Theria and stayed for six months in each one getting to know the people and the rulers. When we returned from our round-the-world journey, Phillip's parents, King Guimart and Queen Tiffonia abdicated the throne and we became High King and Queen."

Aileene nodded in understanding and squeezed the hand I had placed in hers when she first became upset on my behalf.

"How soon will we need to start this journey?" I asked.

"We have some time to prepare," Frieda answered. "But Fritz and I estimate we should begin the journey within the next three months."

"There are some benefits to the rulers across Theria insisting on communicating face-to-face; it takes time to travel there and back to negotiate the items required for a royal visit, and that will allow us to prepare on our end," Fritz commented. "In the meantime, we will plan our strategy and learn as much about the current state of the other kingdoms as we can before we travel. Phillip and Beatrice, I'm afraid you're being called out of retirement already and will need to assume the Throne again because the other rulers only recognize King Alister as the Crown Prince."

"Well, it was fun while it lasted," my father smirked at my mother.

"You're not getting out of spending time with me on a beach that easily," Mother grumbled, "at most this succession business will take a year. After that, you're all mine and we won't have to worry about politics getting in the way."

My royal parents had been ruling Theria for five hundred years and deserved a break. While there wasn't a lot I could do to circumvent the demands from the rulers of the other kingdoms, I would do my best to hurry the process along.

"How do we transfer the powers of the High King from me back to my father?" I asked.

Gustav answered. "You cannot. Even though there isn't unanimous acceptance on this by the other rulers, the fact is you are the High King. An'Ceann affirmed you when you received all the powers associated with this position. You can only transfer these powers to your heir, when it is time for you to abdicate."

"Very well, since I'm still High King, I decree that King Phillip and Queen Beatrice shall act as regents until I can sit the throne without the threat of war hanging over our heads."

Standing up, I looked at the people to my right and said, "If you would, please stand and move one seat to your right—thank you."

After sitting in my new seat, I gestured to the open seats reserved for the High King and Queen and continued. "Father, Mother, since you'll be acting as regents, it's only fair that you get the comfy chairs." I smiled impishly at them while everyone else chuckled.

They rose from their seats and grudgingly took the seats I indicated.

"I was more comfortable when I didn't have to be in charge," Father grumbled but the twinkle in his eye conveyed his humor.

"Well, now that's settled we have two more matters on the agenda," Mother smiled cheerfully, "the first is the birthday celebration for Alister and Aileene, the second is the matter of rescuing our people from Earth. Fiona, please let us know about the birthday celebrations?"

"Of course. In case it slipped your attention, Alister and Aileene will turn nineteen in two weeks. We have a grand celebration planned for this momentous occasion."

"Turning nineteen isn't that big a deal," I muttered.

Mom laughed and turned to me. "No, the momentous occasion is you're both turning nineteen and for the first time in your lives, you have two sets of parents to celebrate your birthday with you."

"Does that mean, twice the cake?" Shelley asked as he air-fived me across the table.

"Sort of," Miriam added. "Because Frieda and I are planning the birthday celebration for you and Bernadette at the same."

"Wait, I didn't know that Bernie and Shelley had birthdays close to ours," Aileene said.

I nodded, "Yes, you and I share the same birthday and they share the same birthday a week later."

Aileene clapped her hands and bounced in her seat with joy. "That must mean that you're true-mates."

Shelley and Bernie blushed while Stavros roared with laughter at the expression on his son's face.

Wanting to spare my friends from further embarrassment I asked, "What will we do about the shifters trapped on Earth?"

Father looked at me with a smile on his face. "The four of you can consider this an unexpected birthday present. We would like you to go to Earth and bring our people home."

I looked around the table at the smiling faces and realized they had been discussing this by thought-speech since we learned our people were on Earth.

"You mean, I'll get to visit Earth and see what it's like?" Aileene asked in wonder.

Mom put her arm around Aileene and gave her a loving squeeze and said, "Alister is the only one who can open and close dimensional gates so he has to go. This business with the other kingdoms helps with this, since Alister can be absent from Theria until he has to meet the other rulers. You will have over two months on Earth to find our people and bring them home."

"Dude, do you know what this means? We'll be on Earth, in July." Shelley exclaimed but then got disgusted when he saw the blank look on my face. "Hero Con is in July; we've always wanted to go and now we'll be able to. It will be epic."

Bernie and Shelley high-fived and I couldn't help laughing at the looks of glee on my friends' faces. We'd always dreamed of going to Hero Con in California when we got older, and now it looked like we'd be able to do so. Shelley was right, this trip would be epic.

The day before the momentous birthday party, my father found me as I was working with Hillaes on a magical shield spell we called *Spheara*. Not only could I place the surrounding shield, but I could expand it to include others in a twenty-foot sphere and keep them from harm.

Today we were working to see if I could cover someone with *Spheara*, even when they weren't standing near me. Hillaes was standing across the room from me and I tried to send a shield to cover her. It helped me in the past to visualize the spell I was trying to create so I did the same thing now. I imagined a soap bubble that would allow air to flow in and out but reject everything else. I then encased Hillaes within that bubble. When I felt the spell was complete, I turned towards my father.

"Hey, could you help us with something since you're here?" He nodded to me, so I continued, "please pick up a stick from the table and toss it to Hillaes."

Father walked to the table, grabbed a stick and tossed it underhanded towards Hillaes where it bounced off the shield about six inches from her outstretched hand.

"Good, now keep tossing them at me a little harder each time until we tell you to stop." Hillaes said and braced herself for his throws.

It took around five minutes to go through all the sticks and by the end, my father was throwing them as hard as he could. They stopped six inches away each time but the harder the throw, the more Hillaes stepped back from the force of the stick striking the shield. Even though the sticks didn't touch her, the inertia from the blow had to go somewhere, and the shield acted like a buffer which pushed her back each time as the wooden missiles shattered against the shield.

"Well, that was a success," I said as Father threw the last stick. "Did you feel any of that Hillaes?"

She beamed at me. "No. Next time we'll practice outside so we can see how far you can throw the shield on someone else. I'm sure the King didn't come here just to take part in our experiment so let's call it a day. I'll even clean up so you can get out of here quicker."

I thanked her and followed my father from the room and spoke to him using thought-speech. *What's up?*

There are some important things I need to share with you before you go to Earth. You can tell Aileene, but I will ask you to keep what I'm about to tell you from everyone who isn't a Royal Dragon.

Intrigued, I followed him down into an area of the palace I hadn't been to before. We walked single file down a narrow passage which ended in a room with nothing but a tapestry hanging on the wall. My father pulled it to the side and revealed something that looked like a fingerprint scanner. He pulled out a dagger and asked me to hold out my right thumb.

"I will prick your finger and you will need to place your blood on the scan pad. This will transfer control of this door to you and will be the only time you must use your blood to open it."

I did what he asked and when I placed my bloody thumb on the scanner, it turned green, and the door moved inward then slid to the right. After we passed through the entrance it closed again and the overhead lights came on. We were in a rectangular room which was twenty feet by forty feet. The room's designer lined the walls with bookshelves, maps and monitors. The enormous table in the middle of the room was a smaller version of the one in the Council Chambers, and there were five holographic globes spinning slowly above its surface. Each globe was labeled. The one in the middle was Theria, then to the right was Claw, then Earth. To the left of Theria, the planets were labeled Grebalar and Dyosonus.

"What is this place?" I asked in wonder.

"Most people believe that we cut ourselves off from the other dimensions over five hundred years ago but that's not entirely correct. The High Kings and Queens have continued to influence and guide each of these dimensions since we learned how to create gates. This room is one of our best-kept secrets and is only accessible to us. Here we monitor activity in other dimensions that could cause problems for our people. If there are issues, we have teams in place to deal with them. I make these teams up of shifters who work for the Crown of Theria and are part of an elite group called Tionchar.

"Unfortunately, your mother and I weren't able to monitor any of this activity while Dimitri held us captive and we waited until now to tell you about this secret. We're so used to being the King and Queen we decided to handle things ourselves, and that's one reason we spent so much time away over the past six months. I was sure we could solve this mystery without including you. It's not that I didn't trust you, I was just convinced I knew what was best; I was wrong. There's a problem with one planet and the threat has continued to multiply for thirteen years. Fortunately, we're sending a team to that planet soon to deal with whatever they find there."

He touched the table and at once a red haze lit up across one of the spinning globes, the one labeled Earth.

"Guess it's not going to be all fun and games on this trip after all," I muttered darkly.

CHAPTER THREE

My father and I talked long into the night about our clandestine operations in other dimensions, and other aspects of being High King. We'd never spent so many hours together at one time, and I loved it. We stayed in the secret support center for hours and then had dinner together in one of the private dining rooms found in the kitchen wing. When I told my friends we had to skip our hang-out session, they were okay with it because Bernie and Shelley were spending time with their parents and Aileene and Mother were together. She was getting the same information I was, just from my mother's perspective.

One of the surprising things I learned was how extensive the Tionchar network was on Earth.

"What does Tionchar mean?" I asked

"Tionchar has multiple meanings but the best words in English are influence, effect, impact and strength. These are all things members of Tionchar do in the dimensions where they're assigned. There are only twenty members of Tionchar on each planet at a time and they blend in with the local populace," my father explained.

"These shifters agree to serve off-planet for fifty years and then rotate back to Theria where they can reintegrate into our society.

Shifters have a much longer life span, so they must move every ten to twenty years to avoid raising suspicion why they aren't aging. The members of Tionchar work in areas where they can have the most influence and monitor military and scientific advancements on their respective planets."

He pressed his hand to one cabinet near the head of the table and nothing happened. "It seems the system has already transferred everything over to you," he muttered. "Son, please put your hand on the scanner."

The cabinet opened when I put my hand on the spot he showed me. He reached inside and handed me a tablet which looked like an iPad.

He saw the look of surprise on my face and laughed. "Before my forced hibernation, I was working with members of Tionchar to introduce tablet technology to Earth's high-tech companies. From your expression, I guess that worked out the way we planned. This tablet will only open for you and gives you information about Tionchar and what they've accomplished on each planet over the years."

"What happened to Middle Earth? How was Minos able to cause so many problems for Buttle?" I asked.

There was a flash from the globe labeled Claw, and it changed the name to Middle Earth. "That's so cool," I breathed.

My father chuckled. "Middle Earth's military and scientific research hasn't advanced in the last hundred years, so I recalled every member of Tionchar from there six months before Dimitri attacked your mother and me. We received a report that Minos died in a shipwreck and we believed it. We even held a nice memorial for that murderer when we thought he'd died."

"Was Minos a member of Tionchar?" I asked.

"No. Minos was part of a scientific team researching whether the magic found on Middle Earth could open a dimensional gate. Since it seems he was working for Dimitri all along, it's a splendid thing their research wasn't successful. Once Tionchar members returned, your Mother and I were reevaluating how many shifters to send to Middle Earth. Before we could send anyone there, Dimitri incapacitated us."

I looked at the tablet and noticed that reports were filed on a regular basis over the past thirteen years from Grebalar and Dyosonus even though they hadn't received responses back from my parents. When I looked at the reports from Earth, I noticed that there were regular reports from all twenty members of Tionchar only for the first ten years after we fled to Earth. However, four years ago all but one reporter stopped submitting.

After scanning the reports, I looked at my father and said, "I have some questions."

"I'm sure you do," he chuckled, "let me see if I can answer them before you ask." He smiled. "These tablets can send messages across dimensions, but only if there is an open gate to facilitate the transfer of information. Tionchar agents on each planet would have been able to send their reports, and assume it had transmitted them but would have only known there was a problem when they didn't receive any responses. How'd I do?"

I laughed. "Good, that was one of my questions. How did you know?"

He rubbed his hands together and continued, "You're my son and we have a lot in common. Let's see if I can go two for two. Alex Farrel is the only member of Tionchar who still submits reports from Earth. He is the current CEO of Rex Industries, which is a multinational conglomeration of companies specializing in high-tech, medical research, space exploration, renewable energy and food production."

He looked at me expectantly, so I had to concede, "You're two for two. Do you want to try three for three?"

"Sure—I don't know."

I looked at him with a puzzled expression.

"I don't know what happened to the other members of Tionchar on Earth, but I'm trusting you and the team we're sending to find out. Even though I can't go to Earth myself, I'm counting on you to find out what happened to our people. Oh, and one last answer to your unasked questions...he's a coyote shifter."

Even though our trip to Earth got more complicated because of the missing members of Tionchar, I had to grin at my Father because he was right, again. I guess he knew me better than I thought he did.

Earth

The tablet was plugged in and resting on the counter of the darkened kitchen. Besides the ticking of the clock and the running of the refrigerator, the only sound in the quiet house was gentle snoring coming from the sole occupant. The silence was broken by a gentle *DING* from the tablet showing an incoming message had been received. The screen lit up—

Sorry for not getting back with you sooner but some of your cousins will come to visit. They'll bring you some things from home and something special from me. They'll let you know when they're in town. Uncle Phillip.

After two seconds the screen shut off and the kitchen was once again cloaked in darkness. The snoring continued from the bedroom.

Theria

Aileene and I were lying on our sides basking in the morning sunlight and she had her head and neck draped over my shoulder. In the distance, Mkali was sparring with Bernie and Shelley at the same time and was doing well. She would shift to her centaur form and use her speed to avoid attacks then shift back into her human form to go on the offensive. She was a very impressive fighter and improved every day. I shouted encouragement in mind-speak and then closed my eyes to enjoy the feel of a full belly, the warmth of the sun on my scales and Aileene draped across my shoulders.

I missed seeing you last night and our nightly ritual with our friends, Aileene sent.

Me, too, I added. *How was your time with Mother?*

It was wonderful. First, I got to spend time with Mom and Mother planning a gift for your birthday. Then Mother and I spent hours alone talking about secret things.

It sounds like you had fun, but you don't have to give me anything.

This is the first birthday we've spent together, and I want it to be special. Lord Moss stopped celebrating my birthday after I turned six, so this will be fun for me, too. Did you get me a gift? Aileene sent shyly.

Of course, I sent. *Just because you don't have to give me a gift doesn't mean I'm not going to get you one. I want you to know how important you are to me.*

Aileene nuzzled her jaw along mine as she sent, *Thank you, Alister, you're important to me, too.*

After a few minutes of contented silence, I asked, *What secrets did Mother share with you?*

Aileene coyly sent, *Some of the secrets are just between us girls but she also talked about Tionchar.*

Yeah, Father talked with me about that, I sighed. *I'm not sure how I feel about all the secrecy and keeping this from our friends who are part of our Inner Circle. I don't have a problem with a group of our people working on other planets in secret, but it just feels wrong that we're the only ones who know about it.*

Aileene didn't answer me right away so I opened my eyes and watched my friends battle one another. Bernie and Shelley were in their natural forms and Mkali was human. She danced away from Bernie's horn and into Shelley's reach. He swiped at her with his huge paw and sent her flying. I had a moment of concern when she hit the springy turf, but she turned it into a roll and sprang back to her feet. She shifted and charged back at Bernie and Shelley, laughing with the thrill of battle the entire time. I smiled at how Bernie could turn such serious training into play for Mkali and closed my eyes again.

How is this any different from the secrets An'Ceann has shared with us about Royal Dragons? Aileene asked.

Cracking my eyelids, I once again watched my friends who had collapsed in a heap on the ground and thought about Aileene's question.

Maybe it's not, but this feels different to me, I sent.

Well, my mate, I will stand by your decision if you feel we should tell our friends, but I think it would be wise to listen to your parents' counsel on this. They've ruled Theria for centuries and know more about this than we do.

As I thought about what Aileene said, a sense of calm washed over me and I felt as though a weight had lifted off my chest. I didn't know why this had bothered me so much but Aileene was right. I trusted An'Ceann and my parents, and knew they had wisdom I didn't have yet. There were reasons for secrets and even though I didn't know them, I could trust that those who love me wouldn't willingly lead me astray.

You're right, my love, thank you. I sent.

Of course, I am, Aileene sent with a snort and shifted into her human form.

I craned my neck and followed her as she walked across my body and hopped to the ground from my chest. "Come with me Alister, let's show our friends what it's like to wrestle with dragons." Aileene grinned and started running towards Bernie, Shelley and Mkali who were already getting into defensive positions. I shifted and took off running after Aileene with a smile stretched across my face. This was the best birthday ever.

The rest of the day was perfect. We stayed in our meadow for hours playing games, taking naps and talking the way best friends do. We talked about the things we wanted to do on Earth, when we weren't searching for our missing people.

"I hope we find a shifter in Kansas," Shelley said.

"Oookay," I drawled. "Why?"

"Because then we could go see the World's Largest Ball of Twine," he said. "I used to have a book with all the unique tourist attractions you can find across the country and I always wanted to go see it."

"Of course, you did, you big goof," Bernie said as she kissed Shelley on the cheek, "I hope there's a shifter in London, I've always wanted to travel there. What about you Mkali, is there somewhere you want to go?"

Mkali blushed and looked embarrassed. "I've always wanted to go to Disneyland and ride the rides."

I held up my hand for a high-five, "That's what I'm talking about, we'll add that to the list, even if there aren't shifters in California. I'm looking forward to Hero Con in Los Angeles, we've always talked about attending and dressing up. We'll check out a lot of things on that side of the country while we're there. What about you Aileene?"

She smiled at our excitement and answered, "Anywhere you three want to go will be fine with me but it would be cool to see some dinosaurs." She laughed at herself, "I know the Jurassic Park movies aren't real, but I would love to meet a T-Rex in person and if it wanted to fight, that would be even better."

We laughed at the image of Aileene fighting a dinosaur and then screaming like a T-Rex after defeating her enemy.

"The dinosaurs in the movie may not be real, but maybe we should visit some museums to look at fossils or check out the Jurassic Park ride at one of the Universal Studios Theme Parks."

"Or all of them," Shelley added.

"Or all of them," I agreed, and we laughed. After all the fear, death and destruction during our last adventures we were looking forward to a vacation where we could act like kids again.

We headed back to the palace in the late afternoon so we could get ready for dinner. After we landed, we went our separate ways and Aileene grabbed my hand as we walked towards her suite where she lived with our parents.

"Hey Mom," I said when I walked through the door and saw my mom loading up a backpack.

"Hi honey, have you had an enjoyable day?" she asked and came over and gave Aileene and me hugs.

"We did," I said as I hugged her in return.

"Hello, you two," my mother said as she walked into the living room with a set of sheathed knives. "Fiona, where would you like me to put these?"

"I'll take them, thanks," Mom said and held out her hands. Mother handed off the knives and then enveloped first Aileene and then me in an embrace, kissing us on the forehead.

"What have you been doing all day?" she asked.

We sat on the couch and told them about everything we'd done so far while Mom continued to pack. Finally, the curiosity got the better of me and I asked, "Mom, are you going somewhere?"

"Yes, I'm coming with you to Earth and so is Miriam and Frieda," she answered with a smile.

"How wonderful," Aileene exclaimed. "What about you, Mother can you come, too?"

"No. Your Father and I must stay behind to stand as Regents for Alister while he's gone." She said with a sad smile on her face. I could tell she was disappointed that she couldn't come.

Father, Fritz, I sent. I*s there any reason Mother can't come with us on our trip to Earth?*

We must stay behind to rule in your absence—Father began.

Nonsense, Fritz interrupted. *You know as well as I do that you can handle things well enough on your own. You just don't want your wife to be absent for so long.*

That's true, Father laughed, *I'm pitiful without her. Very well, why don't you ask her if she wants to go with you? I'll just have to make do with Fritz, Albert and Stavros since we'll all be without our mates. We'll be bachelors again, just like Gustav.*

You are correct, Gustav doesn't have a mate—yet, Fritz commented. *But he has been spending a lot of time with Seraset.*

Isn't she the sphinx he used to date about two hundred years ago? Father asked.

Yes, Fritz mentally chortled, *Gustav told her he was too young to settle down and she told him to see if she was still single when he finally grew up.*

Ummmm, I interrupted, *I'm still on the line here guys. This is probably more information than I want to know. I'll ask Mother if she wants to, and let you know what she says. See you at dinner.*

The last thing I heard was mental laughter from my Father and Fritz before I dropped the mental connection.

Clearing my throat, I asked, "Mother, would you like to go with us? Father and Fritz said it wouldn't be an issue for you to come and they would keep each other company; and tease Gustav about Seraset."

Mother looked delighted as she jumped off the couch and ran

towards her room, "Fiona, help me. If we're leaving tomorrow, I've got to get packed."

"I guess that means she wants to go," Mom said with a smile. "I'd better get her a backpack and help her fill it with stuff. See you at dinner." She waved as she left the room.

Aileene and I laughed at the sound of my mother frantically pulling out clothes for the journey. Even though she wasn't talking to us through thought-speech, her joy and excitement were being broadcast from the other room. We sat back on the couch and Aileene made herself comfortable as she leaned against me and I placed my arm around her shoulders. I thought about this beautiful young woman sitting next to me and sent a silent prayer of thanks to An'Ceann for this amazing partner who would one day be my wife.

"You're welcome," said a deep voice near my ear which startled me. I tried to get up but froze in place until An'Ceann, in his lion form, padded to the front of the couch and sat, looking like a cat who had gotten in the cream.

"You don't have any cream, do you? I adore cream," he purred.

"An'Ceann," Aileene squealed while launching herself off the couch and tackling the grinning lion. Even though she is over six feet tall in her human form, the lion the size of a small elephant dwarfed her. Her momentum carried the two of them to the floor. He laughed loudly and purred, Aileene giggled like a little girl and I smiled. Not wanting to miss out on the action, I jumped into the fray and tackled him as well.

"Hello children, happy birthday," he said after we lay in bliss for a few moments. He cocooned us in a bubble of silence and it felt like we were the only ones in Theria. An'Ceann radiates warmth and I felt energized and refreshed just by being this close to him. Aileene and I lay side by side, resting our backs against his side and we could feel the rumble of his deep voice when he spoke.

"I wanted to spend some time alone with the two of you before you departed for Earth tomorrow. There are a few things I want you to know. First of all, Alister I know you are concerned about keeping secrets and feeling you are lying to your friends. However, as King, there will be times when you'll be burdened with knowledge you can't share with anyone else because you're the King. You always have Aileene to share these things with, that's one reason I give a true mate to each High King or High Queen before they take the Throne. Or, in your case, about the same time as you take the throne." He chuckled.

"You two will know things that only those in your position can handle. There will be other times when you have information first and you will have to decide when others can handle it. Then there will be times you will receive information from others that you will have to decide what to do with. The roles of High King and Queen are both a burden and a joy. By choosing to serve your people, you also bear some burdens alone. Although, you're never alone because you have each other and you always have me. It was my decision to keep Tionchar, well—hidden, from most shifters, even those who are part of this elite group."

"What do you mean?" I asked.

"Once a shifter returns to Theria after serving, they lose the ability to speak with anyone except me and the High King or Queen about what they did while on a mission or about the Tionchar organization."

"That seems cruel to interfere with someone that way," I argued.

"It would be cruel if we did it without their knowledge, however, we give everyone who chooses to be part of Tionchar all these details before they agree to serve. Not only do they agree to these limits when they return, they also agree to have limited knowledge about other teammates while they are on assignment. Each member of Tionchar works independently and only the High King and Queen know the extent of the operations and how they work together."

"So, these shifters volunteer to be part of Tionchar, know that they are isolated while on assignment and when they return won't be able to tell anyone, except the three of us, about what they did while they served; is that about right?" Aileene asked.

"Yes daughter, you are correct," An'Ceann answered softly.

"But why?" I asked.

"Alister, this is one of those times I will ask you to trust me. I have my reasons and they are essential for protecting not only this planet but the other planets in all dimensions."

I nodded. "You've never given me any reason not to trust you; so, I will."

An'Ceann rumbled with laughter. "Thank you, my son."

I laughed also. "You know what I mean. But, I'm still not sure I understand why I can't share this with my Inner Circle."

"If you were to share information about Tionchar with Shelley and Bernie, these limits would bind them the same as anyone else. But they wouldn't have received the training needed before being given the choice to follow the Tionchar path. If you told them, you would take their freedom from them without their consent; and that would be cruel."

The full weight of his words hit me and I broke out into a cold sweat when I thought about how close I had come to ignoring my father's warning and telling my friends anyway.

"And, that's one reason I needed to come see you today. You'd never forgive yourself if you did that to your friends and I wanted to spare you from that," he breathed and enveloped me in his comforting presence. "Just so you know, I've had to have a very similar conversation with every other High King and Queen since I created Tionchar. Royal Dragons don't like to be told what to do," he laughed.

"What else do you want to tell us, not that I'm not content to just sit here, I'm just curious," Aileene said.

An'Ceann roared with laughter, "Oh, daughter, you are so delightful and dragonish, and not at all patient when there's a mystery to solve."

"Yes, yes," Aileene laughed, "I'm not the most patient but I said I'm willing to just sit here, you're the one who brought up you had things to tell us."

"You're right," An'Ceann agreed. "The other thing is while you will face challenges on Earth, I trust you to make the right decisions to protect your people, no matter what."

"That's it?" Aileene exclaimed. "Could you be any more mysterious?"

"Believe it or not, I could but I won't. If I give everything away, where would be the fun in that? As one of my favorite television characters says, 'spoilers'." He laughed.

I got the *Dr. Who* reference but Aileene looked puzzled. "I'll explain later," I said to her. "You like that show?" I asked him.

"Yeah, the weeping angels are creepy. Happy birthday you two, enjoy the party."

And with that he disappeared taking our support away and we tumbled to the floor. I swear I could hear the sound of a disappearing Tardis for a few seconds as we lay on the ground.

"He thinks that's so funny," I grumbled as I stood.

Aileene giggled and wiggled her hands at me so I could pull her up. "It is kind of funny," she said with her ear pressed against my chest as I held her. "I love you Alister and am glad we're in this together."

"I love you, too," I said as I kissed the top of her head, "and couldn't imagine facing any of this without you."

"Then it's good we don't have to worry about that, isn't it?" she grinned mischievously as she looked up at me.

"Yeah, it is," I said and gave her a quick kiss.

Our birthday celebration was fun but they decorated everything for a six-year-old. Mother explained that she had big plans for our sixth birthday because that would have been when Aileene joined us in Theria, and she didn't see any reason to let the decorations go to waste. Bernie and Shelley looked ridiculous in their conical birthday hats, but I suppose I did, too. Aileene looked fabulous as usual, even if she was wearing a Birthday Princess hat with a long pink silk scarf hanging from the top.

The adults dressed themselves in festive wear. Of course, Dad had on a pair of purple sweats. The riotous pattern was a red dragon holding a pink balloon. My father was also wearing a pair. I cracked up whenever I looked at Fritz wearing a unicorn hat which said, I'm a Pretty Unicorn. At first, I was shocked that many of the party favors seem to have come from Earth. But according to the info on the pad I read last night, there were many things found on Earth that were created in Theria, and were taken to other dimensions by members of Tionchar. There were many industries and businesses across the dimensions our covert group had built and maintained.

Dinner was amazing and the Head Chef made many dishes I remembered from my childhood when I lived in the palace. There were pasta dishes, meat dishes and even spicy gambon served in flat bread that looked and tasted like tortillas. Everyone was in high spirits and we ate until we were full. After the meal, we moved into a sitting room talking and laughing until it was time for presents.

Since there were four birthdays being celebrated there were many gifts set out for each of us to open. All four of us received new hiking backpacks since the ones we had taken with us from Earth to Middle Earth had seen better days. Bernie, Shelley and Aileene also received new hunting knives with belt sheaths and I received a new sheath for my father's knife that dad had given me last year.

Shelley gave Bernie a silver necklace with a unicorn pendant and Bernie gave him a comic book she had created titled The Adventures of Shelley the Grizzly Bear. He didn't want us to notice, but he teared up when he opened his gift. I gave Aileene a charm I made for her which connected to her thought-medallion. The charm was layered in magic and matched the one I made for myself. It would create an extra pocket dimension so she could store larger things when she transformed into her dragon. She could access the pocket dimension anytime she wanted. She had tears in her eyes when she hugged me and thanked me for such a thoughtful gift.

"I've got to get your present now, so don't go anywhere," she said as she left the room with Bernie and Mkali in tow.

"Dude, did you see what Bernie made me?" Shelley asked as he showed me his comic book. "I'm in a comic book, and I'm a hero."

"Son," Stavros said as he sat on the couch and put his arm around Shelley, "that's how she sees you. In her eyes, you are a hero."

"Thanks, Dad," Shelley said and gave his dad a hug.

"Alister, close your eyes," Mother said and I could feel Aileene come back into the room through the connection we always shared.

"Please open your eyes," Aileene said and I looked at her. She was biting her bottom lip with her top teeth and her eyes were filled with worry. She had something in her hands, and it took me a bit before I realized what she was holding.

"Is that, soda pop cake?" I asked in wonder.

She nodded her head and said, "I made it for you. Both Mom and Mother said it was your favorite."

Reaching out I placed my hands on the outside of hers which were holding the cake pan and said, "Thank you, it means a lot that you made this for me."

"I hope it tastes okay," Aileene said anxiously.

"It'll taste great," I assured her and she smiled timidly.

Each of the birthday celebrants got our favorite cakes, or in Shelley's case pie. I was pleasantly surprised at how delicious my cake was since it was made with ingredients only found on Theria.

"Would anyone like a piece of my carrot cake?" Bernie asked.

"I'd offer you some berry pie, but it's almost gone," Shelley said with a grin.

"I love you all, but no one better touch my death by chocolate cake," Aileene warned.

Everyone laughed and the chef wheeled out duplicates of each dessert, so no one got hurt. The celebration lasted long into the night because it was the last time we'd all be together until we returned from our mission on Earth.

Since we planned to depart after dark, we had another full day to prepare. Aileene and I spent more time with Father and Mother going over the names of the shifters who were part of Tionchar along with their last known locations. We downloaded all the information about the clandestine organization onto tablets; both Aileene and I had one. Even though Aileene and I weren't married yet, we linked her into the system so she could access the information. Because we would need to communicate while we were on Earth, I experimented to see how small

I could make a dimensional gate and could create one the size of a pinhead.

Father wanted to see if we could use such a small gate for real-time communication, so he composed a message to Alex Farrel using the secure system.

Sometimes the most important paths are hidden ones.

I grinned at the coded message and teased my father, "Really, code phrases?"

"Alex has been in the United States since 1975 and is a big fan of spy movies. It was his idea," Father laughed.

But hidden paths can also be dangerous. The response flashed across the screen.

Greetings Alex, are you well?

Yes, Sire. Why have you been silent for so long?

It's too complicated to go over via message. I apologize for my cryptic response, but it'll be easier to explain the details in person. The team I am sending to Earth will answer your questions, but they will also need your help.

Of course, Sire, what do you need?

Secure transport for twenty including Queen Beatrice and my son, Alister. Beatrice, Alister and four others will need complete identification packets and access to unlimited funds while they are on Earth. They will need a secure location to stay in Maine and access to the corporate jets the entire time they are on Earth. Alister will be my representative so please extend him every courtesy you would give me.

There was such a lengthy pause, I was about to check to make sure the gate was still open before Alex started typing again.

It will be as you say. When will this team arrive?

In ten hours.

This time the pause was even longer and my father grinned at us. "I'm glad we don't have audio; I'm sure Alex is using some inappropriate language." We all laughed.

"Phillip you just can't help yourself, can you?" Mother smiled indulgently.

After five minutes, Alex finally responded. *There will be a*

Trafero Line luxury bus in the South Branch Pond Trail parking lot by seven pm, waiting for their appearance. Please have Prince Alister contact me again when he arrives, and I will give him more details on the secure location where they will stay. Since I am in Arizona, I cannot be there when they arrive, I hope that will be acceptable.

It is. Thank you, Alex, I appreciate everything. He closed the channel and I closed the gate.

"That worked even better than expected," he said as he rubbed his hands together. "We'll be able to stay in contact the entire time you're on Earth because you can open a pinhole gate wherever you are. I'll keep a pad with me at all times."

"I know that look Phillip, you've got plans within plans, what are they?" Mother asked.

Father smiled as he answered, "I might have some suggestions on things you should look for on Earth…"

Once we finished our planning session in the secret room, the four of us returned to our rooms so we could finish packing. Aside from Brarth and Gekur, the ogre shifters standing guard outside my door, I was alone, getting my gear ready for the trip. I would have to buy new clothing once we arrived on Earth since the only things that fit were the clothes created for me on Middle Earth and Theria. If I tried to wear them on Earth, I would stand out. However, I packed some anyway in case I wanted to wear them to Hero Con.

There was a knock on the outer door and Brarth sent, *Sire, Josef is here to see you.*

I was startled when I opened the door and was greeted by a face I'd seen on TV and movies. The shifter standing before me was about six inches shorter than my seven feet but was much more muscular and had golden brown skin. He was bald and had a distinctive tattoo below the left sleeve of his t-shirt. He grinned at me and raised his right eyebrow.

Laughing at my dumbstruck expression, he said, "Hello, Your Majesty. My name is Josef. May I come in?"

"Please do," I replied, and motioned him inside. "Forgive me for asking, but do people ever tell you you look like The Rock?"

He laughed again, "All the time. In fact, I've been Dwayne's stunt double since he made it big."

"Wow, that is so cool," I breathed. We moved over to the couches and sat. "Thank you for coming so swiftly, would you like something to drink?"

"No, thank you," he said as we settled and he relaxed on the couch. "Your father briefed me on the rescue mission but I wanted to check one or two details with you. It's my understanding that we're missing twenty members of Tionchar on Earth and my team and I will look for them, correct?"

"Actually, we're only missing nineteen because we know who the twentieth is, but you are correct. Since you've served on Earth and now serve as a trainer at the academy it makes the most sense that you would lead the rescue effort. I received a message from An'Ceann that he lifted your oath of secrecy so you could lead your team. He told me I can trust you implicitly."

Josef bowed his head in embarrassment. "I am honored."

"I understand that the nine others you will bring with you began Tionchar training on Theria but fled to Earth with everyone else so they never took the oath, correct?"

"Yes, they know enough about Tionchar so they will be effective but aren't under the compulsion to keep everything secret. I trust each one of them and their commitment to the secret group. We will find these missing shifters or find out what has happened to them."

I nodded my head at his assurances and handed him a stack of the encrypted tablets. "These tablets need to be coded to each member of your team through a drop of their blood placed here." I pointed to a scanner near the top of the tablet. "Once the tablet has been synced, that person will be the only one who can access it. Each of these will link back to my tablet and we will work together to coordinate while on Earth. My team will focus on the shifters who were trapped on Earth and your team will focus on missing members of Tionchar."

"Very good," Josef said as he accepted the tablets. "If there's nothing else, I'll finish preparing my team."

We stood and I held out my hand to shake his. Clasping his hand firmly, I held it for an extra second while I thought about my request. "Um, this is embarrassing, but do you think it would be possible to arrange for us to meet The Rock? I know Sirs Arktos and Einhorn and I would love to meet him."

Josef chuckled as he answered, "I'll see what I can do, Sire."

The only people in the meadow when we left were my father and the members of his Inner Circle who were staying behind. There were some guards in the distance, but they couldn't hear what we said. I opened a gate to Earth the size of a baseball, and extended my senses to make sure there weren't any humans near our landing zone. Satisfied we wouldn't surprise anyone on Earth, I closed the gate and hugged both my dad and father and shook hands with the others. We had already said our goodbyes so our company turned towards the north end of the field where I would open the gate.

"How're you doing?" I whispered to Aileene.

"I'm excited to be going to Earth, but I'm nervous, too," she whispered back.

"It'll be fun," I finished in a whisper.

"I like to whisper," Shelley added.

"Whispering's my favorite," Bernie chimed in and we all laughed.

"Okay you goofs, it's time," I whispered to my friends.

To everyone else I raised my voice and said, "C'mon everybody, here we go!"

And opened a gate to Earth.

CHAPTER FOUR

e hurried down the trail through the woods and to the parking lot where we would meet our ride. Since the moon wasn't visible, starlight was the only source of light but with our excellent night vision, that was enough. We were quiet as we traveled and Aileene and I walked hand-in-hand. There were a few times I had to catch her as she stumbled, because rather than look at the trail, she kept looking at the sky.

After another stumble I finally sent, *You're not usually this clumsy. Is there something wrong?*

The stars on Earth differ from those on Theria, she replied and broadcast a sense of wonder through our connection.

Even though I was raised on Earth, I had adjusted to the constellations on Theria but imagined this was a novel experience for Aileene and Mother. Aileene had an enormous smile on her face as she looked up through the canopy of trees over the trail and a warmth spread through my chest as I saw the look on her face. I pulled her to a stop and she looked at me with curiosity. I dropped my backpack, put my arms around my future mate, manifested my wings and slowly flew us above the treetops so she could get a better look. She gasped as the entire sky came into view.

The stars glittered like diamonds against black velvet. I didn't know much about the constellations but knew about Ursa Major, Ursa Minor, Pegasus and Draco. My parents taught me these constellations and now it made sense since they're named after a bear, a winged-horse and a dragon. As we hovered in the air I pointed these out to Aileene and she smiled in wonder. The longer we stared at the stars the more we saw. It was as if we were looking through a telescope and it felt like we were traveling in space. We used thought-speech to describe our experiences to each other.

We hovered in reverential silence until Josef cleared his throat and murmured, "Sire, we should go."

Aileene turned towards me, kissed me and then I lowered us to the trail.

Thank you, Alister, that was beautiful, she sent.

Not as beautiful as you, I answered and was gratified to hear her self-conscious giggle at my compliment.

Oh, Alister, can you please give me a ride next? Shelley broadcast to our entire group and I heard people laugh.

You're just jealous you can't fly, I returned and replaced my backpack.

No, I'm just jealous that Aileene got a hug and none of the rest of us did, he sent.

Whatever, I sent, *let's get going again.*

We started walking again and about an hour later we exited the forest and entered pandemonium.

The parking lot was filled with vehicles belonging to police, rangers and concerned citizens. There were five kids ranging in ages from six to twelve who were missing. Their families were camping nearby and the kids had set out to go hiking that morning but hadn't returned. After hours of searching, the parents had informed the park rangers who then called in the police. A group of rescuers was about to head up the trail we came down, but we assured them we had seen no one as we made our way to the bus. Tobias, a wolf shifter, who had been a police officer in Bangor, Maine when he lived on Earth, walked over to speak with the Officer in Charge while the rest of us boarded the bus.

Tobias joined us thirty minutes later to fill us in. "The OIC will concentrate the search parties along The Traveler Loop since I convinced him the kids hadn't been on the trail we hiked along. They'll probably still check once they have enough searchers, but we could narrow their search for them."

"Are the kids in danger?" Mother asked.

"Maybe. While the weather has been unseasonably cold so far this summer, the low temperature tonight will drop to around fifty degrees. However, the biggest concern is if the kids left the trail they're probably lost and could be injured. From what their parents think, they didn't bring any food or water with them. One of the twelve year olds took his dad's compass and it worries his parents he might try to lead the rest out of the woods using a shortcut. They weren't supposed to leave the campground and unfortunately each set of parents assumed the kids were at the other camping spot until they had been gone for hours."

"Hey, I don't want to sound callous but if we don't leave within the next thirty minutes, I won't be able to drive you to Bangor where you'll be staying," our bus driver Tiffany announced.

"Why is that?" I asked.

"It's the law that I can only drive for ten hours at a time and then I need eight hours off. I've already been driving for six and a half hours today and it will take us almost three hours to get where we need to go. I'm sorry but if you want to get out of here tonight, we have to leave soon."

"The OIC told me to thank everyone for their help and asked us to send our thoughts and prayers for the lost kids, but we're free to go," Tobias said as he took his seat.

Tiffany started the bus and pulled away.

Alister, I don't like the thought of those kids lost and alone in the woods, Aileene sent to me. *We must help.*

We will, I promised, *we just need to be careful. Tiffany is human and we can't afford to let her in on our secret.*

Okay everyone, I broadcast, *we cannot leave those kids in the woods by themselves.*

I agree, Tobias interjected. *The OIC told me they can't get rescue dogs to the park until tomorrow afternoon at the earliest. There was another hiker lost this afternoon along the New Hampshire border and they sent the dogs there. If the kids are on the trail, they should be easy to find, but if they're not, it's unlikely they will find the kids tonight.*

Okay, team, what do we do? I sent.

After a few minutes of quiet thought, Shelley sent. *Hey, isn't there a Tim Hortons about fifteen minutes down the road from the park?*

Yeah, you and Alister wanted to stop there for donuts when we were heading to Middle Earth a year ago. Bernie sent the group.

Why don't we see if Tiffany will stop there for a late night snack and a few of us can head back to the park to help find the kids. Shelley added.

Tiffany won't be willing to wait for us, Josef sent.

Those left on the bus will convince Tiffany that everyone is back on board and then everyone else will continue. Alister can fly the rescuers where we'll be staying in Bangor. Easy-peasy, Shelley sent.

After more discussion in thought-speech we put our plan in action, and I asked Tiffany if we could stop for some food. Thankfully the adults who had left Earth a year ago had their wallets with them so we had plenty of cash to buy food. She was still concerned about her timetable but since we left the park right after her announcement, she told me we could spare twenty minutes at the restaurant. Aileene, Mom and I got off the bus first, got our food and made sure Tiffany saw we got back on the bus and headed to the back. Mother convinced Tiffany to join her in the restaurant and those of us who were in on the rescue hurried into the darkness.

Besides Mom and me, we only brought Shelley, Tobias and Frank with us. Frank was a wolf, too and we needed his keen sense of smell. Once we were away from prying eyes, I quickly shifted, and everyone clambered onto my back. Even though I was longer than a city bus, I silently climbed into the moonless sky and avoided being seen.

We're off, I sent to Aileene.

Rescue those kids, love, Aileene sent, *we convinced Tiffany everyone is on the bus and we just left the restaurant. This is an exciting first night on Earth, I just wish I was flying with you.*

We'll get our chance, I promised.

It only took a few minutes for us to return to the state park. I began to slowly circle over the area where we thought the kids could be. Even though we were a couple hundred feet above the ground, I could see the beams of the searchers' flashlights as they looked for the kids. Thankfully, the moon had already set so no one could see me flying but there was enough light from the stars for me to see to the ground below. We flew over The Traveler Loop but didn't see any sign of the kids. I widened my search pattern and asked An'Ceann for help in finding them.

Below at three o'clock, Mom sent excitedly.

Looking where she told me to, I could focus on five still forms huddled on the ground in a small clearing. The kids were about a mile off the trail and were dangerously close to the edge of a small canyon.

Good eyes, Mom. I must find a spot to land to let everyone off. Mom and I will follow on foot and Shelley, Tobias and Frank will make their way to the kids in their natural forms.

I found another clearing a half mile from the kids and landed. Tobias and Frank quickly stripped and handed me their clothes which I stored in the pocket dimension pendant I'd created. Shelley, Tobias and Frank shifted and took off toward the lost kids.

"Well, I guess we're jogging," Mom chuckled and took off after the others.

It only took us a few minutes to find the kids; they huddled together to keep warm. While we ran, we talked to our rescue crew on the best way to continue. Frank and Tobias would pretend to be dogs and check out the kids for injuries. Once we assessed their condition, we would decide what to do. Frank and Tobias barked as they left the tree line and made their way to the sleeping kids, although Frank's 'woof-woof' sounded forced. The older boys jumped up at the sound of barking and stood protectively over the younger kids who began crying. Even though they had gotten themselves into this mess, I was proud of those boys protecting the weaker kids.

I think they're okay, Tobias sent, *I can only smell a little blood— wait, one boy seems to have a broken leg. We will need your help.*

They smell sickly, Frank added, they're probably dehydrated.

Okay, Mom and I will join you.

I pulled some water bottles and two flashlights out of the pocket dimension around my neck, handed a flashlight and some of the bottles to my mom and stepped out of the trees calling, "Here Frank, here Tobias...what have you found?"

Mom and I walked towards the kids and she got down on her knee and spoke softly to the now crying kids. "Hey, it's okay, we've found you. You're safe now."

"It's all my fault," the oldest boy cried, although it was clear he was trying to be brave. "I thought I could find my way back to camp but then Oliver hurt his leg and it really scared us."

I kneeled next to Mom and passed out the water bottles as I talked to the kids. "Hi, I'm Alister, what are your names?"

"I'm Finley," the self-appointed leader said and pointed to the rest of the kids. "This is David, Scotty, Kristen and my brother Oliver."

"Hi guys, you've already met our dogs, Frank and Tobias—"

"Those aren't dogs, they're wolves," Kristen declared. "I read a book about the differences between dogs and wolves and they look like wolves."

"Are they going to eat us?" Oliver asked but sounded more excited than scared.

"No. They're friendly and so is my friend Shelley," I answered with a laugh as Shelley stepped through the trees and walked towards us.

"Are you sure he's safe?" David gulped as he backed away from the enormous grizzly bear. Kristen launched herself at Shelley and he fell to the ground and lay on his back. Soon all the other kids, except Oliver, were crowding around Shelley and petting him like he was an overgrown puppy. He lifted the side of his mouth and showed his teeth in a grin, the kids laughed.

Mom and I kneeled next to Oliver and I asked him if I could see his hurt leg. His eyes welled with tears and he whimpered from the pain, but he bravely let me wrap my hand around his injured leg. I whispered *Relevium*. It was a tough decision to not repair the bone in his leg, but I was concerned it would raise too many questions. I did the next best thing and I used the *Relevium* spell to take away the pain. Oliver's eyes grew larger as he saw the glow coming from my hands and he felt the immediate relief from his pain. He looked at me in wonder and I winked at him.

"Can I carry you, Oliver?" I asked.

At his nod, I picked him up and cradled him in my arms. Mom lifted Finley, Kristen, Scotty and David on Shelley's back one at a time and we headed back towards the trail where the rescuers were searching for the kids. Shelley was gentle as he walked along and soon the kids grew sleepy. Mom steadied them so they wouldn't fall off and we soon came within sight of the trail. We could see the searchers' flashlights in the distance and we gently laid the kids beside the trail.

"Are you for real?" Kristen asked sleepily.

"No, honey," Mom answered, "we're part of an amazing dream after a terrible scare."

I whispered *Somnum* and the kids fell at once into a deep sleep. Shelley transformed and joined Mom and me as we crept farther into the forest until we came to a small clearing where Mom and I could transform. Tobias and Frank stayed in their wolf forms so they could watch over the sleeping kids but were well hidden in the underbrush. Before I transformed, I pulled Frank and Tobias' clothes out of the pocket dimension and put them on the ground.

After fifteen minutes, we could hear shouts of joy from where we left the kids. Within moments, Frank and Tobias came running into the clearing and quickly got dressed after transforming. Shelley and Tobias crawled onto my back while Frank climbed onto Mom's and we took off.

Excellent work, team, I sent and adjusted my heading, so we were flying towards the others. I could always sense Aileene through the connection we shared. *Aileene, can you please let everyone know the kids are safe and we're on our way back to you?*

Absolutely, she sent. After a few minutes Aileene came back on our mental connection. *Tiffany said we should arrive at our destination in about twenty minutes.*

I relayed the information to the rest of my team, and we took our time flying towards the others. Aileene and I kept in constant contact and I told her everything we did to find the kids. She laughed at my description of Kristen and said, *she sounds like my kind of person.*

We were about twenty miles away from the rest of our friends when Aileene once again broke into my thoughts. *We've stopped in front of an exceptionally large house and Tiffany said this is where we'll be staying. Josef said this is one of the many properties owned by Rex Industries and will be a safe place for us to stay. There is a huge wall around the entire property and gates that can be closed. He said you can land on the large lawn behind the house and walk to the front to join us.*

I relayed the information to my companions and the property soon came into view. This was the only house for miles around so we would have our privacy during our stay. We landed on the back lawn as instructed and soon joined the others by the bus, which they just finished unloading.

"Okay, folks," Tiffany said, "I'll park the bus and head to bed. I'll be sleeping in the apartment above the garage if you need me. However, I won't be driving anywhere for at least eight hours. Mr. Farrel had the place tidied up for your stay. You will find everything you need inside. I'll say goodnight." With that she climbed back on the bus and slowly made her way towards the garage.

"Let's go inside," I said. "I don't know about the rest of you, but I could use something to eat."

"You don't have to tell me twice, Stretch," Shelley said as he raced through the front doors in search of food.

"I'll carry your backpack for you, shall I?" Bernie asked with a grin as she picked up his gear.

"Thanks," Shelley shouted from inside the house.

We laughed as we followed my hungry friend.

Portland, Maine

The theme from the X-Files TV show coming from his telephone awakened Neil Paterson. He had been dreaming of the night he had been camping in the forest and hundreds of people appeared from thin-air. Ever since that night he was obsessed about finding the truth of what happened to him. He didn't know if aliens had abducted him or not. He couldn't remember being taken, but then again he wouldn't if they wiped his brain after they performed their diabolical experiments.

Neil fumbled for the phone and knocked over a glass of water on his nightstand. No matter, the maid would clean it up in the morning.

"Yes, who is this?" Neil demanded.

"Mr. Paterson, this is Kurt Abbot," said a nervous sounding man through the phone.

"Who?"

"Kurt Abbot, I work with Dr. Brent in Research."

"Ah, yes—you better have an excellent reason for calling me this late at night."

"Sir, Dr. Brent wanted me to inform you that the sensors we set up in Baxter State Park last month picked up anomalous readings about three hours ago."

Neil jumped out of bed and paced as he spoke rapidly into the phone. "I knew they'd be back; I just knew it. All those people who doubted me will grovel at my feet when I show the world that I've been right all along."

"Sir—," Abbot tried to interrupt.

"Hah, they'll invite me to all the talk shows and I'll show the world the truth. Maybe I can bring a head with me to show everyone what a real alien looks like. No, that may be too much for television, even late night TV. Even better, I'll travel with the body of a frozen alien, so it won't be so gross. Even though it'll be dead, no one will care because it's an alien..."

"Sir—," Abbot tried again.

"I gave my strike team specific instructions to capture one male and one female alien alive but take out the rest, they're too dangerous to let loose on Earth."

"Sir," Abbot shouted into the phone, finally breaking into Paterson's diatribe. "I've been trying to tell you that even though we noticed the anomaly, your strike team could not get to the meadow to initiate contact."

"Why?" Neil asked.

"There were unforeseen complications. Some kids went missing earlier today and the police set up a roadblock and weren't letting cars into the park after they started the search," Abbot finished lamely.

"Why was the strike team outside the park? For the amount I'm paying them to wait in that campground, that should be their number one priority."

"They ran into the nearest town to buy food and, um, see a movie." Abbot's voice trailed off as Paterson screamed into the phone.

For the next few minutes Kurt Abbot held the phone away from his ear and heard some creative cursing and even heard some unfamiliar words. He waited for Paterson to wind down from his tirade before he tried speaking again.

"Sir," he began, and Paterson interrupted him.

"Don't sir me, inform those former employees of mine they're fired and will be lucky if they ever work again. You're lucky you're just the messenger or you'd be out of a job too," Neil took a deep breath and continued. "Do you have any positive news for me?"

"The sensors worked and if there is another blast of energy in Baxter State Park, we'll know about it." Kurt finished.

The silence continued for so long on the other end of the phone Kurt looked at it to see if the connection had been lost.

"You will tell Dr. Brent to report to me at ten in the morning, at my home; do you hear me?" Paterson demanded and ended the call as he stormed into the walk-in closet in his bedroom that was as large as a two-car garage.

He stomped up to the enormous portrait of his parents which was painted two months before their deaths. The man was tall, imposing and wore a supremely tailored black suit with a red tie. The artist did an amazing job capturing his piercing gaze and arrogant expression of superiority. The man's hand was on the shoulder of the woman seated in a chair next to him. The woman's expression was just as severe as the man's but the way her body was positioned suggested that if the hand were removed from her shoulder, she would bolt out the chair to charge whoever was standing in front of the painting.

Based on their clothing and the jewelry the woman wore, they were wealthy but not people you would want to spend time with. Most people assumed he kept the portrait close to his bedroom because he loved his parents and was grateful for the vast fortune they had left him when they died. That wasn't why he kept the portrait there.

"You didn't believe me when I told you about the aliens I saw while camping in the woods. You never supported me, but had me checked into an asylum for my delusions. Well, I was right, and you were wrong. Aliens exist and they are back on this planet. I'm the only one who can stop them. Now, I bet you wish you'd supported me and given me the money I asked you for, so I could protect every human on the planet. If you'd supported me, maybe you'd still be alive or maybe not. I don't know. At least I wouldn't have had to kill you to get the money that should have been mine." He spent the next thirty minutes alternating between crying, screaming at the portrait of his parents and repeating how much he hated them until he felt better. Once he had exhausted himself, he turned off the light and crawled back into bed with a smile on his face. Aliens existed and soon he would have his own to experiment on. Then he would show the world the truth.

"Hey, Alister, we made the paper," Shelley shouted as he burst into my room waving the newspaper above his head. We hadn't gotten to bed until four in the morning and I was still tired.

"What time is it?" I asked.

"Nine o'clock," Shelley grinned when he heard me groan. "Sucks to be woken up before you're ready, doesn't it?"

"How long have you been waiting to do this?" I asked with a chuckle.

"Months," Shelley answered, "and it was totally worth the wait. Anyway, breakfast is almost ready, and you and your Mother must meet with Axel Farrel who will be here in an hour. I doubt he got enough sleep either since he had to fly here from Phoenix."

"Yeah, you're right," I said as I got out of bed and walked to the bathroom. Since I had to walk by Shelley to get there, I decided it would be a splendid idea to punch him in the arm on my way. He must have thought it was a superb idea too because he punched me right back with a gigantic smile on his face.

"Hurry up, Sire," he mocked. "Aileene and Bernie are almost ready and won't leave you any food if you're not ready in ten minutes."

That was enough to motivate me to hurry but I kept our conversation going in thought-speak as I showered.

Did my mom go to the bank already?

Yeah, your mom, my mom, Bernie's mom, Tobias and Josef took one of the SUVs in the garage and went to the bank to empty the safe deposit boxes.

It's amazing that they kept the IDs, cash and documents they got from the shifters who came back to Theria at the bank, I sent as I washed my hair.

Yeah, it's even more amazing that there are millions of dollars in cash in there, too; and we get to use those funds while we're here on Earth. Dude, we're totally rich—cha-ching, Shelley sent with enthusiasm.

Well, technically, I own Rex Industries and all the other companies around the world that are part of that business. It's all part of the Royal Treasury, I sent back.

Okay, so, you're totally rich, Shelley amended. *By the way, how much do I get paid as one of your knights?* He asked.

"You don't get paid," I said as I stepped from the bathroom to the bedroom and rummaged through my backpack for some clean clothes. "It's an honor to serve the King as one of his knights," I said flippantly and stumbled forward from the force of the pillow Shelley threw at me.

"Yeah, it's an honor to serve you, Your Majesty," Shelley said with a mocking bow, "you look so regal in your royal towel."

Laughing, I walked back into the bathroom to finish getting ready. *You know, I haven't thought about how much to pay you and Bernie, I suppose I need to pay Mkali, too. We didn't have to think about money in Theria. How much should I give everyone?* I sent as I dressed.

Let's ask your mother, she was Queen for hundreds of years before you took over.

"Wonderful idea," I said when I finished dressing and walked back into the room. "I know we need to meet with Alex Farrel to give him information about what's been going on but I'm looking forward to beginning our road trip."

"Me, too. Have you tried to connect with the shifters on Earth yet, so we'll know where to go?" Shelley asked.

"Not yet, I want to wait until after we've met with Alex. I feel like we need to keep most of our plans to ourselves."

"Have you had another dream about this?" he asked.

"No, it's just a feeling. I don't know if it means anything but figure it won't hurt to keep this within our Inner Circle."

"Sounds good to me," Shelley answered and opened the door for us.

"By the way, what did the newspaper article say about the rescue?" I asked.

"I'll tell you on the way to breakfast. I'm hungry and if I hadn't had to wait for your sorry self to get ready, I'd already be eating heaps of bacon," Shelley answered with a chuckle.

"Bacon, why didn't you say so?" I exclaimed and quickened my pace.

CHAPTER FIVE

J liked Alex Farrel the moment I met him and my opinion of him continued to improve over breakfast. He had roguish charm and reminded me of a young Han Solo as he regaled us with tales of his exploits over breakfast. Josef joined us since he had been Alex's mentor, but the rest of the Tionchar rescue party ate in another part of the house. Josef wanted to leave with his team following breakfast because he wanted to keep our two missions separate.

Alex was in awe of Mother and kept stealing glances at her throughout the meal. Shelley retold the story of how we rescued the kids the night before. He added so many embellishments, I almost didn't recognize the events of the previous night. Everyone shared freely with Alex except for Aileene who was unusually quiet.

What's wrong, my love? I sent to her.

I'm not sure. But, I am cautious about sharing too many of our plans with anyone on Earth, she sent.

Do you have a problem with Alex? I asked.

Not really, I am just more suspicious of strangers when I first meet them.

That's true, I teased, *you tried to kill me the first time we met.*

Aileene snorted a laugh in a very un-lady like fashion while I laughed out loud. The rest of the table looked at us curiously and I waved off their questioning glances.

I'll trust your instincts, I sent and squeezed Aileene's hand under the table.

The rest of the meal was uneventful, but both Mother and Aileene took great delight in pouring as much real maple syrup on their pancakes as they could. They devoured great stacks of the soggy breakfast food. I think they had an eating contest but I'm not sure who won.

When we finished eating, Josef said his goodbyes and gave Alex a long embrace and kissed him on both cheeks. "It is good to see you again, my son, your time on Earth seems to have agreed with you. I look forward to when we can spend time together on Theria and maybe catch some of those fish we are always threatening to."

"It's been marvelous to see you, too, Josef. You are like a father to me. I know you well enough to know you are on some secret mission for King Phillip; contact me if you run into trouble." Alex said and turned away from Josef with a tear in his eye.

After Josef left, Mother and I took Alex into an office off the dining room so we could inform him of why we were on Earth. We also wanted to get his report on what had been happening while he was out of contact with Theria. The rest of our team was going with Tiffany on the bus into Bangor to buy clothes and other necessities we would need for our cross-country adventure.

Have fun, I sent our team as they left the house.

We will, honey, Mom sent back, *I'll bring some clothes for you as well, if we can find anything in your size.*

I'm looking forward to choosing clothes for you to wear, my mate, Aileene added with a laugh as they left. Even though Aileene could have stayed for the meeting with Mother and me, for some reason she didn't want Alex to know she was a Royal Dragon, or we were true-mates. I thought she was being overcautious, but I didn't tell her that.

Once everyone was out of the house, we briefed Alex on everything that had happened over the past fourteen years and told him we were on Earth to find the missing shifters. Mother reminded him that we would need complete identification packages for herself, me, Aileene, Bernie, Mkali and Shelley since none of us had official identities on Earth. Alex listened attentively to our tale and took notes on his tablet which he used to go over points when he needed more clarification.

"Of course, Ma'am, it is my pleasure to serve," Alex said solicitously when Mother had finished speaking. "But, please accept my heartfelt sorrow that you and King Phillip had to face such horrors. And you, Prince Alister, I am at your disposal to do whatever I can do to assist you on your quest," Alex finished with a smile.

I didn't correct the assumption that my father was still High King but nodded at Alex's assurance. "My Father indicated there were some problems on Earth that Tionchar usually takes care of, but I'm not sure of the extent of the problems."

Alex took a deep breath before he began. "I'm not sure either but I can tell you what I know. About a year ago ads ran on TV, radio and internet browsers warning against aliens and other paranormal creatures and the threat they represent to humanity. At first everyone treated these ads as a joke, but they became more sophisticated and generated fear among distinct people groups. Before long, a few state and federal congressmen and senators appeared on news channels calling for laws to protect 'decent folk.'

"Rex Industries has an extensive research department, and media and marketing experts and we started digging to see who was behind the fear campaign and counteracted the damaging ads. My team followed the money and discovered an organization called Hominum Primus, has funded the media blitz and has made generous contributions to each of the politicians calling for these laws to protect human interests."

"Is this organization dangerous?" Mother asked.

"Yes, and the more we dig into it, the more concerned I become. Not only is Hominum Primus running the overt ad campaign, they are also running a covert ad campaign on the dark web offering a substantial reward for proof of either an alien or a paranormal creature. It doesn't matter if the creature is dead or alive."

"Where did this group come from?" I asked.

Alex swiped the screen on his tablet and started typing. After a moment of this our tablets lit up as Alex sent all the information to Mother and me. I looked at my screen and saw a picture of a man dressed in a suit. His skin was tan, his hair was blond and he was looking at the camera and smiling. His smile didn't meet his eyes and I had the impression of the dead eyes of a great white shark. Even through the photograph I could feel the intensity of his stare.

Alex continued. "It took more digging but we found out this man is behind Hominum Primus and their activities. His name is Neil Paterson and he's the head of Paterson Munitions. Neil's great-great-grandfather founded Paterson Munitions during World War One. This was one of the most successful companies at war profiteering, because they sold weapons and protective equipment to every side in the war.

"The company grew over the years by taking over their competition by any means necessary. They are one of the largest suppliers of weapons to every country in the world. Most of the current US defense contracts are being serviced by Paterson Munitions or one of their shadow companies. They also have an army of mercenaries for hire that supports company interests in other countries around the world. It is an enormously powerful company and many of their business dealings are shady, bordering on illegal. Neil Paterson inherited sole control of Paterson Munitions after his parents died in a car accident five years ago.

"However, one of the most important items we discovered about Neil Paterson occurred thirteen years ago. Please hit the tab labeled Ashton Center at the bottom of the tablet. According to public records, Neil Paterson entered the Ashton Center thirteen years ago for drug rehabilitation, but it's more concerning than that. I'll play a recorded excerpt from a session with his doctor for you."

Good morning, Neil, and how do you feel today?

Feel? How do I feel? I feel betrayed by my family for sending me here because I told the truth, and I'm terrified that aliens are taking over the Earth.

Yes, aliens—let's start with that. Why do you believe aliens are taking over the Earth?

I've already told you a dozen times and you take notes every time. You're probably recording each of our sessions. I'm not stupid you know.

No, you're not. In fact, you measure at the genius level on all your IQ tests and are one of the youngest graduates ever seen at MIT. But sometimes great intelligence can place a burden on other centers of our brains and lead to a disconnect from reality. Your brain is unique, but I hope that with the proper treatment we can help center you in reality once again. Please tell me your story again.

Fine. After graduating from college, I felt restless and tired of taking standard classes from stuffy universities. So, I took a journey of discovery around the world. After years of searching, I made my way home and camped at one place I loved as a kid, Baxter State Park. One night I woke up because I had to go and I headed into the trees to do my business. Suddenly there was a sound like a tear and then there were hundreds of people standing in the meadow where there had been no one before. They walked towards the trail and disappeared until there were only seven adults left holding three sleeping children. I don't know what they did to close the tear but before it closed, I saw a dragon, a bear and a unicorn standing on the other side.

Alex touched the tablet and the recording stopped playing. I sat back on the couch and thought about what I'd just heard. This man, Neil Paterson, had seen our exodus from Theria all those years ago and became convinced aliens had invaded the planet.

"Well, this is a problem," Mother commented.

"I'm not sure what the other members of Tionchar have been doing to counteract the damage Paterson's been doing. But I've been using the resources of Rex Industries to counter the stories coming out about aliens. I've also been trying to calm any growing hysteria amongst the population. Unfortunately, some people look for excuses to express their hatred towards people different than they are and have embraced the messages coming out about aliens and paranormal creatures.

"So far, there has been limited violence in this country but other countries around the world have passed laws to protect humanity. Unfortunately, these have been used to further erode basic human rights in countries that were already known for oppressing their citizens. Perhaps if you would give me the names and locations of other members of Tionchar I can help coordinate an effort to counteract Hominum Primus and what they're trying to do," Alex finished.

I shook my head, "I appreciate your willingness to coordinate efforts but there is a reason they have organized Tionchar the way they have. Now that we're on Earth, we'll be able to coordinate our response and get to the bottom of everything here. Thank you for the information you've gathered and for your faithfulness."

"Well done, Alex," Mother said. "We will keep you informed on what we discover and how you can help us in our efforts."

"Very well," Alex answered and for a microsecond I could see an expression of anger and frustration cross his face. Almost immediately, the solicitous expression he had been wearing the whole time we'd been speaking soon replaced that flash of irritation.

"You've explained why you need new identities for yourselves and," he looked down at his tablet, "Mkali, Bernie and Shelley, but who is this Aileene? Why do you need a new identity for her?" Alex asked.

Mother opened her mouth to speak but I jumped in before she could. "She is a representative from Eutheria and is traveling with us because of a boon I owed Lord Moss. She is part of his Court and it overjoyed him when we informed him she would come with us."

Alex looked at me shrewdly. "I see there is more to this story, but it's not my place to ask for details you don't wish to give. Very well, I will plan for your new identities." He looked at the expensive watch on his wrist and continued. "A man named Sinclair will be here in two hours to create your documents. In the meantime, we should make sure you have access to bank accounts and the resources you'll need while you're on Earth."

For the next two hours we handled paperwork on our tablets and Alex gave Mother and me access to Rex Industries. He gave us access as Beatrice and Alister Rex because we would use our actual names when our identities were created. I shared Aileene's concerns about revealing she was a Royal Dragon with Mother using thought-speech. So we decided to give Aileene the name of Aileene Drake for her identification. I wanted to surprise Bernie and Shelley, but I gave their last names to Alex and he laughed as he made a note of my choice. We also decided that Mkali's last name should also be Rex for her new identity but would ask her when she returned.

Theria

Royal Palace

Phillip

I could hear the crowd laughing and cheering but couldn't see them because I was on the bottom of what my friends called a 'dog pile.'

"Get off me, you big oaf," I shouted as I shoved the butt of the grizzly bear sitting on my chest. Stavros grunted as he rolled off my aching body. Albert was grinning as he offered his hand to help me up. I couldn't help groaning as I stood and stretched my back, thankful for my fast healing ability.

"I thought we agreed that we wouldn't shift into our natural forms while we played this ridiculous game," I moaned.

"No Phillip, we all agreed that you wouldn't shift into your dragon, we never said the rest of us wouldn't shift." Fritz said with a laugh.

"But—," I began.

"It's not our fault you didn't double check the wording of our agreement before we started playing." Stavros laughed as he shook a finger at me.

"It's still your ball," Gustav said as he handed me the instrument of so much of my pain.

"This game of football makes little sense to me. So far it just seems like someone yells 'hike' and the rest of you jump on top of me. If I'm not mistaken, on the last play Stavros was bouncing up and down on my chest in his grizzly bear form," I grumbled.

"Again, it's not our fault you don't know how to play. Weren't you the one bragging you could beat us at any game we came up with?" Fritz asked.

I sighed in resignation because my boasting was coming back to haunt me. "Do we really need to have this crowd here to watch the game? It's humiliating."

"On Earth, they always play the game in front of a crowd. Now, are you going to keep whining or are you ready to try again?" Albert asked.

"Okay," I moaned. "I'm ready." I was determined to score a point, so this time I tried another tactic. When Gustav yelled 'hike' I started running backwards trying to gain enough room to run around my friends. Unfortunately, they anticipated my intentions and rushed me from four different directions. Before I could jump over Stavros who was rushing me from the front, Fritz dove at my legs, Albert hit me from the right side and Gustav hit me from the left. Stavros laughed as he jumped in the air and turned one-hundred-eighty degrees as he changed into his bear. As I fell to the ground, Stavros landed on my face with his big, hairy, butt.

I could hear the crowd cheering as I shoved my friend off me, again.

"The score is twenty-five to zero." Stavros shouted after he shifted back to his human form. "It's your ball again, Sire," Gustav laughed as he handed me the ball.

A child in the crowd diverted my attention as he talked with his dad.

"Dad, what game are they playing?"

"The Historian told us they're playing football with the King."

"It doesn't look like any football game I ever saw on Earth," the boy remarked.

There was a sinking feeling in my stomach and when I looked at the grinning faces of my four friends, I knew I'd been had.

"Oops," Fritz laughed. "It looks like he figured out our ruse."

"I'm going to bring the pain," I shouted and launched myself at my friends with an enormous grin on my face. The crowd may have come to watch a football game, but we treated them to a royal rumble between the five of us that hadn't been seen for hundreds of years. We laughed like boys again as we reveled in the joy of friendship and being alive. When we finally exhausted ourselves, we were beaten, bloody and laughing so hard, tears streamed down our faces.

"Whose idea was this?" I gasped as we lay on the grass.

"Fritz," the others confessed.

I leaned up on one elbow and lifted an eyebrow at the most strait-laced member of our group. "You?" I asked incredulously and Fritz just shrugged. "What's gotten into you?"

"Alister," Fritz, Stavros, Gustav, and Albert answered at the same time with a laugh.

Lying back down in the grass, I listened to the crowd disperse as servants invited them into the palace for an after-game celebratory feast. I'm not sure what they were celebrating except watching me get beaten by my friends, but at least they would enjoy a superb meal. I was grateful for their friendship but realized that they knew more about my son than I did and felt despondent about that.

"Hey Grumpy, what's going on in that head of yours?" Stavros asked lightly.

"Grumpy?" Albert asked.

Fritz snorted as he added, "Grumpy—I'd forgotten we started calling Phillip that after Beatrice came to live at the palace. Phillip would feel bad for the way he treated Beatrice, but instead of talking to her, he would just get grumpy."

"You want me to talk?" I ground out. "Fine, I'll talk." I placed my hands under my head and stared up at the fluffy white clouds moving across the sky. My friends silently waited for me to respond, but it still took me a few minutes to gather my thoughts.

"I've missed so much of Alister's life and you all know my son so much better than I do. I'm grateful that you cared for him so well and have helped him grow into the man he is today, but I wasn't there for him."

"Well, that's just stupid," Albert said beside me. Before I could respond he continued. "Did you choose to leave your son as you and Beatrice lay comatose for thirteen years? No, you didn't. We know that and Alister does, too. I may have had the honor of raising Alister for the same thirteen years, but you and Beatrice spent the first five years of his life showing him the right path and you let him know how much you loved him. Fiona and I only built on the foundation you started."

"That may be true, but once again, Alister is off cleaning up another one of my messes and I'm not with him. I'm grateful that Beatrice gets to spend time with our son on Earth, but can't help feeling that he will resent me for piling another of my problems on his shoulders when he won't be prepared for it," I admitted with a sigh.

This time Gustav broke the silence, by laughing.

"How can you laugh at my pain?" I demanded.

"Don't misunderstand me, my friend," Gustav countered. "I'm not laughing at your pain, but at the notion that Alister isn't prepared. While on Earth, he will have complete access to Miriam, Frieda, Fiona and Beatrice. Not only that, Josef has his group he's trained to help find the missing shifters.

"Let's not forget Aileene, another Royal Dragon and Bernadette and Sheldon who have already faced down more dangers than we ever did at their ages. Oh, and one more thing, the most important of all, An'Ceann has taken such an interest in Alister that he appears to him often."

"An'Ceann appears to Aileene as well," Albert added.

"Alister is more than prepared for whatever problems he will encounter on Earth," Stavros said.

"Then I suppose he really doesn't need me at all, and I don't have any hope of building a relationship with my son," I added glumly.

"Don't make me sit on you again, you idiot," Stavros growled. "Just because Alister is capable doesn't mean he doesn't want a relationship with you."

"Phillip," Gustav said softly. "I can only imagine the pain you're going through, but I will encourage you to trust us when we tell you that Alister has an amazing ability to love the people around him and draw them into his circle. You are his father and even though you weren't there for the past thirteen years, you have more years ahead to build the relationship you want with your son."

"Alister always knew that he was adopted by Fiona and me. He knows we couldn't love him more if he'd been born to us, and he loves us. He also hoped to one day meet his birth parents and have relationships with them. Thanks to your son, and everything he did to defeat Dimitri, and save you and Beatrice, you can build a new relationship with him. Don't let your fear and guilt push you away from what can be, because you focus too much on what you lost," Albert finished.

Could it really be that simple? I wondered to myself. Could I choose to move forward with my son and build something new?

Yes, a deep voice said into my mind. *It won't be easy, but it is that simple.*

An'Ceann? I asked timidly.

You are correct, he answered with a chuckle. *Alister also wants to have a relationship with you. If I may suggest, when you communicate with your son while he's on Earth, talk about more than the details of the mission; get to know who he is.*

I will, thank you. And, thank you for taking such wonderful care of Alister.

An'Ceann laughed again. *You're welcome, my son, he's fun to watch. Almost as much fun as it was to watch you play football earlier. The look on your face when you realized those four had tricked you, was priceless; you made my day.*

An'Ceann dropped the connection and once again I was alone with my thoughts of rebuilding my family and adding to it with Aileene. For the first time in months, my heart felt light.

"Thanks guys, I'm grateful for your friendship and for helping me remember what's important," I said to my friends.

"You're welcome," Albert answered for everyone. "Are you ready to play football the real way now?"

"No, I think I'd rather hear about how Gustav is getting along with Seraset. You've been out on a few dates, right?" I asked.

Gustav stood up and walked away. "I'd rather talk about anything else," he hedged.

"Oh, no you don't," I said as I stood and tackled him to the ground.

"Dogpile on Gustav until he tells us everything," I shouted and the rest of my friends were laughing as they piled on us. Stavros shifted into his bear and his hairy butt was once again in my face. I knew everything would be all right.

Alister

Earth

The others returned from their shopping trip just after I had gathered sandwich makings in the kitchen. Mother, Bernie, Shelley, Mkali and Aileene each met with Sinclair and he took their pictures for their passports and other identifying documents. Mom helped me prep lunch and she told me a few stories about their shopping trip. It bummed me that I missed seeing Aileene's reaction to her recent experiences but knew the issues we covered with Alex were essential to our mission.

Once they had finished with Sinclair, everyone sat around the large island and I made sandwiches based on what they wanted. It surprised Alex that I would make a sandwich for him, but he finally accepted one after I insisted. He thanked me repeatedly for the kind gesture; it was embarrassing. Shelley complained, good-naturedly, that I hadn't given him enough meat on his, so I smacked him in the back of the head and took a bite of his sandwich before handing it back to him.

"That'll teach you to complain," Bernie elbowed Shelley in the ribs as the rest of us laughed.

"Man, you ate half my sandwich in one bite," Shelley said as he rubbed the back of his head.

"And if you're not quiet, I'll eat the other half," Aileene grinned evilly.

As we ate, I watched how well Alex interacted with my friends. I wondered what it must have been like for him to live in isolation for so many years on Earth; both before my parent's capture and the years when there weren't any answers from Theria. He enjoyed making everyone laugh and asking about the details of their lives. He was really interested in Mkali and the experiences she had growing up on Earth. When she finished her tale, he asked if he could give her a hug and she cried a bit because of his tenderness.

Aileene watched how Alex connected with everyone and smiled at his antics. When he asked more about her, she shared amusing stories about her life in Eutheria but never let on that she was a Royal Dragon. Shelley was describing the battle with Dimitri to Alex when Sinclair stuck his head in the kitchen to let us know he finished our documents.

He was surprised when I asked him what he would like on his sandwich and was very polite as he requested a peanut-butter and jelly sandwich with the crusts cut off. As Sinclair ate, Bernie asked questions about his profession.

"How did you get into the document forging business?"

"Miss Bernadette, I'm not a document forger. I create authentic documents, which will pass the scrutiny of any government on the planet; I just create them without their knowledge," Sinclair said primly as he dunked his sandwich in his glass of milk.

"My apologies," she said. "How did you get into the document creation business?"

Sinclair looked to Alex, who nodded, before he continued. "It's a family business, you could say, which goes back generations. Even though we are human, we know about Theria and have dedicated our lives to help Therians here on Earth. Although we work for the King of Theria, most of my family members work exclusively for Rex Industries to create what's necessary."

"And you serve well, Sinclair. I don't know of anyone else who does work half as good as you do," Alex praised the gentle man who continued to consume his sandwich.

When Sinclair had finished his last bite, he dabbed his lips with the paper napkin I had given him and then folded it five times and stuck the small square in the briefcase he had brought into the kitchen. "Thank you for the sandwich," Sinclair said as he bowed from the waist.

He took six manila envelopes from his briefcase and handed them to us as he gave us our alternative names. "Beatrice Rex, Alister Rex,

Mkali Rex, Aileene Drake, Bernadette Dufus and Sheldon Goofay. Inside your envelope you will find bank cards, drivers licenses and credit cards for each of the adults. Miss Mkali, inside your envelope you only have school identification and a passport. The Rex family have passports from Canada complete with entry stamps. Miss Aileene, you have a British passport complete with an entry stamp into the US and others from trips you have taken within Europe. Mr. Sheldon and Miss Bernadette have US passports.

"Not only do you have these physical documents, but your identities have been well documented electronically also. If anyone investigates your past, they will find digital footprints from the day you each were born in your respective countries. I am quite pleased with this work. One more thing," he reached back into his briefcase and handed each of us the latest smartphone. "Each of these are untraceable and have the best encryption capabilities possible. This technology is decades ahead of the best any government on Earth has at this time." Sinclair looked at Alex and said, "I hope I didn't overstep sir because I didn't ask your permission first, but I thought it would be prudent to give these to our guests."

"And you were correct," Alex said with a smile. "That's why you are so valuable to the company Sinclair, thank you."

Sinclair nodded and continued, "Do any of you have questions?"

Shelley nodded as he asked, "Why did you pick Goofay for my last name and Dufus for Bernie's?"

Sinclair looked flustered for a moment before answering. "Those are the names Mr. Farrel gave me to use for you. He said Mr. Alister chose them for you."

Shelley and Bernie looked puzzled at my enormous grin and it took them a moment to work it out for themselves. Mom got it first and stifled a laugh with her hand over her mouth.

Bernie's eyes grew wide, and she spluttered. "My last name is doofus and his is goofy?"

Everyone, including the prim Sinclair, burst out laughing at her indignation. Shelley was torn between being offended and laughing; he gave in to the laughter. Eventually Bernie saw the humor and joined the rest of us.

"I guess I can't blame you," Shelley added when he finished laughing. "If I changed your name, I probably would have made it worse."

After Sinclair finished passing out our new identities it didn't take him long to load his equipment into his van and drive away. Before he left, I gave him ten thousand dollars cash to thank him for his service. He was surprised and grateful. As he was driving away Alex looked at his watch and said, "I've got to get back to Arizona tonight, so I need to be on my way. Here is all my contact information," he handed me a business card, "please contact me for updates on the Paterson situation."

I surprised him with a hug as I thanked him for his help. "I'll keep you informed if we run into any trouble with Paterson."

"Please let Josef know I missed saying goodbye to him and if he has time to visit me in Phoenix, I would enjoy having a meal with him."

"I will let him know," I said then added mentally, *When we return to Theria, you are welcome to come back with us. We will have another member of Tionchar take your place so you can come back home.*

Thank you, Sire, that is a kind offer. Alex answered and wiped his hand over his face, trying to hide the emotions that had surfaced there. Without another word, he got in the back of his car and the driver drove them away.

We spent the rest of the day at the house and told Tiffany that we would start our journey the next morning. Aileene showed me all the things she had bought for herself while she shopped and showed me the things she had picked out for me. She told me how helpful Bernie and Shelley had been to show her the clothes I would like best.

She admitted it surprised her I liked flowery shirts so much but bought me each of the ones our friends had shown her. Once I saw the shirts Bernie and Shelley picked out, I didn't feel bad about the last names I chose for them. She was excited to see me wear one shirt she picked out for me, I changed into one right then. It was covered in pink, yellow and purple flowers on a black background. Aileene smiled so proudly, it became my new favorite, even though I hadn't been a fan of flowery shirts before this.

After dinner we found ourselves in the media room preparing to watch a movie on a screen almost the same size as a regular movie theater. Shelley informed us that we would finish the third Hobbit movie since Aileene still hadn't seen it. They outfitted the media room with a movie theater popcorn popper and soda fountains. Once everyone had the snacks they wanted, we started the movie.

This time Aileene didn't destroy the room when Smaug was killed; but Mother almost did.

CHAPTER SIX

eil Paterson

I reread the article about the children rescued in Baxter State Park and screamed out my frustration. If those idiots I hired had been where they were supposed to, I would have an actual alien to show the world. But they left the campground and I had nothing to show for it. The only thing that cheered me up was another article lower down on the front page reporting the freak explosion that claimed the lives of three men after they stopped for gas. At least I wouldn't have to give those idiots their last paychecks.

My phone buzzed and I answered, "Yes."

"Mr. Paterson, this is Caine," came the voice over the line.

"Do those kids know anything about who rescued them?" I asked.

"No," Caine answered, "I interviewed them using my FBI identity and they know nothing. For the record, that cover is compromised so I cannot use it again."

"That doesn't matter to me," I snarled, "those kids must know something, and I want you to use any means necessary to get information out of them."

"That won't be necessary, sir," Caine answered. "The children knew nothing, but the parents remembered seeing a group of about twenty hikers board a Trafero Line bus and leave the park two hours before they found the children."

"Where is that bus now?" I asked.

"The manager of the local branch of the bus line is unwilling to provide that information," Caine replied.

"I'm sure if you apply the right amount of pain, the manager will gladly provide it then," I seethed.

"Sir, I know how to handle this situation and want to caution you about leaving a trail of bodies behind. Whoever you hired to take care of the men with the explosion was sloppy and left too much evidence behind. Not only were the three former employees killed but many bystanders were also injured. That will bring our activities to the attention of the authorities and we don't want that."

"Don't you dare tell me what to do or how to do it. If you're not willing to follow my orders, you just think about how I fired the last people who failed me," I screamed. "Do your job, find that bus and then bring me those aliens. I don't care if they're dead or alive. Do I make myself clear?"

"Yes, sir, you are perfectly clear. I will do what you ask, but I will do it my way with a minimal number of casualties. Caine out."

I looked at the phone in my hand for a moment and thought about what Caine said. He's been useful to me in the past, and has carried out every task I've given him so maybe I would do things his way. "Caine you're good, but it never hurts to have insurance," I muttered as I searched through my contacts on the phone and called the number listed. "It's me, here's what I want you to do—"

Alister

Maine

We left the house outside Bangor, Maine at ten in the morning. Everyone was excited to get on the road. Before we left the house, I asked Tiffany for a map of the US so we could plan our route. After she gave me the map, she walked out to get the bus ready for travel.

The rest of us gathered in the dining room as I tried to find our missing people through my ability to connect with all shifters. It wasn't necessary for me to close my eyes to connect, but I found it hard to concentrate as Shelley made goofy faces at me.

I opened myself to the connection with other shifters, and was at once filled with an infusion of strength from those surrounding me. Aileene and I are always connected because we're mates but it had been a while since I'd done this with others. So the added power was a pleasant experience. I pushed my awareness outward, and could feel other shifters connecting with me one at a time. Each connection flared with a flash of light in my mind and then settled into a steady pulse, like a heartbeat. I sent a feeling of hope, along with a slight amount of my energy, towards each shifter I was connected with, so they would know they weren't alone.

I opened my eyes but kept the connections active in the back of my mind. "Well, the wonderful news is I can sense all the shifters on Earth and including those of us in the room there are sixty-one; but the grim news, I'm not really sure how we can locate them."

"Can you sense direction and distance?" Miriam asked me.

I thought for a few moments as I looked again at the connection I had with the shifters. It was easy for me to sense the people with me in the room and a group of ten shifters who were moving away from our location; that would be Josef and his group. "Yes, I can sense the direction and can feel which shifters are farther away," I finally answered.

"Great," Miriam nodded encouragingly, "I want you to point in the direction where you sense the closest shifters."

Smirking, I quickly pointed my finger to those in the room with me.

"Hilarious," Mom muttered.

I laughed and concentrated on the next closest group of shifters, apart from Josef and his team, and pointed. Then I shifted my hand a slightly as I pointed to a second group of shifters. "There are two groups close together along these paths. The second one has five shifters but the first one only has three."

"You pointed at two distinct points to the southwest," Miriam said as she aligned the map with my pointing finger and drew lines from Bangor, Maine to the Gulf of Mexico. "If I'm correct, we will find our missing shifters somewhere along this route."

"And I'm sure you're correct Miriam," Mother interjected. "You are a master tactician."

Miriam smiled at the compliment and looked at the map again and traced a path. "If I may suggest, why don't we head towards Hartford, Connecticut and we can make adjustments to our route as we get closer to our missing people."

We agreed to that and left the house to give Tiffany our destination.

"This is a very comfortable way to travel," Aileene sighed next to me where she cuddled under my arm. We'd been on the road for almost six hours and except needing to stop for food three times, we'd been driving the whole time. The bus was luxurious with two bathrooms and a choice of games and movies on the extra-large tablets at each of our seats. Aileene and Mother had never traveled this way before and were fascinated by being able to sit in comfort while we flew down the road at sixty miles an hour or more. It was pleasant to sit and relax with Aileene sitting by my side. My tablet chimed to show an incoming message from Josef. I kissed the top of Aileene's head and apologized for moving and reached forward to grab my tablet from my backpack.

"I was comfortable," Aileene growled good-naturedly and I chuckled until I read the message from Josef, which sobered me at once.

Danger, Sire! You and the others may be compromised. What is your location? How far are you from Hartford?

Grabbing my tablet, I moved towards the front of the bus to speak with Tiffany. As I walked, I broadcast a message to the others on the bus. *Josef sent me a warning that we may be compromised. Gather your things. We will leave the bus quickly when we stop.*

I sat in the front seat to the right of the driver and asked Tiffany where we were.

"Specifically? We're on the I-84 about ten miles out of Hartford. Do you want to stop for an early dinner?"

"Probably, let me check something," I answered as I typed the answer furiously on my tablet.

Take the Simmons Rd. exit, head south and park in The Home Depot lot. We'll meet you there. Stay alert.

After giving Tiffany the new instructions, I made my way back to my seat, and I explained what was going on to those sitting around me. We must have been close to the exit Josef had given me because I could feel the bus slowing as I stuffed my belongings into my backpack.

I laughed when I saw the expression on Aileene's face and instead of anxiety I saw eagerness. "You hope someone tries to interfere with us, don't you?" I asked.

"Oh, yes," Aileene smiled widely. "I have enjoyed this drive in comfort but would prefer to stretch my wings against an enemy." Her face grew serious as she narrowed her eyes. "These are our people, they are ours to protect. No one will harm those in our care."

Since everyone on the bus, except Tiffany, could hear what Aileene said, they cheered at her statement. It's a splendid thing Tiffany's such a skillful driver or she might have crashed at the sudden noise from the previously quiet passengers. When we stopped five minutes later, Tiffany looked confused when we filed off the bus and I asked her to open the luggage compartments. As she worked, I talked to her.

"Tiffany, I'm afraid I have some grim news."

She looked startled at my statement but finished what she was doing. "What kind of grim news? Does it explain why you're getting off the bus?"

Josef walked up to us while Frank and Tobias led the others away towards a nearby restaurant. *Sire, do you mind if I speak with Tiffany?* Josef sent.

Not at all. Turning to our driver I said, "Josef will answer you. I want to give you my assurance that we will take care of you."

"Hello Tiffany," Josef said. "I will be happy to answer your questions but I'm afraid the answers may cause you more problems…"

As I walked towards the restaurant, Shelley walked up beside me. Gone was my goofy friend and in his place was a Knight who took his job seriously. "What's going on?" he asked.

"We've got someone tracking us and they're not afraid of getting their hands dirty. Josef sent me two files just before we stopped. The first file showed a story about three men dying when their car mysteriously exploded at a gas station close to Baxter State Park. The second file showed an explosion at the Trafero Bus Line primary office in Bangor. Josef feels like we're being hunted, and I agree with him."

"But who even knows we're here?" Shelley asked.

I told Shelley about Neil Paterson as we made our way to the restaurant.

Shelley's expression was grim when I finished. After a moment, he brightened and smiled his cheeky grin. "You know, in a way, we are aliens."

"Yes, we are," I agreed. "But I don't think Paterson will like the outcome if he gets close to us."

Caine

"Mr. Paterson, this is Caine."

"Do you have a status update for me?" Paterson asked stiffly.

"I do, but before I report you need to know that your secondary team is hampering my efforts to locate our quarry," I said into the phone with barely restrained fury. "If you continue to use the bumbling idiots who insist on blowing everything up in their path, me and my crew will disappear like a fart in the wind."

There was silence on the other end of the phone for a few minutes and then Paterson spoke so quietly I had to turn up the volume on the phone to hear him.

"Caine, you seem to be laboring under the delusion that I work for you and that won't do. While I will concede that you are fantastic at what you do, you aren't the only one I can rely on. If you ever speak to me in that manner again, you will displease me. And since I've sent you to visit many people in the past who have displeased me, you know exactly what you can expect if I give an order for your termination. Do you understand me?"

My tone was more respectful when I resumed speaking to Paterson. "My apologies sir, I'm just frustrated that the secondary team made such a mess in Bangor by blowing up the Trafero office and killing everyone inside. This has drawn the attention of the authorities."

"Yes, yes—I will deal with their enthusiasm," Paterson said placatingly. "Now, let's try this again, what do you have to report?"

"Trafero bus number twenty-fourteen departed Bangor, Maine on June eighteen en-route to Baxter State Park to pick up nineteen passengers who had been camping in the park. They were taken to a private, walled estate near the Bangor City Forest and continued their journey today, June twenty. The receptionist at the Trafero office gave me the name of the driver. Her name is Tiffany Krewe and she has been with the company for ten years. She reported their destination was the downtown Marriott in Hartford, Connecticut. The bus is scheduled to arrive at six this evening."

"That's the information I received from the secondary team leader. It appears the receptionist told you the truth. Every employee confirmed that information in the office before we eliminated them. The delightful news for you is that none of those you spoke with this afternoon will ever be able to identify you. Isn't that fortunate?"

I answered respectfully, "Yes, sir, but I don't think it was necessary to eliminate anyone."

"I don't pay you to think, I pay you to do what I tell you to do." Paterson screamed into the phone. "We're dealing with aliens here, Caine. I don't think you understand the danger these beings present to humanity. We do not understand the technology they have or their ability to follow our movements. It's unfortunate for those people that they were in the wrong place at the wrong time, but I'm willing to sacrifice anyone to protect humanity from this deadly threat."

"Yes, sir," I replied.

Paterson took a few deep, cleansing breaths before speaking again. "Where are these aliens now?"

"I believe they are still en-route to the hotel in Hartford although we could not connect with the bus driver via radio or cell phone. It's also possible they heard about the slaughter at the head office and are in the wind. I will confirm with you once I have more information."

"Are you familiar with baseball, Caine?" Paterson asked. "Because you are at the plate with two strikes against you. Fail me one more time, and you're out."

Paterson ended the call and I was sure his next call would be to his secondary team leader. I'd have to watch my back.

Paterson

"I want you to gather information on this bus driver, Tiffany Krewe, and use it to find her. I don't care who you must kill to get the information, but I expect you to be more circumspect. It would be inconvenient if the FBI got involved in my affairs. Oh, and one more thing. Caine is being a bit of a problem; I expect you to carry out his termination at the proper time." Paterson sat back in his chair with a smile on his face as he reached for his drink.

Alister

Hershey, Pennsylvania

We pulled into the parking lot of the Hershey Park Hotel shortly after seven pm. Even though the group of shifters in New York was closer to Hartford, Josef suggested we head to Pennsylvania because he was concerned it would be easier for Paterson to find us in New York. Josef had obtained two identical tour buses which were even more luxurious than the one we had been on.

When I asked him about it, he just smiled and said, "It's good to have access to unlimited funds."

These buses didn't have a company name written on the sides and each pulled a Ford Expedition behind them. For all intents and purposes, they looked like privately owned vehicles.

Josef had convinced Tiffany to travel with us for her own safety. Thankfully, she didn't have any family to worry about, so she will remain with us for the time being. I'd contacted Alex Farrel and he was sending a private jet to Hershey the next day to take Tiffany wherever she wanted to go. Neither Josef nor I wanted Paterson to find Tiffany, for her sake.

Two of Josef's team members, Jason and Todd, had the licenses so they could drive our buses. Jason drove the bus my team was on and I could give adjustments to the directions as we got closer to the five shifters we were searching for. Miriam also helped with the directions and could use the map to plot our course. When we knew where we were heading, Frieda made room reservations.

When Mkali found out we were heading to Hershey she was beside herself with excitement. She shared that she had always wanted to visit the area when she lived on Earth, but never had the chance. She told us about the amusement park, the water park and the zoo with hundreds of animals. It was great to see her enthusiasm as she talked to us about the attractions. Even though our primary mission was to find the missing shifters, I was determined that we would also have fun; while staying alert for danger.

Our moms were excited about the chocolate factory tour and visiting the hotel spa. Mother was caught up in the excitement, even though she didn't really know what everyone was talking about. Aileene and I were searching for information about Hershey and the parks. When Aileene saw videos of the roller coasters she was giddy with excitement.

"Even though I can fly faster than that, it looks like such fun. Please tell me we can ride this together, my love," Aileene said while looking earnestly at me.

I smiled and answered, "I can't wait."

"Awww, look at you two," Shelley sniggered as he leaned over the back of our seats. "I think it's cute how you want to ride together on the roller coasters."

"Who will you be riding with?" I asked with a smirk.

"Bernie, of course," Shelley boasted.

"Is that so?" Bernie countered. "For your information, Mr. Assumption, I'll be riding with Mkali since she was thoughtful enough to ask me."

"But—" Shelley spluttered, "you're my girl."

"I am, but you've still got a lot to learn about relationships and it looks like I'm the one to teach you," Bernie said with a smile.

Shelley opened his mouth to respond so I took pity on him and interrupted. "Dude, I'm learning about relationships, too, but I know enough that the proper thing to say right now is, yes, dear."

Shelley looked at Bernie who just nodded her head. "Yes dear," he said woodenly.

Bernie kissed him on the cheek and the rest of us laughed.

Josef, Mother, Aileene and I met in Mother's suite after a late dinner where we discussed our plans for the next day. I also created a pinhole gate to Theria so we could keep Father updated on our progress. The information we'd uncovered about Neil Paterson and Hominum Primus concerned him. He relaxed once we assured him we were taking precautions and he suggested Josef liaise with Alex Farrel to stop this threat. I messaged Alex the address to our hotel so he could send Josef ten of the untraceable phones. He quickly responded that they would be aboard the plane he was sending to pick up Tiffany.

The next morning, Josef and his team, except for Tobias who would stay with Tiffany, would leave from the airport to seek members of Tionchar who had stopped reporting in. I had given Josef the names and locations of each of the shifters and his team would check each one. Josef and his team would also remain vigilant for any sign that Paterson was on our trail. We weren't taking these threats lightly, but the lack of contact convinced us we had given Paterson and his goons the slip.

After Josef left, Mother and Aileene talked at length about getting me more clothes because they didn't think I had enough. I tried to argue that I only needed one pair of pants, but my objections were ignored, and they talked about me as though I wasn't in the room. Since my life was being discussed without my input, I contacted the shifters who were living nearby. I opened my connection with them so I could speak with them via thought.

Hello, I sent, this is Alister Rex, can you hear me?

After a few minutes there was a tentative reply, *Prince Alister, is that really you?*

It is, who's this?

Dag Foim.

"Pardon me, but I contacted the local shifter, he says his name is Dag Foim," I informed my mother.

She clapped her hands in glee and laughed musically. "Oh, they're friends of mine and your father. It will be wonderful to see them again."

Nodding to her I asked, "What type of shifter are the Foims?"

"They're brownies," she answered matter-of-factly.

"I love brownies. We had many of them living throughout the castle in Eutheria. I am looking forward to meeting them," Aileene grinned.

"This may be a dumb question but what exactly is a brownie? I'm assuming you're not talking about the chocolate cake, right?" I asked.

"No, silly," Aileene laughed. "A brownie is a type of fairy that loves to cook, clean and is helpful. They have special abilities that allow them to keep homes in order and clothes clean and in good repair."

"We had troops of brownies at the palace in Theria and they oversaw housekeeping. Dag and Fal retired from service shortly before we left to visit Dimitri and were going to live in a cottage near the palace. Please inform Dag that I cannot wait to see him and his lovely wife, Fal," Mother said and then turned back to the project she was working on with Aileene.

Dag, Queen Beatrice sends her greetings and—

The Queen lives? Dag interrupted me.

My Mother and Father are both alive and well. Unfortunately, this isn't the right time to go into everything that happened, I answered.

My apologies for interrupting you, Sire, what message do you have from the Queen?

My mother wants me to inform you that she's looking forward to seeing you and your wife, Fal. Who else is with you?

Even across our mental link, I could sense Dag's immense sorrow as he responded. *Please thank the Queen for me. Unfortunately, my lovely bride is no longer with us but our son Tunn, his wife Meid and their children Teith and Abhold are.*

I am terribly sorry for your loss, Mr. Foim. Since we were connected mentally, I sent a pulse of love and comfort to him before I continued. *We have come to Earth to find those of you who we'd left behind when everyone else returned to Theria.*

You mean you're on Earth, and the Queen is as well? Dag sobbed through our connection.

We are and we want to bring you home, I replied.

The moment I walked into our room, a pillow hit me in the face. It took me a second to get my bearings and by that time, Shelley had thrown another pillow at me and was following up with the one in his hand. I did the only thing I could and lowered my shoulder and rushed the pillow wielding fiend, tackling him to the bed. For the next few minutes we were in a full out brawl complete with pillows, kicks, punches and major wrestling moves—and plenty of laughter.

Shelley ordered room service as I took a shower and got ready for bed. When I finished getting ready, Shelley took his turn and I answered the door to let in the waiter with the food. Before Shelley came out, I ate all the food we'd ordered and put the covers back on the plates. The look on Shelley's face was priceless, when he noticed I'd eaten all the food. I was laughing so hard, it was difficult for me to tell him I'd already placed a second order and it would be delivered shortly. He calmed down even more when the knock sounded at the door again with the second delivery. It was a marvelous way to finish the day.

Alister, are you asleep? Aileene's voice sounded in my head.

Not anymore, I sent with a laugh, *what's up?*

I'm having trouble sleeping because I'm so excited about tomorrow, can we talk for a while?

Sure, do you want me to come up to your room?

I would like that, but don't want to wake Mother. Why don't we just talk this way? Aileene suggested.

We talked via thought-speak about everything we'd experienced so far since coming to Earth. I could sense her anger through our connection when we talked about Neil Paterson and all the things Alex Farrel had shared with me. She was incensed about the people who were murdered to find us and wanted us to hunt down Neil Paterson right away.

It's better for us to take out enemies before they have a chance to gain strength and come for us, Aileene sent when I suggested we wait.

I know you're right but since we're not on Theria we need to be cautious of how we handle things. We're aware of Neil Paterson's agenda and know he's looking for us. We'll keep our eyes open and if any of his people come after us, they'll be sorry.

That appeared to calm her, and we talked about our plans for the next day for about an hour until we were both exhausted.

Goodnight, Alister, I love you, Aileene sent.

I love you too, sleep well, I answered sleepily and closed our mental connection.

Neil Paterson

Once again, I was awakened by the sound of my phone. I was groggy as I answered tersely, "What?"

"Sir, it's Caine and I've got unpleasant news to report. The bus never arrived in Hartford and the driver Tiffany Krewe has disappeared. I've spread the word throughout the Hominum Primus members to be on the lookout for the Trafero bus but we've hit a dead-end."

"Do not contact me until you have pleasant news for me, Caine. I don't care what you have to do, find those aliens," I shouted and hurled my phone against the brick fireplace in my room, shattering it. I was breathing heavily as I lay back down on my bed and tried to go back to sleep. Caine had outlasted his usefulness and I would make a call tomorrow that would guarantee he would never fail me again. That thought put a smile on my face and I could go back to sleep as I imagined the terrible day Caine would have tomorrow.

Alister

Hershey, Pennsylvania

Bernie, Shelley, Mkali, Aileene and I finally got into Hershey Park after a busy morning. Shelley and I were rousted out of our beds by my mother barging into our suite. She informed me that a tailor would measure me for new clothing before breakfast. Since I was so tall, it was almost impossible to find pants in my size in a store, so she was getting everything made for me by a tailor.

She also informed me she had been in contact with Dag Foim and Alex Farrel via phone and they were arranging the sale of Dag's home in Hershey. Rex Industries would buy his home through the real estate division, but everything would take about three days to carry out and we would wait at the hotel until they completed everything. She smiled brightly when she finished sharing all her information and walked out the door.

"Well, you can tell that your mother's used to being in charge,"

Shelley murmured and I laughed as I dressed in the only proper clothes that fit me. Before we left for breakfast there was a knock at the door, and I opened it to admit the man I assumed to be the tailor. It was clear by the shock on his face he wasn't expecting me to be as tall as I was. It was embarrassing for me to stand there while the tailor took my measurements to fit me for fresh clothes. He had to stand on a chair to measure my arms.

Shelley didn't help matters with his teasing. He was enjoying my discomfort so much I had to get back at him. After Mr. Randall had finished with me, I insisted that he fit Shelley for some clothing of his own. Shelley sobered at once and stopped laughing at me. That was fine by me, because it was my turn to laugh at him. Mr. Randall completed his measurements and told us he would put a rush order on the clothing and would have everything ready for us in a couple days.

"Thank you, Mr. Randall, but shouldn't I see some clothing samples so I can pick out what I like?" I asked.

"There's no need for that, Mr. Rex. Your mother and Miss Drake made the choices for you so you didn't have to worry about things like that."

"Great, I can't wait to see what they chose," I muttered sarcastically.

"You will look fabulous, I promise," he enthused as he left us.

"That went well," Shelley snickered and we both laughed.

The first ride we went on when we finally got into the park was Candymonium. This is the newest roller coaster in the park and there was a lengthy line to get on. We let Mkali pick the rides we would go on since she had waited so long to go to Hersheypark. The moms would enjoy a spa day and Jason had opted to come with us so we would have an even number for the rides. Bernie used to have problems with roller coasters but since she spent so much time training on the back of Aileene's dragon, she didn't struggle with motion sickness as much.

After waiting over an hour it was finally our turn to get on the ride. There were four seats per row so Bernie, Mkali, Aileene and I sat on the front row and Shelley and Jason sat on the second. I was worried I would be too tall for the ride, but the operator assured me it wouldn't be a problem. Candymonium was an amazing ride and I had as much fun listening to Aileene scream during the ride as I had on the ride itself. The drops, twists and turns were amazing and according to the ride operator, we reached seventy-six miles an hour during one turn. It wasn't as fun as flying, but it was still amazing.

We would ride one ride, get something to eat and then race to the next one. We played and laughed together, and we all took turns riding with Mkali, so she never had to sit alone. The park was about to close when Shelley suggested we visit the Kissing Tower.

"And why do you want to go to the Kissing Tower?" Mkali asked innocently.

"Well, um, because I'd like to see the entire park from the top of it" Shelley added lamely.

Mkali giggled as she added, "I'm just teasing you Shelley, I know you want to go to the tower so you can give Bernie a kiss."

"That sounds good to me," Aileene added. "I would also like to give Alister a kiss."

The view from the top of the tower was breathtaking as we looked over the rest of the park, and the town of Hershey. The top of the tower slowly rotated and Aileene and I stood on the opposite side of the tower from our friends, holding hands in the silence. I looked at Aileene and she had a serious look on her face.

"You know, Alister, I've loved having fun with you all day. Thank you for taking me to such an amazing place. I never thought riding roller coasters would be so much fun. I'm glad we get this chance to be alone so I can give you a kiss," she whispered as she leaned her face closer to mine. Just as I was moving in to place a gentle kiss on her lips she smiled brightly as she held up a silver-wrapped Hershey's Kiss in front of my face. Her action took me by surprise, so I barked out a laugh as I looked at her mischievous, blue eyes dancing with glee.

"You got me," I finally responded.

"I sure do," she said and stepped into my arms for an embrace. I got an actual kiss from Aileene after all.

CHAPTER SEVEN

$\mathcal{C}$aine wearily rubbed his face after getting back into the black SUV he'd parked across the street from where Finley and Oliver Smith lived with their parents. He'd taken a chance in using his FBI cover again, but felt it was worth the risk. The badge impressed the Smith parents, and the ruse worked. It frustrated Caine because this second interview was also a bust and he knew Paterson would send his clean-up team to take care of the family.

Too bad, the kids were kind of cute, even if they weren't much help because they still knew nothing. The youngest, Oliver insisted wolves rescued them, along with an angel, a giant and a bear named Shelley. The older kid, Finley still felt guilty that he led the others into the forest but he could give the name of one of his mysterious rescuers: Alister.

"What a waste of time," Caine muttered to himself as he updated his notes from the interview. He was interrupted when his phone buzzed with an incoming message from John, his second in command.

Paterson ordered your termination. Time to bug out.

As Caine reread the message he swore and composed a coded group message to the rest of his team telling them it was time to disappear.

Kappa, Rho, Alpha, Pi. We have struck an iceberg and are sinking by the head.

Satisfied he'd done everything for his team, he composed another message which would destroy the psychotic Paterson. This message contained a link to a secure server which held evidence he'd collected on every crime committed by Paterson and his organization Hominum Primus. He allowed himself a mean smile as he thought about the trouble Paterson would face once the news outlets and government agencies received the information packet.

"Try to stab me in the back, will you?" Caine said through gritted teeth as he continued typing his message with his right hand. He leaned to the side and pushed the start button with his left hand because it wasn't smart to stay in one place too long.

The resulting explosion blew out the front windows of the houses on both sides of the street.

Alister

The TV was playing in the background as I looked through the clothing that Mr. Randall delivered that morning. It was amazing how quickly he had everything made and had to wonder how much Mother paid him to put such a rush on it.

Alister, can we come in? Aileene sent.

I crossed to the door and opened it widely. Not only was Aileene standing in the doorway, everyone else was, too. I grinned and gave Aileene a quick hug and kiss and stepped aside to let them in.

"Oh look, Fiona, Alister's new clothes are here," Mother said as she brushed past me and kissed me on the cheek.

"Good morning, Son," Mom said as she gave me a hug and brushed past me to sort through the pile on the sofa.

"Well, good morning to all of you," I laughed as I shut the door once everyone entered. Our suite wasn't as spacious as Mother's but there was still enough room for everyone to sit comfortably.

"Is Shelley awake yet?" Bernie asked.

"No, he's still sleeping; can't you hear the snoring?" I asked with a smile.

"C'mon Mkali, let's go poke a sleeping bear," Bernie grinned, grabbed a bottle of water off the counter and led her squire into Shelley's room.

"Try not to get water everywhere," I called after them.

When I turned around, everyone was staring at the TV, so I grabbed the remote and turned up the volume.

I'm standing in front of the home of Michael and Jessica Smith, the parents of Finley and Oliver Smith, two of the children miraculously rescued in Baxter State Park after getting lost in the woods. Behind me you can see the broken windows of their home, but their windows aren't the only ones. Last night an explosion killed a man claiming to be an FBI agent. His vehicle exploded shortly after he interviewed the family about their ordeal on June eighteenth. An anonymous FBI source has confirmed that the person killed was not part of any ongoing investigation; his identity is still undetermined.

This is the third unexplained explosion in as many days, and both the FBI and Homeland Security will coordinate in a joint investigation. We will keep you informed with the latest news and information as we continue to investigate the truth and give it to you. This is Courtney Street with WXRG channel six, back to you Peter.

My phone chimed with an incoming message from Alex Farrel.

I'm sure you've seen the news of the explosion; I've got connections inside both the FBI and Homeland Security and will get information to you ASAP.

Thank you, Alex. Can you please also keep Josef in the loop on this? He is better equipped to deal with these matters.

Will do, Sire, enjoy your day. We'll take care of this.

I appreciate it Alex, good luck. I messaged and put my phone back in my pocket.

"Both Alex and Josef are working on this, so we need not worry about it, other than to stay alert for anything suspicious. What's on the agenda for today?" I finished.

Mkali, Bernie and a soaked and disheveled Shelley joined us at that point. "I vote for breakfast," he growled.

"I agree with breakfast first, but then suggest we hit the water park today," Mkali said enthusiastically.

Bernie added, "After all, Shelley already got a head start on getting wet."

"Sounds good to me, any objections?" I asked and looked around the room; everyone shook their heads. "Shelley, the rest of us will head down to breakfast while you dry off. We'll try to leave you some."

When Shelley joined us for breakfast it looked like he'd fallen in the gift shop and clothing from the reject rack fell on him. A floppy silver hat shaped like a Hershey's Kiss, complete with the tag that looked like a little flag covered his curly hair. He wore a pair of neon-green oversized sunglasses shaped like the little chocolate treat. A hot pink t-shirt barely contained his barrel chest. It was at least one size too small with silver sparkly letters that read, "I charge for hugs, but kisses are free." He was wearing a deep purple pair of board shorts covered with images of all the candy bars made by the Hershey company. To finish the outfit he was sporting a pair of black socks pulled up to his knees and Birkenstocks on his feet.

I froze with my fork halfway to my mouth and could only move after he leaned over to Bernie and kissed her on the cheek while saying, "Good morning, dear."

Each of us at the table erupted with laughter, drawing the stares of the other patrons in the restaurant who also began laughing. Shelley stood proudly, turned towards the others in the restaurant and bowed with a flourish. "Thank you," he exclaimed, "I'll be here all week—don't forget to tip your waitress."

He finally sat to a chorus of cheers and a round of applause.

"You aren't going to wear that ridiculous outfit today, are you?" Bernie asked while she palmed her face.

"Absolutely. Not only that, I'll be by your side all-day-long. I'll be the most devoted boyfriend in history today," Shelley finished with a grin.

"I guess we shouldn't have thrown water on Shelley to wake him up this morning." Mkali said with a giggle.

Bernie turned pleading eyes to Miriam who sat across from her, "Can't you do something?"

Miriam laughed, "Sorry, dear. I'm just his mother and the sooner you learn how to deal with him, the better." She continued with a twinkle in her eye, "Besides, I think he got his fashion sense from his father."

"C'mon beautiful," Shelley stood and pulled Bernie up with him. "I need to get some food from the buffet and need an extra set of hands to help me carry everything."

"At least my life isn't dull with you in it," Bernie laughed as she walked hand-in-hand with Shelley to get food.

"Ladies, what do we want to do today? Should we go to the water park with the kids or should we take another run at the spa?" Mother asked.

"Am I considered a kid, or a lady?" Jason asked with a smirk.

Mother leaned over to pat his hand. "At my age, I consider almost everyone else a kid. What do you want to do?"

"I've never been to a water park, it looks fun," Jason answered.

"I think we should all go," Mom said.

"We took the kids on a trip to Bar Harbor when they were around ten. There was a water park nearby," Frieda added.

"Do you remember how loudly Stavros yelled the first time he went down the slide?" Miriam laughed in remembrance.

"Do you think I'll like it?" Aileene leaned towards me and asked quietly.

"Absolutely," I answered and put my arm around her shoulders, "they're like roller coasters but with water."

"That's settled then," Mother exclaimed and bit into another piece of bacon.

"We must get swimsuits," Mkali leaned forward and whispered, "humans give you funny looks if you swim naked."

"We're all going?" Shelley boomed as he sat down with two plates piled high with food. "I know just the shop to get our suits, they have a great selection."

Bernie set the plates she was carrying in front of Shelley, also, and added, "I'll pick out my swimsuit if you don't mind. Your taste in clothing is questionable."

Shelley looked down at his outfit and shrugged. "You may be right, but I make this look good."

"Whatever you say dear, whatever you say," Bernie said as she patted his hand.

Josef

I crouched on one of the eagle heads on the Chrysler Building thinking about the last two days. Alex Farrel sent one of Rex Industries corporate jets to pick Tiffany and Tobias up in Hartford, Connecticut to take her back to Phoenix. Steve, Robert and Rick traveled with them. We decided that both Rick and Tobias would stay with Tiffany, and take her on a vacation to Hawaii to keep her safe. It thrilled Tiffany, especially since it would be an all-expense paid trip and they would travel in style in another of the corporate jets.

Steve and Robert would meet the rest of us in New York City with the Gulfstream G500 corporate jet which has a range of over seven thousand eight hundred miles. That would be enough to fly us anywhere we needed to go in the US or around the world. Alex wanted to resist when I requested the jet, but when I reminded him everything belongs to the King of Theria anyway, and I was on a mission for him, he relented.

Todd drove Scott, Dwight, Frank and me to New York where four members of Tionchar were living undercover. King Alister had given me the classified information on each member and their identities on Earth. I had the access codes King Phillip and King Alister had given to me so I could contact each shifter using our encrypted tablets. I'd received messages from Phanes, a griffin, and Lilly, a pegasus and we'd agreed to meet on the roof of a building just west of the Chrysler Building at ten-thirty at night.

My phone was hanging around my neck but I had to transform my hands so I could use it to check the time; it's tough to open my phone with clawed hands. Even though I was a gargoyle, I didn't resemble any of the small statues on the Notre Dame Cathedral but looked a lot like Goliath from the Disney Gargoyle cartoon from the nineteen-nineties. There was a message from King Alister that must have come in while I was flying asking me to update him after the meeting. We had spoken earlier in the day after the news report of the most recent explosion in Maine. I hope he could enjoy his day at the water park after I told him my team and I would take care of it.

I stood and stretched to my full height of eight feet and expanded my wings. From tip to tip, my wings measured ten feet and were so black they seemed to swallow the light. One thing the myths got correct, my skin is tougher than granite but I don't turn to stone in the daylight. I snorted at the ridiculous notion that flesh could turn to stone and saw two griffins gliding in to land on the roof of the building south of my position. I jumped off my perch and made my way over, but was confused because I was expecting to see a griffin and pegasus, not two griffins. They were magnificent creatures with the bodies of lions, and the wings and heads of eagles.

I landed on the roof at the same time as my two new friends and spoke to them through thought-speak. *Greetings, sometimes the most important paths are hidden ones.*

They answered in unison, *but hidden paths can be dangerous,* and transformed.

Before me, a man and woman stood tall, proud and unashamedly naked. Since it is shifter courtesy to transform when others do, I took my human shape. Even though it was significantly colder on the roof, our natural body temperature kept us warm, even though we weren't wearing any clothing. Each of us carried a duffel bag with clothes and we threw those on as we talked.

"My name is Josef and the King sent me to Earth to collect the members of Tionchar who stopped reporting in."

"I am Phanes and this is my mate, Lilly," the man said as he pointed first to himself then to the woman standing next to him.

"Has anyone ever told you that you look like The Rock?" Lilly asked with a smile.

Chuckling I answered her, "I've heard that a time or two. In fact, I was Dwayne's stunt double for the past ten years."

"You evidently know the code for Tionchar so you must be one of us. Are you here to explain why King Phillip was silent for so long?" Phanes asked with suspicion as he crossed his arms across his chest in challenge.

Nodding my head, I summed up the events surrounding Dimitri's betrayal and Alister's rise to the throne. They both sagged in relief and Phane's expression softened.

"Congratulations on finding your true-mate," I smiled at Phanes and Lilly.

"Thank you," Lilly beamed as she intertwined her fingers with Phanes'. "Even in the middle of this uncertainty we've been able to find happiness."

"I'm glad you've found each other, and I'm not criticizing or condemning, but can you please explain how you got together if you followed standard undercover protocol?" I asked.

"About four years ago we each received a message on our tablets, using the proper codes, with instructions from King Phillip for us to come to the gate location in Baxter State Park. I doubted the message because it was counter to everything they had taught us in the academy, but journeyed to Maine anyway. Along the route, I would cast thought-speak out just to see if I could connect with any shifters in the area. Apparently, I wasn't the only suspicious one because as I got closer to the park, I received messages from other shifters gathering at a rest stop about twenty miles outside the park. When I arrived, Lilly was already there along with eight others."

"Even though it violated our training, those of us who were already at the rest stop shared our names and our current assignments," Lilly added.

I pulled out my tablet and opened it to the list King Alister had given me. "Who was already there?" I asked.

Lilly ticked the names off her fingers as she answered, "Andy the leprechaun and Lucas the kelpie, both from Chicago, Sophia the anemoi and Yukio the kitsune, both from Los Angeles. There was also Pippa the banshee and Liam the barghest from the UK, Gunter the kobold from Germany and Colette the cockatrice from France, and then I was there and Phanes joined us."

Phanes continued the story. "When I arrived, the rest had already been debating what to do for quite some time. The supposed message from the King instructed us to meet at the gate location within an hour. No one in our group thought the message was really from King Phillip, but we needed to know what was going on. Those of us who could fly headed to the meeting place but stayed in the air until we knew it was safe. Those who couldn't fly would hide in the woods close enough to communicate via thought-speak but far enough away they would be safe if something went wrong.

"Since I have excellent sight in my griffin form it was up to me to watch what was going on in the clearing and report to the others. I could fly high enough in the sky that I wouldn't be spotted, so it made the most sense for me to be the lookout."

"Our cars were the only ones at the rest stop, so we felt safe enough to transform there and implement our plan," Lilly added.

"It only took us a short time to fly the distance to the park and get into a safe position in the woods. When it was close to the meeting time, I took off again and circled the meadow high enough I couldn't be seen from the ground. There were eight people gathered in the middle of the clearing and they appeared to be talking to one another. I soared in a circle for about five minutes and was about to tell everyone else it was safe to join the others in the clearing when gunfire erupted from the surrounding woods. The shifters in the meadow were surrounded and didn't react quickly enough.

"I sent the warning to the others to escape as I watched in horror as people dressed in black stepped out of the trees and continued firing at the defenseless shifters. Everything happened so fast, no one shifted before the hidden assailants gunned them down. The last thing I saw was the gunmen walking among the fallen and shooting into their prone bodies," Phanes added sadly.

"The moment Phanes gave us warning, we rushed back to the rest stop and each shifter changed to their human form, got in their cars and quickly drove away. I waited for Phanes to make sure he was safe, so I hid in the woods. About five minutes after everyone else left, another car came up the road from Bangor and turned into the rest stop. Whoever was driving the car drove slowly past our parked cars and then parked in a spot away from the lights.

"The driver never got out of the car, but I heard a male voice in my head asking, 'Is anyone out there?' but I was wary because of what Phanes had reported so I didn't answer and stayed hidden. After another five minutes, the car started up again and drove back the way it came. I only came out of hiding when Phanes landed by his car and started to get in."

"Lilly told me what she had seen, and we left the cars where they were and flew back to New York and had a service pick them up the next morning. We've been together ever since," Phanes finished their story.

As I digested what they told me, I realized we needed King Alister to join us so we could contact Theria and plan our next moves. I picked up my phone and dialed King Alister. I hoped he had a splendid day at the water park because I was about to ruin his night.

Alister

Even though we have amazing healing abilities as shifters, the non-dragon members of my team were still feeling the effects of terrible sunburns; we dragons love fire in all its forms, including the sun. We had an amazing day at the water park but had forgotten about the need for sunscreen—big mistake. Bernie had offered to heal people who were in pain, but Shelley and Jason decided to see who could tough it out longer; the rest of us were tiring of their moaning. We were in my mother's suite and Shelley was moaning but refused to let Bernie put her hands on him to heal the burn.

I answered my phone when I saw it was Josef calling. "Hey Josef, what's up?"

"I'm sorry to disturb your night, Sire, but how quickly could you, Aileene and Queen Beatrice join us in New York?"

"How far away are you?" I asked.

"About a hundred and fifty miles," he answered.

"We can be there in about an hour if you need us to get there quickly."

"Yes, Sire, it will be better for me to explain everything once you get here," Josef finished.

"Ok, we'll be there soon." I ended the call and looked at Mother and Aileene. "As you probably heard, that was Josef and he needs the three of us to get to him as quickly as we can." As I spoke, I gathered my phone and tablet and placed them in the dimensional pocket I wore around my neck.

Mother and Aileene were also gathering a few of their things and placing them in the pocket on Aileene's necklace.

"What do you want the rest of us to do?" Mom asked.

"I think it would be best for you to enjoy your day tomorrow as planned in case we're not back in time. If we need to stay in Hershey an extra day, we will. Otherwise, we'll still plan on sending the Foim family through a gate the day after tomorrow. And, Bernie, please heal Jason and Shelley so you don't have to hear any more whining." I gave Shelley and Jason a hard stare when they opened their mouths to argue. "That's an order."

"We're ready, Son," Mother said as she started for the door.

"I'm so excited I get a chance to fly on Earth," Aileene beamed. "And, I bet we can make it there in less than an hour; it's only a hundred and fifty miles away."

I laughed at her excitement and followed her out the door.

It only took us forty-five minutes to make the journey and Aileene led the way until the last few miles so I could follow my connection to

Josef to find his location. He wasn't in the city as I expected, but in a campground near a lake.

Josef, we're coming in for a landing, I sent.

That was fast.

Yeah, Aileene wanted to race. I could hear her snicker in my mind and the three of us shifted into our human forms as we came in for a landing. We walked to where everyone else was sitting around a campfire in chairs.

Two shifters stood as we approached the fire and bowed deeply. "Your Majesties, Lady Aileene, it's an honor to meet you. I am Phanes and this is my mate Lilly."

Aileene laughed as she poked me in the ribs. "Don't be too honored to meet these two slow-coaches, I could fly circles around them."

"Watch yourself young lady, you're not too big for me to take you down a peg or two," Mother laughed and put her arm around Aileene's waist.

"Don't mind them," I said as I smiled at the two gaping shifters. "Without Fritz and Frieda around to help us with proper protocol, they revert to children."

I walked up and embraced each of them in turn. "Thank you for your loyalty to the Crown and the shifters of Theria, you are a credit to your profession."

Lilly wiped a tear from her eye and Phanes stood taller at my words of encouragement. Steve stood from his chair and motioned Robert to do the same as Mother and Aileene sat in the vacated seats. Steve and Robert brought over three chairs and sat again, and I joined them. As soon as I sat, I opened a pinhole portal to Theria and used my tablet to send a message to my father while everyone else engaged in small talk. Once Father came on the line, I opened the video app and turned the tablet around so everyone could see his face.

Josef, I sent, *I think it's time for you to bring us up to speed on everything you learned tonight. It may violate previously held procedures, but I think we should brief everyone on your team, too. What do you think?*

Josef nodded and reported on everything he'd learned as well as filling in Phanes and Lilly on what we'd learned about Neil Paterson. Father would interrupt occasionally, with clarifying questions so it took some time for Josef to give his full report.

"Beatrice, what do you think?" Father asked.

"It appears we can identify eleven of the twenty missing shifters who are members of Tionchar and we know eight died in that clearing. Even though it seems like Neil Paterson is a formidable enemy, I don't believe he had anything to do with the shifters being killed; this looks like an inside job."

"Another betrayal," my father said sadly.

"It seems so, dear," Mother answered lovingly.

"How did we miss so much?" Father wondered in a melancholy voice.

It hurt my heart to hear the pain in his voice as I remembered that Dimitri had been one of his closest friends and I wished I could give him a hug. Deciding to try something, I turned the tablet so I could see his face and connected with him through the pinhole gate using my gift from An'Ceann, and sent him my love and the sense of an embrace. I could tell by the surprised expression on his face it worked, and he smiled at me.

"Thank you, Son, I'm amazed at how quickly you've learned to use your abilities as High King. I love you and am proud of you."

Aileene suddenly shoved her face next to mine so she could look in the camera. "Hello Father, when I find the shifter who has betrayed us and caused you such sadness, I'm going to bite him in half. We're having a splendid time on Earth. I've ridden many roller coasters and rides at the water park and eaten many, many churros. Love you," Aileene said brightly and sat on my lap.

"Daughter of my heart, I love you, too," Father said while laughing at her antics. "Thank you both for helping me feel better; we'd better get back to work. We won't know every name of the murdered shifters until we learn the identity of the one in the car. Alister, can you reach out with your senses to pinpoint any shifters close to your position? I'm looking at the list of Tionchar members and I've marked those we've already identified along with their assignment location.

"We're missing people from New York City, Seattle, Italy, India, two in Japan and two in China. Are you able to pinpoint people around the world with that kind of accuracy?"

I thought about his question and some of the spells we used when we flew across Middle Earth. Gustav and I had experimented with various mapping spells before we perfected the one I used. One of my favorite subjects in school was geography; Bernie, and Shelley used to make fun of me because I asked for a globe for one of my birthdays. Closing my eyes, I tapped into my magical reservoir and cast the spell *Saeclum,* which created a magical globe that hung in the air in front of me.

From the gasps I heard, others could see it too, so I opened my eyes to look at the perfect replica of Earth slowly rotating in front of me.

"That's impressive, Son," my father responded from the tablet when he saw the magical sphere I had created. "But, can you add the shifters you sense?"

"Let me try," I answered then closed my eyes and connected to all the shifters across the globe. Every shifter popped into my mind; counting them again I still came up with sixty-one. I placed those of us sitting around the fire on the globe in my mind and then added those who were in Hershey. After that, it was easier to add the glowing dots to the map every time I figured out where another shifter was. Once I placed everyone in my mind, I transferred the mental image to the globe spinning in front of everyone then opened my eyes.

"That's amazing Alister," Aileene breathed in my ear as she hugged me. I kissed her on the cheek and looked at the globe and noted where the glowing red dots were, and where ones should have been but were not. There weren't any shifters in Italy, India, China, Japan, or Seattle however there was another dot in New York, and I reported that to my father.

"I'm sending a message to the tablet of the other Tionchar member assigned to New York, using an even more exclusive code phrase to prove the message is from me." We could see my father typing for a minute before he looked back at the camera.

"There, he knows you're on Earth, and I've sent the phrase I used to your encrypted tablet. You can use this new code when you contact him. Let's hope this is our missing Tionchar member. That's all we can do for now, but I recommend you take Phanes and Lilly with you and then send them through the portal tomorrow night. We'll worry about closing down their identities on Earth later," Father finished.

I looked at my watch and noticed he was correct because it was almost three in the morning on June twenty-third and we were spending one more day playing in Hershey.

"Sounds good, Father, but I better get going so we can get some sleep while it's still dark out." Mother and Aileene said their goodbyes and then I stored the tablet back in the pocket dimension. After we said farewell to Josef and his team Aileene grinned at me and ran toward the lake shouting, "Last one to Hershey has to wear a silly hat to the zoo."

Mother grinned at me and took off running after Aileene. I looked at Phanes and Lilly and said, "Hurry you two, we don't want to be the last ones to Hershey, I've seen some of the ridiculous hats in the gift shop." The three of us sprinted into the darkness trying to catch up.

CHAPTER EIGHT

Aileene opened the door, took one look at me and then laughed so hard she had to lean against the frame to stay upright. "You don't have to wear the hat anymore; you already wore it all day at the zoo," she said between fits of laughter. Grinning, I pulled off the monstrosity and held it in my hand. She took it from me and tossed it into the room behind her before closing the door.

Since Aileene beat us back to Hershey, Phanes, Lilly and I had to wear the matching hats she picked out for us. She picked out something that was a cross between a rainbow Hershey Kiss, Ice Cream cone and poo emoji. There was a silly face on the front of the kiss/cone and for some reason there was a long red cape attached to the back which trailed down the back of my neck. The hat included a pair of built-in sunglasses, so it covered part of my face and the only way to keep it on my head was to tie the attached neon-green ribbon under my chin.

She reached up and smoothed my hair as she smiled at me. "I had a wonderful day with you, Alister, thanks for being such a good sport about the hat. I've got some impressive pictures."

"Hey, a bet's a bet; but I will get you back," I said evilly as I hugged her and gave her a kiss on the forehead. "Are you ready to go to dinner?"

"Yep," she said as she grabbed my hand and headed down the hallway to the room my mom was sharing with Miriam and Frieda. The door opened before we got there, and Mom stepped out. Aileene smiled and tapped the side of her head to let me know she had already let Mom know we were on our way.

"I don't know about you two, but I'm starving," Mom said as she shut the door and joined us.

The restaurant was crowded but since we'd made a reservation they showed us to our table, but only after the Maitre' d inspected the clothing I was wearing to make sure I met the dress code; which I barely did. He wasn't afraid to tell me about my wardrobe choices, and I had to listen to his opinion longer than I wanted. I squeezed Aileene's hand warningly as I felt her tense at the insulting tone the man used as he spoke to me. Thankfully, Mom is fluent in snooty and could defuse the situation before roast Maitre' d was added as a special to the menu.

It was my fault since I wanted to treat Mom and Aileene to a special meal and picked this five-star, award-winning restaurant over the pizza and burger place I would have picked. However, since I had access to a lot of money now, I figured more expensive would be better. It wasn't in this case. While we had an enjoyable time chatting with each other over dinner, each of us felt we had to be more restrained in our laughter and enjoyment of one another. The food was delicious, there just wasn't much of it, so we were all still hungry when we finished and hit the pizza and burger place after all.

Over the next two hours we consumed three large pizzas and about twenty burgers and all agreed the experience was much better than the snooty restaurant. Mom told stories about me growing up and she and Aileene had a grand time laughing at my expense. Since the stories were funny, I laughed, too. It was great to see these two women who were so important to me laughing together and cementing their relationship. However, towards the end of our meal, I could tell something was bothering Mom and she was having trouble bringing it up.

"Okay Mom, you've told enough stories about me. How about I tell the one about the time there was something you wanted to talk to us about, but you were too nervous to bring it up?" I asked while looking pointedly at her.

She looked startled for a moment but then laughed. "I keep forgetting you're not a little boy anymore. That's one of the tough things about being a parent; when you look at your child you see every stage of their life in layers and it's difficult not to default to treating them like tiny kids." She sighed before continuing, "I'm stalling again —here goes—you're going to be a brother."

Overjoyed with the news I blurted, "You're pregnant? That's great."

Mom looked around and switched to thought-speak. *Technically, I was pregnant until I laid my eggs. Now your siblings will finish developing until they hatch.*

Aileene perked up at this revelation and asked, *How long will they be developing?*

They will still be in their eggs for another six months. The entire process takes about a year for fire drakes. The mother is pregnant for six months and the children develop in the shell for another six months.

Wow, I'm going to be a brother, this is awesome, I thought but then said aloud, "This calls for a celebration. Let's get a pizookie."

"Or two," Aileene added.

"Or three," Mom finished with a smile.

Shelley and I were waiting in the lobby when Dag Foim and his family arrived at our hotel. Alex had arranged for the sale of their home and the movers had taken away everything they weren't bringing with them to Theria. As far as anyone knew, Dag accepted a job offer in Las Vegas and would work for a casino. After we introduced ourselves to the Foims, we led them behind the hotel where the others were loading the bus.

"Mr. Foim," Shelley began, "how did your family end up in Hershey?"

Dag smiled ruefully as he answered, "Please call me Dag."

At Shelley's nod, he continued, "When we came through the gate we stayed in Maine for a few months until we decided where we wanted to go. One day Fal was excited about a place named Hershey and told us all about it. She had been shopping in the market and was talking to a fellow shopper about how much she loved Hershey chocolate. The woman told Fal that if she liked the chocolate so much, she should visit the town of Hershey where the candy was made. When Fal came home, she told us about the town made of chocolate and we packed up that day and moved here." Dag smiled fondly as he thought about his wife.

"I like candy, too," Shelley said, "but it seems a bit extreme to move just because a place makes chocolate."

Dag laughed, "You don't know much about brownies. We love our families, we love to cook and clean, but we especially love candy. I admit we were disappointed to arrive and find out the town wasn't made of chocolate but the delicious smell permeates the town and there are candy shops everywhere. But, when we saw the hotels and found we could get jobs in them cooking and cleaning rooms; we knew we found our home on Earth."

"Why didn't you come through the gate to Theria when everyone else did?" Shelley asked. Dag had already shared this part of the story with me but I figured it might be good for him to share it again.

Tears gathered in Dag's eyes as he answered. "We were given notice that everyone was heading back to Theria but when it came time to leave for Maine to join everyone we couldn't leave because my beautiful wife was killed in a car wreck."

The tears were streaming freely down Dag's face and his son and daughter-in-law put their arms around him in a comforting embrace. I steered Dag over to a chair in the lobby and had him sit.

"Here, drink this," I said and handed him the glass of water I poured from the dispenser on the counter. "If you'd rather not talk about this right now, that's fine."

"No, it's good for me to talk about Fal, just give me a moment," Dag said then finished his water. His son and daughter-in-law, Tunn and Meid, rubbed his back while the children climbed on his lap and placed their heads against his chest. He looked at Shelley then continued his story.

"Fal was excited about going back to Theria but wanted to get some of her favorite snacks to take with us. She drove to Costco fifteen miles away to do some shopping. I offered to go with her but she wanted me to stay behind to pack with the rest of the family. After she had been gone for three hours we joked that she must have wanted to go shopping to spend some time by herself. It wasn't until I couldn't reach her on her phone that I began to think something was wrong.

"Tunn and Meid had put Teith and Abhold to bed when there was a knock at the door. My stomach dropped and I was instantly nauseous because I suspected something was wrong. When I opened the door there were two State Troopers on the porch. The moment the taller trooper told me how sorry he was, I knew my lovely wife was gone. I don't remember much else from that night but I do remember him telling me that Fal was on the highway and a big rig crossed the median and hit her car head on.

"I'm sure our friends meant to be kind when they told me she must have been killed instantly and didn't suffer but their words gave me little comfort. She was gone. We couldn't make it to Maine in time to leave with everyone because we held her Celebration of Life service the same day. We were sad that we couldn't return to Theria but we resigned ourselves that we would make our life on Earth."

"I am so sorry, Dag," Shelley sobbed and hugged the grieving brownie in the chair.

We sat in the hotel for another twenty minutes before Dag said he was ready to board the bus. When we got outside, I thought Dag would faint when he saw my mother. He kept telling her he was grateful she was alive and that we came to Earth for them. We didn't want to cause a scene in the parking lot so we rushed the family into the bus and pulled away as quickly as we could.

My mother sat with the Foims near the front of the bus on the drive so she could hear about everything they had gone through on Earth. The children were so cute, and Mother was so good with them as she let them sit on her lap. When the children boarded the bus, they transformed into their natural forms.

Brownies are small by nature and the largest adult will only stand about three feet tall. Since Teith was only eight, he was only about two feet tall and his little sister, Abhold, was only about twelve inches tall since she was only two. Both children had long agile fingers, large pointed ears and brown curly hair on their heads. Like most shifters they weren't concerned about their lack of clothing but their mother Meid had brownie-sized clothing for them to wear for the journey; they made the clothes from distinct shades of brown cloth.

The children were excited to be on the bus and wandered from person to person and sat on laps so they could see out the windows. They were cautious of Aileene and me until she murmured to them in another language and gave each of them a piece of chocolate. After that, Abhold settled on my lap and fell asleep almost at once. I stayed still because I didn't want to wake her but relaxed as I saw Aileene's laughing eyes and her beautiful smile as she saw me holding this tiny girl.

About an hour later, their dad Tunn came back and looked at me holding his sleeping daughter and he put his hand on my shoulder and looked me in the eyes, "Slainte mhor agus a h-uile beannachd duibh," he said then gently picked up his sleeping daughter. Both Tunn and Teith walked to the front of the bus and sat with the rest of the Foim family.

"What did he say?" I asked Aileene. "It sounds like the same language you used to speak to the kids earlier."

"On Earth, the language is Gaelic and spoken in Scotland and Ireland, we use the same language in Eutheria. Tunn gave you a traditional blessing that means good health and every good blessing to you. The way you showed love to his daughter moved him," Aileene said and leaned over to kiss me on my cheek.

The rest of the ride passed quickly and I was able to contact the missing shifter when we stopped in Portsmouth, Ohio for an early dinner. Jason unhooked the Expedition from the bus and we drove to Shawnee State Forest to pick up Harry. Bernie, Shelley, Mother and Aileene accompanied Jason and me on the journey and everyone else stayed behind at the restaurant to eat and let the kids play at a nearby park. Mkali stayed behind because the park had a rock wall and she was determined to climb every surface. Phanes and Lilly assured me they would keep everyone safe in our absence.

The plan was to enter the forest, pick up Harry and find the best place to create a gate to send everyone through. It was four hours until sunset and I didn't want to send anyone to Theria before dark. We drove up to the gate and the park ranger informed us that all the campgrounds were full, but we could park in the day-use area to walk the trails. We had planned to come back with the bus and book a camping spot, but we'd have to adapt.

We paid the fee for day use and drove around until we found a parking spot. As we stepped out of the car we noticed the trails were crowded with hikers and people enjoying the spectacular weather.

Harry, we're in the park and are about to walk the Lampblack trail, I sent.

I'll find you, he replied.

"Okay team, let's hike, Harry will find us," I said. Since we didn't want to be overheard, we switched to thought-speak.

What type of shifter is Harry? Bernie asked.

He didn't say, I replied.

He's a sasquatch, Jason interjected.

How do you know about — I asked but Shelley interrupted.

Wait—Shelley laughed, *he's a sasquatch and his name is Harry; that's awesome.*

I don't understand, Mother sent.

Queen Beatrice, there was a movie called Harry and the Hendersons about a family who found a sasquatch and named him

Harry. We used to watch the movie over and over when we were kids, Bernie sent, her thoughts laced with laughter.

Can we buy copies of these movies you watched as kids? I would like to watch them, Mother asked.

"I would like that," I said and gave her a hug; which wasn't easy to do as we walked along.

I can see you on the path, Harry sent to me. *Veer off to the right into the forest after you pass the enormous boulder.*

We followed Harry's instructions and walked about two hundred yards into the forest from the path and into a small copse of oak trees, so they screened us from sight. An enormous man stepped out of the shadows and walked up to Jason.

"Hello, cousin," he growled before he punched Jason in the nose, knocking him to the ground.

"I guess that explains how he knows about Harry," Bernie muttered.

Jason hit the ground but bounced up almost immediately transforming into his sasquatch form, shredding his clothes as he did so. I'd seen pictures of Bigfoot just like everyone else, but the creature Jason turned into was much more ferocious than any depiction in movies. He was over eight feet tall with brown fur and looked a lot like Sully from *Monsters, Inc.* He snarled and showed his four-inch-long canine teeth at Harry, who had also transformed. Harry raised his arms above his head threateningly and showed the wickedly curved claws on his upraised hands. They were both moments away from attacking each other when I'd had enough.

"Shift," I commanded and instead of two enraged sasquatches there were two naked humans who suddenly realized they were exposed and standing in front of Queen Beatrice, Aileene and Bernie. Even for shifters used to casual nudity, this was too much. Embarrassed, they both covered themselves with their hands and tried to shield their bodies behind nearby trees. Fortunately for them, we had brought some extra clothes for Harry in case he didn't have any when we met him.

As I dug in my backpack for a pair of shorts for Jason and

sweatpants for Harry, Mother was scolding them like little children in a hoarse whisper.

"What foolishness is this? Why did we bother to use thought-speech to stay quiet when you two act like pen-channas and attack each other at first sight? What do you have to say for yourselves?"

As Harry put on the shorts, he blushed then bowed and answered. "My apologies Your Majesty, I let my anger get the better of me when I saw my cousin for the first time since he stole the woman who was to be my mate."

Mother looked at Jason who quickly put up his hands in surrender and spoke rapidly as he saw her thunderous expression. "Queen Beatrice, my cousin is mistaken. Before we escaped to Earth, I was spending time with my cousin's mate-to-be, but I wasn't wooing her. Ilona had asked me to help her choose the perfect wedding gift for Harry and that's all we were doing. Unfortunately, Harry has always had a quick temper and instead of letting me explain he ran off the moment we came through the gate from Theria and disappeared. I couldn't follow him because I had to take care of Ilona and our other family members when we found ourselves stranded on Earth.

"Once I established a residence on Earth, I could not find him again, but continued to search whenever possible. Ilona was so distraught about what happened that she ended up escaping into the wilds with her parents and other members of the family. We only reunited when we returned to Theria." Jason finished as he looked pleadingly at Harry.

"Do you mean, I've missed out on all these years with Ilona because of my anger and jealousy?" Harry asked quietly.

Jason nodded and Harry fell to his knees and wept with his face in his hands.

Aileene walked over to me and put her arm around my waist and Mother stood next to Harry and put her hand on his shoulder.

"I do not know if Ilona will take you back or not, but you will find out when we send you back through the gate to Theria once it's dark. You and Jason have things to discuss so, we will head back to the vehicle to wait for you there," Mother finished.

Josef

New York City

Frustrated, I pushed through the rotating doors to exit Rockefeller Center. For the past two days, my team and I had been searching for the missing member of Tionchar. I'd checked in with King Alister many times to confirm Bruce was still in New York City. After checking in with each of my team members, I walked to the closest Starbucks to await further instructions. I grabbed a cold brew coffee and sat at a table. I turned on my tablet and drafted my report before contacting the King.

Sire, we have been searching for two days and Bruce hasn't contacted us yet.

While waiting for a response, I studied the people seated around me, unaware of the danger they faced. If Bruce was the traitor, he had the training and abilities to disrupt the way of life for these humans. While their weapons were formidable, a shifter of power could use subterfuge and deceit, and the vast almost unlimited financial resources available through the Tionchar network. Since there was a message sent to the members around the world, I had to assume the traitor also had access to the Tionchar financial accounts on Earth. I wiped my face in weariness because I hadn't slept in almost three days.

"Can I get you a refill on your drink?" a pleasant voice asked.

I looked up in confusion at the red-haired Starbucks employee, her name tag read Jessa. "Pardon me?"

"You look tired, I just wanted to know if I could refill your drink for you." She smiled.

I smiled back in gratitude. "That would be amazing, thank you."

"My pleasure," Jessa replied and took my drink to the counter for a refill.

As I considered that simple act of kindness, I smiled and renewed my determination to do whatever necessary to thwart the traitor's plans. My tablet buzzed, with an incoming message.

We are waiting until dark before sending our friends home. When

I'm finished here, we'll continue to our next stop, and I'll come to New York from there in a few days. I will find Bruce one way or another.

Thank you, Sire. Perhaps he will respond to you where he continues to elude me and my team.

What is your next step?

We need to find out why Alex Farrel didn't tell us about the meeting in Maine and see if he can explain how he avoided the trap that caught the others who died.

Do you think he could be the traitor?

I do not believe so, but unfortunately Bruce and Alex are the only ones whose whereabouts during the deadly meeting are unknown.

Be safe, Josef, I do not know the endgame of this traitor, but he is not above killing his own. You also need to be on the lookout for Paterson and his crew.

Thank you, Sire, I will be careful. We'll spend a few days resting before going to Arizona.

Sounds good, keep me posted. Thank you for everything you're doing to solve this mystery to keep our people safe.

I smiled to myself as I gathered my things and prepared to leave. King Alister is already an outstanding leader; it will be interesting to see how much more he'll grow in the years to come. As I walked by the tip jar on the counter, I added five-thousand dollars and thanked Jessa for the refill as Iwalked by her. There was a squeal behind me as the girl behind the counter noticed the overflowing tip jar. I'm glad I could brighten someone's day.

Alister

There weren't any people around us as we walked down the path to the place I would open the gate to Theria. It was shortly after ten at night and the sun had set about an hour before. We were silent as we walked, and once we stopped Aileene cast her senses outward, the way I taught her, to see if there were any people near us.

All clear, she sent and stepped close to me and took my hand in hers. When we'd chosen this spot earlier, I'd opened a pinhole gate and sent the coordinates to my father.

"Okay, I will open a gate and my father will be on the other side to receive you," I said as the people who were going back to Theria gathered their belongings to take with them.

"Sire, before you open the gate, I want to again apologize for my earlier behavior," Harry said in a subdued voice.

"I appreciate that Harry but the people you should apologize to are those you abandoned, and Jason of course," I admonished.

Harry hung his head in shame. "I've got a lot to apologize for."

"Cheer up, dude," Shelley interjected. "You have a lot of years ahead of you to grovel. If I were you, I'd see someone about that temper of yours before you do something that can't be forgiven so easily."

It hardly took any effort to open the gate to Theria and in a moment, we could see our loved ones we'd left behind. Mother rushed to my father and threw herself into his arms and kissed him soundly. Mom did the same thing to dad and before long, Miriam and Frieda were also kissing their spouses as though they'd been gone for months instead of just six days. After a few minutes of the enthusiastic welcome, I cleared my throat to get everyone's attention and smiled widely.

"Father, it's good to see you," I said as I gave him a hug. After that, I gave my dad a hug, too, and shook hands with Fritz, Stavros and even Gustav who was wearing a backpack. "Let me present to you this group of shifters who were left behind. Phanes and Lilly Nasir, Dag Foim, his son Tunn, his wife Meid and their children Teith and Abhold, and finally Harry Shampe."

Father welcomed each of the shifters as though they were long, lost friends and made them feel right at home. We helped place the suitcases and boxes of keepsakes on the ground in Theria and Gustav stepped through to join us on Earth.

Father spoke to me in mind-speak as Aileene, Bernie and Shelley crossed to Theria to hug everyone on that side. *Son, I agree with your plan to go to New York City to find Bruce, but I want Gustav to join your group as you continue to search for the missing shifters. When will you go?*

I'll go to New York after we pick up our next group of shifters near Lexington Kentucky. I've marked the location of each shifter on this map, I sent and handed him the map of the US I had notated for him. I also handed him maps of Europe showing the location of the shifters living there. *Josef sent you a copy of his report and the reports from the rest of his team analyzing the problem with the traitor and Neil Paterson. Please look them over and tell me what you make of things,* I sent as I hugged him again.

"Don't you two know it's rude to use thought-speech when other people are standing nearby?" Mother said with a laugh.

"Sorry my dear," my father responded as he put his arm around her waist and kissed her on the temple.

I walked over to my mom and dad where they were talking with each other. Dad was wearing purple sweats with pink and blue dragon eggs on them. "Very subtle, Dad," I laughed, "I'm really excited that I will be a big brother."

Aileene bounced up to us and threw herself at Dad, thankfully he was ready and caught her. "I'm thrilled and can't wait to spoil them rotten," she squealed.

"I hate to break things up," Gustav said, "but it would probably be best to close the gate and leave this area right away."

"You're probably right Gustav but when did you get as serious as Fritz?" Father asked teasingly.

"I think Gustav makes a valid point," Fritz sniffed and the rest of us laughed.

"Okay, everyone. Let's get going. We're going to Kentucky next but won't open another gate for three days; see you then," I said, then closed the gate.

Neil Paterson

"This better be important," Neil grumbled sleepily as he answered his phone.

"Sir, this is Kurt Abbot, I work with Dr. Brent." The voice sounded nervous as it came across the line.

"I know who you are," Neil snapped, "do you know what time it is?"

"Yes, but Dr. Brent thought this was important enough to wake you," Abbot stammered.

"And I notice he's not calling me, but you are. Very well," he huffed, "what is it?"

"Sir, two hours ago we recorded another anomaly and have narrowed the incident to an area of only two hundred and fifty thousand square miles." Abbot exclaimed proudly.

The silence lasted so long, Abbot thought we had lost the connection. "Sir?"

"You mean to tell me we've had another alien incursion and you wait two hours to tell me about it and then the best you can do is narrow the search area down to roughly the size of Texas?" Neil screamed into the phone.

"Sir, understand that this is an incredible feat because we've been able to calibrate sensors on a satellite above the planet to monitor this activity," Abbot said lamely.

"You know what would be incredible? If we could capture an alien so we can stop their continued incursions on our planet. It would also be incredible if we had a faster response time than two hours and a search area smaller than an entire state." Neil seethed. "I'm warning you, Abbot, my last employee that didn't deliver results was retired permanently. If you don't know what I'm talking about, watch the news about the recent incident in Maine. The next time you call, if you don't have better information for me, it will be the last call you make. Do I make myself clear?"

"Yes, sir," Abbot answered.

"Pass the message onto Brent and anyone else on the team who needs a pep talk to do better," Neil screamed as he ended the call. Fuming, he got out of bed and entered his closet so he could scream at his parents' portrait. After about thirty minutes of his hate-filled tirade he had calmed enough to place a call.

"It's me, we may have to clean the house at my research facility in New York, set things up but wait for my go-ahead. And this time, try not to draw so much attention to yourself," he said and ended the call. Pleased that he had contingency plans in place, he turned off the light and went back to sleep.

Alister

We were thirty minutes from our hotel when Bernie and Shelley sat across the aisle from Aileene and me.

"You're not asleep, are you?" Shelley asked with a smirk.

"Not anymore," Aileene grumbled. She had been dozing on my shoulder.

"Oh, good," Shelley replied undeterred. "Bernie and I have been debating and we need Alister's help."

"What a surprise," I said and smiled at my friends. Bernie stuck her tongue out at me in response. "What can I help you with?"

"We've been researching knights and wonder why you call both of us Sir. Online we've found, men are called 'Sir' and women are called 'Lady' or 'Dame'" Bernie explained.

"So, what's the debate?" I asked.

Bernie gave Shelley a sideways glance and said, "I think it has to do with you watching the Star Trek series and they call female officers 'Sir'."

"And I think you're just too dumb to know the difference," Shelley smiled good-naturedly.

"And I think, I'm going to punch you so hard, your mom will say 'ouch'." Aileene said as she shook her fist in Shelley's direction.

"Bring it, flame-breath," Shelley laughed.

"You gave me a nickname?" Aileene said in wonder.

"Of course, you're like the sister I never wanted," Shelley smirked.

"Annnyway," I drawled, "would you like to know my reasons or not?"

After receiving nods of agreement from my friends, I continued. "You're both kind of right. When I first knighted Bernie, I called her Sir Einhorn in part because of what I'd seen in Star Trek, but also because of a book series my dad likes. The primary character is female, a Hero of the Realm and is called Sir Daye. Dad always taught me both men and women can be heroes and even though we have differences, we should all be valued equally. After I knighted both of you, I asked Gustav if I'd made a mistake by calling you Sir Einhorn. He told me that both male and female knights had been called 'Sir' on Theria for thousands of years because heroes should be treated the same regardless of gender. Besides, if I've learned anything; female shifters can be as fierce, if not more so, than male shifters."

"Especially Royal Dragons," Aileene growled as she smiled at Shelley, showing all her teeth.

"Especially Royal Dragons," Mother echoed from the front of the bus.

"And centaurs," Mkali whispered from the seat in front of Bernie and Shelley and he held up his hands in surrender.

"Oh, and Shelley," I said pleasantly, "I will get you back for the 'too dumb to know the difference' comment when we find a spacious place to wrestle."

"That's what I was counting on Stretch," Shelley smiled and folded his hands behind his head.

CHAPTER NINE

We stayed in a castle near Lexington, Kentucky. Frieda was excellent at booking our accommodations, and she wanted to pick the best places for us. The castle was a unique place to stay and was luxurious. They were expecting our late arrival so they extended breakfast hours for us, and we could sleep in until ten the next morning. During breakfast we discussed what we wanted to do the next two days we'd be in Kentucky.

Shelley had money burning a hole in his pocket and wanted to visit a Best Buy in Lexington to get movies and new TVs to take back to Theria. Mother also wanted to go so she could see which movies we watched as kids and which movies she might want to get for herself. Miriam, Frieda and Mom also went. Jason unhooked the Expedition from the bus so Mom could drive her crew into town.

Mkali asked if she could go to a thoroughbred heritage horse farm that was owned by former neighbors who had been nice to her family. Aileene and Bernie wanted to go with her and Jason agreed to drive them so that just left Gustav and me.

I needed to leave for Blanton Forest, about three hours away, to connect with the two shifters living there. Jason would drop Gustav and me off at a car rental company so we could have our own vehicle.

We agreed to meet for dinner in Lexington. Once Mom drove her group away in the Expedition, the rest of us boarded the bus to go into town.

Please keep an eye on Bernie, Mkali and Jason while you're out. Have you been practicing the Spheara *shield spell I taught you?* I sent Aileene as we pulled away from the castle.

I've been practicing with Mother and we're probably both as good as you are, but we don't have the magic reservoir you do. Did An'Ceann give you a warning or are you just being overly cautious? she sent back.

Just being cautious but remember, Paterson has shown little restraint when he wants to cause mayhem. Not only that, but we have an unknown traitor out there who has caused death and destruction for our people.

You're cute when you worry, you know that? Aileene teased.

Humor me, okay? I have had no warnings, but I sense danger creeping closer to us.

Okay dear, I'm sorry for making fun of you. I will keep my eyes open. If I must transform into my dragon to protect those we love, I'll do so.

I put my arm around Aileene and gave her a hug. Even though we were true-mates and created for one another, I liked who she was and how perfectly we complimented each other. *I love you Aileene, and am grateful you're in my life.*

I love you more, Alister.

That's impossible, I chuckled.

Well, I love you more than I love to hunt, she sent me smugly.

Wow, that's a lot, I admitted and she dug her fingers into my side to find my ticklish spot.

"That's not fair," I laughed as the bus came to a stop.

"Who said I've got to be fair? Both Mom and Mother told me that as a female, it's my prerogative to keep you guessing about what I'll do next." She smiled at me with a mischievous twinkle in her eye. "By the way, I may love you more than I love hunting, but I appreciate how you'll take me hunting tonight."

"I will?"

"Thanks for agreeing. Have an exceptional day, love." She gave me a kiss and pushed me out of my seat.

I followed Gustav off the bus not exactly sure what just happened. After the bus pulled away, I looked at my mentor and he must have been able to read the confusion on my face because he held up a hand and said, "Don't look to me for answers. I'm often in conversations with Seraset and I do not understand how I agreed to do something I had no plan to do; ever. For example, the other day we spent the afternoon picking wildflowers near the palace. In all the years I've lived there, until the other day I never thought to myself, 'I think today would be an outstanding day to pick flowers.' And yet, it was wonderful and I enjoyed my time with her," he finished with a goofy smile on his face.

Josef

New York

There's something soothing about fly fishing—the repetitive movement of casting, the line slicing through the air and the fly landing gently on top of the water to float with the current. It was almost hypnotic. Since King Alister had instructed us to relax for a few days before returning to Arizona, I'd taken my team fishing. We would take the jet to Arizona the day after tomorrow so I could see Alex's face as I asked him about the message that led to so many shifters' deaths.

The sound of a splash and feline scream of rage broke the silence. I turned my head and looked downriver to see Scott splashing and spluttering as he tried to regain his footing. "I thought this was supposed to be relaxing," he yelled as he struggled to his feet.

"It is relaxing," Robert called from across the river, "you're just not doing it right. You're supposed to use the line to fish, not keep diving into the water trying to catch it with your leopard paws."

"I'm having a blast," Dwight called from farther down river from Scott.

"That's because you're a bear, and bears love water," Scott grumbled as he threw his gear up on the bank and sloshed up on shore so he could empty his hip waders; again.

"What's wrong with a little water?" Todd asked as he reeled in another fish; his third in the last thirty minutes. As a tiger, Todd loved the water, too.

"Water's fine for drinking but I would rather stretch out on a tree limb in the sun than wade around an icy river," Scott huffed.

"You can always join me on the bank," Steve called from his camping chair on the grass slope leading to the water.

Scott sloshed out of the water and sat in the chair next to Steve with a sigh.

Guys, there are some humans on their way to the river so be careful of what you say. Frank sent to the rest of the team. He had opted to remain in wolf form so he could keep watch to make sure the rest of the guys could relax.

Scott, if you hate fishing so much, why don't you and I switch places so I can fish? Frank sent.

That works for me, how far out are the humans? Scott broadcast.

It'll take them about five minutes to get to the river from where they are.

I'll be right there. Scott stood, quickly removed his wet clothes and transformed into his leopard form. He stretched and then ran to the woods where he scampered up a tree and lay on a limb out of sight.

After a few minutes, Frank made his way out of the trees and over to the fishing gear Scott had left behind. He looked at the snarled line and shot an annoyed look to where Scott had disappeared. "Thanks for making a mess for me to clean up," he muttered under his breath but loud enough for the rest of the shifters to hear him. They laughed at his injured tone.

About that time four men came down the trail and the man in the lead called out. "How're the fish biting?"

"You'll have to ask Todd, he's the one with all the luck," I called from my position in the river. As the men wandered over to Todd to see which fly he was using, I turned back to the task at hand and started casting out my line again. Saturday when we'd fly to Arizona would come soon enough. Today and tomorrow I was determined to relax as the King commanded, and I would make sure my team did the same.

Alister

Gustav told me he rented a Dodge Challenger for us because he likes the way it looks, and it has enough room for us even though we're both over seven feet tall. It would take us over two and a half hours to drive to where the two shifters lived, but I was happy to have the day to spend with Gustav.

"You know, Alister," Gustav broke the silence as he was passing a slow car, "even though I had the pleasure of watching you grow up, I'm amazed at the man you're becoming."

"Thank you," I replied. "You've always been an enormous part of my life and your influence has helped me tremendously, especially this past year." As pleased as I was by the compliment, I broached another subject. "So, how's Seraset?" I laughed.

"She's good," Gustav couldn't stop the smile that overtook his face as he answered. "I'm sorry you didn't have time to meet her before you returned to Earth."

"That's okay, from what I hear, I will get the opportunity when we return to Theria," I said and waggled my eyebrows at Gustav.

Gustav laughed. "You heard correctly. Centuries ago, Seraset wanted me to marry her but I was foolish and used my job as Historian as an excuse to put it off. I figured I'd always have time later since we're so long lived. Seraset left the palace shortly after I told her of my decision and we only connected again once we came back to Theria. I've gotten wise in my old age and finally proposed. She agreed and we'll get married once I finish this adventure with you."

"Congratulations," I laughed excitedly, "I'm thrilled for you."

"We're thrilled, too. Seraset also wants to have kids right away, she says we've wasted too much time already. I'm looking forward to being a dad," Gustav breathed.

"I think you'll make a great dad," I said. Even though Gustav didn't respond, I could tell my comment pleased him and we rode in silence for a bit, just enjoying each other's company. It reminded me how my dad and I would take road trips when I was younger, and we would ride in silence. Occasionally, he would reach over and pat my knee. When he did that, I would always answer, 'I love you, too, Dad' because I knew what he was saying with that simple gesture. I never had to guess where I stood with my dad, he was good about showing me affection and telling me how he felt.

"Gustav," I said, breaking the silence. "I know I said it earlier, but I really want you to know how much you mean to me. Even though I always respected you as my favorite teacher, you are also part of our family and taught me a lot as I grew up. It wasn't until we went to Middle Earth that I finally understood what you added to my life. If it hadn't been for you, Stavros, Miriam, Fritz, Frieda and my parents, I wouldn't be who I am today. Thank you. Even though my father and mother are back in my life, I still need your guidance."

"Thank you for saying that Alister. It has been my pleasure to walk with you through your childhood and I'm looking forward to the years ahead. It's fun watching you work, and observing the things you, Shelley and Bernie get up to. Now that you've added Aileene to your group, it's fun to watch her, too."

I learned something about my mentor on that drive; he really likes to drive fast. Occasionally, he would ask me to see if there were any humans near us and if I told him there weren't he would open up the Challenger and drive it as fast as he could until I warned him there were people nearby. He did that so many times we cut a lot of time off our trip and even though we stopped for a pleasant lunch, we arrived at the entrance to Blanton Forest before three in the afternoon.

Using the connection I had to the two nearby shifters, I could guide Gustav to the parking area closest to where they were.

As he parked, Gustav remarked, "Phillip wasn't able to pinpoint shifters the way you do. As King he also had the connection with the other shifters on Theria, but An'Ceann has given you a level of control that's astounding." He held up his hand to stop me from dismissing his comment. "I realize you feel uncomfortable receiving compliments but it's important you understand this. An'Ceann has given amazing gifts as a shifter and you possess control over magic that goes way beyond anything we've ever seen before."

"Thank you, Gustav," I responded.

"You're welcome," Gustav answered. "But you want to be careful you don't let your uniqueness turn into unhealthy pride. I know you already understand this but the more gifts you're given, the more opportunities you take to serve and help others. You do this well, but I wouldn't be an excellent mentor if I didn't point this out to you."

Gustav's words and his concern for my well being moved me. However, Shelley's irreverence must have rubbed off on me because I replied, "Thank you Gustav, you are my Obi-Wan."

Gustav chuckled and asked, "Is that the Obi-Wan to Anakin or Obi-Wan to Luke?"

"Oh, definitely Obi-Wan to Luke, he didn't do such a brilliant job with Anakin." I laughed.

We got out of the car and started down the path into the forest. The section we wandered in was part of the old growth and according to the internet, many of the trees were hundreds of years old. Gustav and I stopped in a small clearing surrounded by trees. Sunlight filtered down through a gap in the leafy canopy. I could sense the shifters nearby, so I called out to them using mind-speak and included Gustav in the conversation.

Hello, this is Alister Rex, High King of Theria, are you there?

Alister? But you're just a boy.

No, sister, he was a boy, but we've been here so long he must be ancient by now.

Are you sure, sister? We've only been in this forest for days.

You must be mistaken; we've been here for centuries.

Pardon me, ladies, may I have your names?

Yes, Your Majesty, my name is Clovella, but you may call me Ella.

Seannafair is my name, Your Majesty.

"Sire," Gustav said reverently. "Clovella and Seannafair are dryads and are guardians of the woods."

A tall woman with skin the color of cornstalks stepped out of the trunk of a sugar maple tree. Her hair was also green but highlighted with the purples, yellows, reds, and oranges found in leaves in the fall.

"Sire, I am Clovella and I remember when young Gustav here would climb the branches of my tree so he could pounce on his friends."

Another woman stepped out of the trunk of a hemlock tree and she looked identical to her sister, except her piercing eyes were a brighter green than Clovella's.

"And I am Seannafair, Sire, and have been watching over your family since Dóchas and Síocháin united all of Theria; have you come to bring us home?"

"We have, I am so sorry that we left you here," I apologized.

"How many centuries have passed since we fled to Earth?" Seannafair asked.

"It has only been fourteen years since we fled through the gate from Theria," I answered.

"Then these friends of ours have sheltered us well," Clovella said brightly as she reached her arms up to the trees in the circle. The trees appeared to bow towards the dryads and their branches reached out like a child wanting to be picked up.

"Grow well, my friends. You are protected here in this wilderness. Be strong, and healthy and shelter the animals of this place," Clovella said in a melodious voice.

Seannafair continued, "Stand tall until your roots are unfettered, and you can dance the dance of An'Ceann." Their words swept through the trees like a rushing wind and I could hear tinkling bells mixed with a chorus of voices raised in a song without words that trailed off in joyous laughter. When I turned back from looking at the trees in wonder, Seannafair and Clovella had transformed into their human forms and I quickly looked away while I dug into my pack for clothing for the two women.

After they dressed, I looked at them and tried to figure out which woman was which since they were identical except their eye and hair color. "I'm Clovella," said the woman with brown hair and green eyes.

"I'm Seannafair," the woman with green hair and brown eyes said as she smiled at me, "and ready to return to Theria."

Alister

Middle Earth

After we met for a human-sized dinner, I opened a gate to Middle Earth in a wilderness area near Lexington to take Aileene hunting. I didn't think farmers would appreciate it if their livestock went missing. It had been over a week since any of us had eaten in our natural forms, so I took everyone with us, including Clovella and Seannafair. As I watched Mother and Aileene dive towards the herd of sleeping bayak I thought of a question for my mom.

Hey Mom, how did you, Dad and the rest of our friends eat in your natural forms for thirteen years on Earth?

*Hmmm...*Mom sent as she arrowed towards one member of the now-frightened herd which had stumbled as it tried to flee the hunting dragons. Once she settled down to consume her kill, she answered me.

We bought a dairy farm about an hour away from our home in Maine and we would go there every few weeks to eat. Some of our friends from Theria ran it for us.

Wow, I never knew.

Mom chuckled in her mind, *That's kind of the point, we had to keep everything secret. It was such a relief to finally tell you the truth. Aren't you going to eat?* Mom asked.

Yes, but I'm waiting for everyone else to get theirs first, I sent as I continued to soar in lazy circles above the herd.

Do you remember that time your dad and I took a business trip to South Africa when you were ten years old?

Yes, I was able to stay with Shelley for two weeks. That was the summer the three of us decided we wanted to be stuntmen and a stuntwoman when we grew up. We practiced our moves every chance we got. Frieda put a stop to it when Bernie kept practicing falling down the stairs in their home.

Mom laughed at the memory. *I'd forgotten about that. Anyway, when we were in a village in South Africa, we went to a primary school named after MOJA MORAGO -'The King Who Eats Last'. He is still admired because of his willingness to serve his people and put their needs above his own. You're like him; I'm proud of you, Son.*

Thanks, Mom, I sent and then saw that everyone else was eating. Frieda and Bernie were in their unicorn forms grazing on the lush grass while Miriam and Shelley were nearby eating a bayak each. Mother and Aileene were also eating, but were far enough from each other that their natural territorial instincts didn't kick in. Mkali was in her centaur form, Gustav was in his sphinx form and they were walking towards a distook Mkali shot with her bow and arrow. She would cook her meal over the fire she'd started. Jason had also transformed into his sasquatch and would share the meal with Mkali and Gustav.

I processed all this within seconds and spotted two running bayak about to escape into the tree line on the far side of the meadow. With a mighty beat of my wings I crossed the distance to the fleeing animals and roared as I dove towards them. As usual, I didn't want my meals to suffer so I dispatched them quickly and settled down to eat.

As I ate, I wondered about the things happening on Earth. My original plan was to take a mini-vacation and take our time picking up the missing shifters, but that was before learning about the enemies surrounding us. Maybe I should send everyone else home to protect them—maybe we should just return to Theria to deal with the problems arising there—maybe I should.

"Hello little dragon," An'Ceann said as he emerged from the woods. He stood looking at me for a few moments and then fell to the ground laughing. His laughter was soothing and was so full of joy the air felt charged the same way it does after a lightning strike. Even though An'Ceann was laughing at me, I wasn't offended but joined in his laughter even though I wasn't sure what we were laughing about. Each time he would look at me, he would start laughing again and I joined in until hot tears rolled down my face.

This went on for a minute until I finally asked, *What are we laughing about?*

An'Ceann sobered, then snorted when he looked at my face and chuckled again. "You really are a messy eater. You remind me of a toddler eating spaghetti, I think you have more bayak on your face than you do in your belly."

Then I'm glad I don't have a mirror to— I stopped sending because a gigantic mirror suddenly appeared in front of me and I could see exactly what I looked like. I couldn't help myself as I snorted fire after seeing the image.

I've got to work on that, I muttered in my mind. *Give me a minute,* I sent and used my long tongue to clean my face.

"While you get cleaned up, I want to talk with you about a few things—you missed a spot above your right eye—you got it. First, why are you tying yourself into knots about what you should do rather than asking those who love you to help you decide?"

I'm not sure, I guess it's because I don't want to disappoint anyone.

"I hate to tell you but when you lead, you will always disappoint someone. You can't lead by trying to please everyone. It will drive you crazy and you won't be leading. Why did you come to Earth?"

To bring home the shifters abandoned on Earth and reunite them with their families.

"Has that mission changed?" An'Ceann asked.

There's more danger than I expected—but, no, the mission hasn't changed.

"So, you still need to bring the shifters home?" I nodded in agreement and he continued. "If you build your kingdom on *Protect the Weak,* who are the weak in this situation?" An'Ceann asked me seriously.

The missing shifters and the members of Tionchar who are trapped on Earth. I responded.

An'Ceann nodded but continued to look at me. "And...?"

It puzzled me for a moment but responded when I worked out what he was getting at. *And the humans who could be harmed by the traitorous shifter if he's allowed to continue whatever he's doing.*

An'Ceann nodded again but looked expectantly at me as he waited for me to work out whatever point he was trying to make.

And the humans who will be hunted by Paterson if he's allowed to continue to spread his lies about aliens on Earth. But why do I need to be the one to stop him, isn't this a human problem?

"I agree, it is a problem, but it's not entirely a human one. When Neil Paterson saw the shifters come through the gate to Earth fourteen years ago, it started a chain of events that led to where we are today. Since shifters helped to cause this problem, it is up to you to deal with it," An'Ceann answered.

Maybe I should just kill him and be done with it, I answered flippantly.

An'Ceann stared at me and I felt ashamed by my words and my attitude. *I'm sorry, I shouldn't make light of killing someone, even if he deserves it. He's responsible for the deaths of at least six people since we've been on Earth.*

"He's responsible for more deaths than that, and it's possible you may have to kill him to stop his evil; but never make light of having to do so. When you treat others as less than yourself, even if they are enemies, you move a step closer to becoming like them," An'Ceann said with a gentle reproach.

Forgive me, I thought with my head bowed.

An'Ceann moved closer to me and placed his cold nose between my eyes. I was immediately filled with warmth as though An'Ceann hugged inside and out. "My child, I forgive you. But please, tell me what else is bothering you."

There is so much to do and I wanted to take Aileene and the rest of my crew on a vacation and see some fun places on Earth. I didn't expect to have to fight enemies and deal with traitors. Humans are getting killed, they killed some of my people and I'm afraid I won't be able to protect the people with me and they might die.

"That's entirely possible," An'Ceann said seriously, "but tell me Alister, which member of your team would hesitate to put their life on the line to protect others? Which one would stand by and see someone killed to protect themselves?"

None of them would, I answered, affronted that he would imply such a thing.

An'Ceann smiled at me. "Alister, just as you have risked your life many times since finding out who you are, each of your friends is also willing to lay down their lives to protect those weaker than themselves. Whether you like it or not, they are also prepared to lay down their lives to protect you and each other. As much as you want to keep everyone safe, you cannot do that without also taking something precious away from them—their ability to choose."

I saw things clearly, the same way you can see your face clearly in a mirror after the steam dissipates. *You face the same difficulty, don't you?* I sent.

"Yes," An'Ceann said seriously. "If I kept everyone safe by always protecting them from themselves and others, I would take away their freedom to choose their own way. I would rather people always choose the right path, but sometimes they choose the wrong path. If they do, I'll wait for them farther along the road of their life, for them to turn the right way again. The wonderful thing about it when someone does that, that person doesn't have to start from the beginning again but can move forward from that point."

But what if they never choose the right path?

"Then I will respect that choice, as much as it pains me to do so." An'Ceann sighed. "Neil Paterson is probably too far down his own path of evil to turn aside from that, but maybe not."

And what about the traitorous shifter?

"Decide that when you find and confront him."

You can't tell me who it is?

"Oh, I can—but I won't." An'Ceann chuckled.

Why?

"I have my reasons." He held up his paw to forestall my objections. "I'm not doing this to be cruel, but there are lessons you need to learn along the way for your growth and if I give you too many spoilers," here he smiled again, "it will hinder that growth. You're just going to have to trust me."

I sighed but knew he was right. *Very well, is there anything else you can tell me that will help me make the wise choice on what I need to do?*

"Yes, talk to the people with you about what's bothering you and let them help you. If I remember correctly, Aileene was rather perturbed with you the last time you tried to do everything on your own and almost killed yourself. Ask for help. Do the things that only you can do and then trust others to do what only they can do. Also, I'm here for you, even if you can't see me; and you won't see me again until this adventure is over. Remember I love you and am proud of you." An'Ceann said and rubbed his golden mane on my face in a lion's kiss.

Thank you, An'Ceann, I sent.

"You're welcome," An'Ceann said and turned towards Clovella and Seannafair who had sneaked up on us without me hearing them.

"Ceannársa," Clovella addressed An'Ceann.

"Ceannnaofa," Seannafair greeted him as well.

"An'Ceann," they said together and bowed low before the lion.

"Alister, I will take Clovella and Seannafair with me to Theria, so you need not open two more gates tonight. I suggest both you and Josef move forward now rather than wait another day. Are you ready ladies?" An'Ceann asked.

Both the dryads turned to me and bowed again.

"Young King, stay your course," Clovella said as she lay her right hand on my cheek.

"Don't be dismayed when you find yourself tested beyond what you've faced before," Seannafair said as she lay her left hand on my other cheek. Both dryads buried their other hands in An'Ceann's mane, and they faded away.

I was staring at An'Ceann as he smiled and spoke to me. "One last thing, Alister. You still have a chunk of bayak in your teeth. You look silly." An'Ceann laughed as he faded away.

Thanks a lot, I sent and felt along my teeth with my tongue.

Dr. Phillip Brent

New York

"Dr. Brent, we've recorded another spatial anomaly," one of the new technicians said to me, interrupting my musings.

"Where and when?" I asked, my attention sharpening.

"It was recorded one hour ago, within the perimeter of 36° 11'18" N, 81° 28'17'W—"

"I don't want to work out the coordinates; just give me the geographical location and the search area," Dr. Brent snapped.

"Yes, of course," the tech stammered. "The search area is roughly sixty-nine thousand square miles and overlaps the states of Virginia, West Virginia, Tennessee, Ohio, Indiana, Illinois and Kentucky."

Dr. Brent was silent for a few minutes while he digested this information. Suddenly, he laughed and clapped the surprised technician on the shoulder. "Excellent," he exclaimed. "That buffoon Paterson may not appreciate this accomplishment, but I can. We've further narrowed the search area down to one fourth of the earlier anomaly. Well done."

"Does that mean, you will inform Mr. Paterson about our progress?" the technician wondered.

"No," Dr. Brent added hastily. "Not until we have a smaller search area and more rapid response time to give him. Paterson isn't known for his patience."

No, I am not, thundered a voice from the speakers mounted in the four corners of the room. *Did you think I wasn't checking your progress Brent? Did you really expect me to only receive my information from your lackey Abbot? You're a fool. The only thing keeping you from permanent retirement is the progress you've made today. I expect results soon. Oh, and one more thing Brent, I won't forget the buffoon comment.*

Dr. Brent was pale and felt light-headed as Paterson's words reverberated in his head. The only thing that could save him from his employer's wrath would be immediate results.

"We must hope that we record another anomaly soon so we can further refine our instruments," Dr. Brent said shakily to the technician.

"Thank you for your work—I'm sorry, I seem to have forgotten your name."

"Wayne, sir," the technician replied.

"Thank you, Wayne. Keep working while I lie down in my office for a bit; I don't feel well," Brent stammered.

"Very well, sir." Wayne said and went back to work.

CHAPTER TEN

*E*arth *Traitor*

He held the tablet and ground his teeth in frustration as he reread the message.

Immediate Extraction—Protocol Tionchar Erasure—Authorization —Phillip 42QBTHX1138—Contact initiation to be made by Josef Shoals or Alister Rex.

He knew what the message meant and how he was expected to respond. He was being recalled to Theria at once and would either receive contact from Josef or Alister for further instructions. Every member of Tionchar would have received the same message and would already enact plans they had in place so they could leave Earth. He would not let that happen.

He swept his arm across his desk, knocking everything to the floor and knew his plans were balancing on the edge of ruin. He had to act decisively or this order would destroy everything he had built. Even though he was loath to do it, he knew he had to enlist the help of someone outside his circle. He sat in his custom made chair behind his desk, unlocked the top drawer and pulled out a piece of paper with a name and a number.

His lip curled in disgust when he saw the name but entered it on the burner phone he retrieved from the drawer anyway. He typed the message to the person who would get him out of one mess. But, he would take care of the other one personally.

Alister

Schenectady, New York

Mother and I were sitting in a booth at The Water's Edge Lighthouse near Riverside Park in Schenectady, New York. We were waiting for Bruce, the only member of Tionchar unaccounted for. The waitress walked by our table again to ask us if we needed anything.

"No, thank you," I said, "but we'll order when our friend gets here."

As she walked away Mother remarked, "You know she's flirting with you, don't you?"

Her words surprised me but I answered honestly, "I suppose she's cute and all but why would I look at someone else when I have Aileene?" I asked.

Mother smiled at me and patted my hand, "I'll tell her you said that."

I smiled absently and thought back to the conversation I'd had with my team on Middle Earth.

Middle Earth

Two Days Prior

I shared with them everything An'Ceann had told me and asked them for their thoughts, but also apologized for ruining their vacation.

"What are you talking about?" Shelley asked. "Driving around in a bus for hours at a time is exciting and all, but since I've got the movies I want, the only thing I still want to do is go to Hero Con next month. Hopefully, we'll have everything wrapped up by then, but if not; at least we'll get to fight."

"What my wordy boyfriend is trying to say is, we're with you Alister and will back you no matter what," Bernie said as she put her arm around Shelley.

"What she said," Shelley said as he rolled his eyes.

"I don't understand the problem," Mkali added. "You're the King so what you say, goes."

Everyone else agreed with her statement so I continued. "We still have three shifters in Georgia. Two near Atlanta and one in Savannah. There's one in New Orleans, and nine in Port Aransas, Texas. There are seven total in Florida, one in Orlando and six in the wilderness near Lake Okeechobee. Also, one in Arizona and one in California. Plus, Mother and I need to meet with a shifter in New York. How do we get all of them in the shortest amount of time?"

We were silent for a few minutes while everyone considered the problem. Finally, Gustav cleared his throat and spoke. "We may not like it, but we must split up to accomplish everything in the shortest amount of time. I suggest Miriam and I go to Texas."

"Fritz and I have spent a lot of time in New Orleans, I can start there," Frieda offered.

"I'll take Georgia," Mom offered.

"What about me?" Aileene asked.

"I think you should go with Bernie, Shelley, Mkali and Jason on the bus to Florida," I said.

That way I can protect everyone on the bus, Aileene suggested and I nodded. *What about Josef and his team? I notice you didn't mention any of the members of Tionchar.*

After I finished speaking with An'Ceann, I created a pinhole gate and spoke with Father. He sent a pre-arranged, coded, message to every member of Tionchar recalling them to Theria. When we get back to Earth, I'll call Josef to fill him in and have him leave at once to pick up the shifters in Chicago, then go to Phoenix to meet with Alex. After that he needs to pick up Tionchar shifters in Los Angeles, then fly to England to join our people there. We can always gate to Eutheria then open a gate to Earth from there so we can send our people home. We'll make that decision once Josef has reunited with our people. What do you think of the plan we came up with?

That makes sense. You'll be careful, correct? If you end up in a coma again because you've overextended yourself, I will be vexed with you, Aileene sent before giving me a kiss.

I will do my best, my love, I chuckled.

"Eww...Alister and Aileene are kissing again, gross," Shelley exclaimed.

"Well, if you think kissing is so gross, you won't want any more of my kisses," Bernie huffed.

"Um...no, that's not what I meant. You know what—you got me," Shelley smiled and gave Bernie a kiss. "Mmmm, that was nice," he finished, waggling his eyebrows.

"You're impossible," Bernie laughed and slapped him on the chest with the back of her hand.

"I suggest the rest of us use commercial flights to get to our destinations," Miriam suggested. "We've been traveling on the road since coming to Earth so this will help throw off our enemies if they are close by."

We all agreed that her idea was sound and after completing our plans I opened the gate to Earth and we returned to our hotel for a few hours of sleep.

Alister

Schenectady, New York

Present

It jarred me out of my reverie when Mother placed her hand on my arm. Thinking about Aileene made me miss her so I widened the connection we always have between the two of us to let her feel how much I loved her.

Thank you, Alister, I love you, too, she sent.

Momentarily stunned that we could communicate across more than thirteen hundred miles, it took me a few moments to respond. *Can you hear me?*

Yes, she sent excitedly. *Mother told me we might be able to communicate from this far away. I'm glad we can.*

I miss you; we haven't been apart since we met, and I haven't seen you in two days, I sent.

That's true, except for the two times you were comatose from your injuries. Besides, it hasn't been two days, we saw each other yesterday morning.

But that was at five so that doesn't count, I sent. *Were you able to contact the shifter in Orlando?*

Yes, her name is Malonne Farhana and she's an elf. She wasn't willing to come with us yet because she instructs children with autism and must prepare them for her departure. We've arrived in Lake Okeechobee and will pick up the Patel family soon and then will return to Orlando. How are things going with you? Aileene asked.

Bruce finally made contact yesterday after multiple messages from me. He told us he would meet us at a restaurant, but he seems to be late. If all goes well, Mother and I will get on a plane tomorrow morning and join you in Orlando.

Sounds good, my love. I can't wait to see you tomorrow, Aileene sent me a hug through our mental connection and I sent one back.

Goodnight, I sent to Aileene and muted our connection.

"Things are going well in Florida," I spoke softly to Mother. "The team is picking up the Patels in Lake Okeechobee."

"Tagas and Kistha are such lovely nagas, but it sounds like they might have had children. Who was in Orlando?" Mother asked me.

"An elf named Malonne Farhana—" I stopped speaking when I saw the look of shock on my mother's face.

"My foster mother? How is she on Earth?" Mother wondered.

Before I could ask her for more information, I noticed a muscular man about six-feet-three inches tall with close-cropped black hair and green eyes walking towards our table. Even though we had been speaking quietly I was momentarily concerned about how much he may have heard of our conversation with his shifter hearing. He moved with a cat-like grace and it was evident that he was a fighter by the way he carried himself. His skin was chocolate brown and his suit tailor made.

He stopped next to our table and bowed slightly before gently saying, "Queen Beatrice and Prince Alister, it really is you. I apologize for my caution and for making you wait for me."

"Please sit, Mr.?" Mother began.

"Please call me Wayne," he said as he slid into the other side of the booth. After the waitress returned to take our food and drink order, we began again.

"Wait," I said, "you call yourself Wayne Bruce?"

Wayne chuckled, "What can I say? I'm an enormous fan."

"Who are you?" I asked in a scared voice.

"I'm Batman," Wayne said in a low, menacing voice and we both laughed.

Mother just looked confused, so I promised to explain everything to her later.

Since my mother knew Bruce from before he came to Earth, I let them catch up while we ate. I'm sure the food was delicious, but I ate mechanically as I considered whether the man sitting across from us was the traitor we were looking for. There was enough ambient noise in the restaurant that people couldn't hear our quiet conversation as Mother told him everything that had happened over the past fourteen years.

"I'm sorry, I didn't know any of that happened," Wayne said with a look of concern on his face.

After our waitress served our desserts and coffee, I asked him about the mysterious circumstances surrounding the deaths of the members of Tionchar four years before.

"I suspected the message when it came through but since it had the proper code words, I investigated anyway. I planned to drive to the meeting place but got a later start than I'd planned because of some, ah, unforeseen complications that arose before I could leave." For the first time in the conversation, Wayne appeared uncomfortable.

"What were those complications?" Mother asked in a tone that made it clear he had to answer.

"Well, since I've embraced my name of Wayne Bruce, I've also embraced his alter ego and do what I can to stop criminals in New York City as a vigilante. I wear a mask and since I'm a gargoyle, I also use my wings to intimidate the criminal element." His confession embarrassed Wayne, but I laughed good-naturedly which made him smile. "I realize this violates the spirit of Tionchar but once communication from Theria stopped, I couldn't sit on my hands and ignore those who were being plagued by criminals." He chuckled and continued, "I could argue that it's my mentor, Josef's fault. When he lived in New York City, he met a writer named Bob Kane and influenced him to create Batman."

"While this is very interesting," Mother said dryly, "it doesn't answer my question about complications."

"My apologies, my Queen. On the day of the meeting, I helped the police by tracking down the leaders of a drug cartel and waited to make sure the police were uninjured when they arrested the criminals. By the time I got on the road, I was running late and tried to make up the time by driving very, very fast. As I neared the entrance to the park, I was overwhelmed by a feeling of danger, so I pulled off at a rest stop to let the feeling pass. This has never happened to me before or since, but I could sense another shifter at the rest stop, so I called out using mind-speech.

"As I drove slowly through the parking lot, I kept calling out, but no one ever answered. I parked and waited for a few minutes, but dread continued to build within me. Instead of getting out of the car, I turned back towards New York and drove straight home."

"That doesn't explain why you've been ignoring the messages from my father and me," I said accusingly.

Wayne acknowledged my rebuke by nodding his head before answering, "I again apologize for that. I have become extra vigilant since that night and even more suspicious of messages from home. It wasn't until I received the extraction code, which is only known to the King and Queen of Theria, that I took the chance to meet you."

"I suppose that makes sense," I agreed.

"There is one other reason I've been reluctant to communicate; I infiltrated one of Neil Paterson's research facilities as a technician so I could monitor his activities. Unfortunately, one of his scientists, Dr. Brent, has developed a way to find the energy signature from a gate when it's opened, and he is trying to track your movements. I've been doing everything I can to widen the search parameters and delay the tracking time, without bringing suspicion on myself, so I felt I was of more use to you there. I only agreed to meet with you tonight because the entire system is offline so Dr. Brent can figure out why the system is glitching."

"Thank you," Mother said. "It seems we owe you a debt of gratitude."

"Nonsense, Your Majesty, I serve the Crown and people of Theria," Wayne responded quietly. He glanced at his wristwatch. "I apologize but I need to leave soon to get back to the research lab. Even though I don't need to be there until tomorrow morning, it would look suspicious if I didn't show up tonight to check the progress of the system reset."

"Thank you for meeting with us and clearing up a few things. We will contact King Phillip to let him know that we are suspending your extraction order until you've concluded your business with Paterson and Hominum Primus."

"Thank you, Majesties," Wayne said as he bowed to Mother and me after standing. "I've already taken care of the bill. Thank you for a lovely evening. I look forward to going home to Theria very soon," he concluded and walked away.

After a few minutes of silence, the waitress wheeled the dessert trolley back to our table and said, "the gentlemen informed me you would like another dessert."

Mother smiled brightly at her and clapped her hands like a little girl. "Yes, that would be lovely."

Eastbound, Over the Atlantic Ocean

Josef drafted his report but was unsettled and didn't know why. His interview with Alex Farrel went well and Alex had answers for each of his questions. He claimed he ignored the message four years ago because he was sure it was a hoax and didn't bother to respond or go to Maine. When Josef told him about the deaths of the others, because it had been a trap, Alex appeared to be upset at the news.

Josef looked at the in-flight map and saw they were halfway to England and would land in just over four hours. He finished his report, including his misgivings and hit send. Even with advanced technology, without a signal the report wouldn't get to King Alister until later. This Gulfstream G500 is a comfortable jet but Josef needed to get up and stretch his long legs. Perhaps a walk to the galley to see if there was something to eat would be a good idea. He unbuckled his seat belt, stretched, and at once felt a shudder pass through the aircraft.

After a few minutes Steve's voice came over the intercom. "We've got a bit of a problem up here; it appears we've run out of fuel even though the gauges show full tanks."

What does that mean for us? Josef broadcast through mind-speech, including everyone on the jet.

If we were close to an airport it would mean we'd have to land quickly to refuel. Unfortunately, since we're in the middle of the ocean, it means we're going down in about 20 minutes and we'll hit the water so hard our chances of survival are non-existent.

Well, that's a bummer. Dwight sent and everyone chuckled nervously.

There should be enough parachutes for each passenger along with life rafts. We can abandon the aircraft when we get below ten thousand feet and take our chances floating on the water.

On it, Todd broadcast and moved towards the back where the parachutes were stowed. *I've got good news, and awful news,* Todd sent after a few moments. *The good news is there are enough parachutes for everyone. The awful news is they're useless because someone slashed them to bits; it's the same with the life rafts.*

Well, now we know who the traitor is. Alex was so insistent his mechanic do a onceover on the plane I should have been suspicious of his intentions, Josef sent and amended his report and hit send once again. Even though he might not get the report prior to the plane crash, the King would know what happened. That is if the tablet's not destroyed in the crash.

Are you able to radio in our position? Josef broadcast.

The saboteur did something to the radio since it went out at the same time we used the last of our fuel. Robert sent from his position as co-pilot.

All of the highly trained shifters aboard the doomed aircraft retook their seats and fastened their seatbelts so they could compose last messages on their mobile devices.

I hate getting wet, Scott grumbled which caused everyone else to laugh.

Twenty minutes later as the jet approached the surface of the ocean, the right wing clipped a wave and it was torn off as though it were made of tissue paper. This caused the nose to dip down into the water and the forward momentum continued to propel the jet forward end over end. Even though the crash occurred on the water, the damage was the same as though the plane hit the Earth. In moments, the rest of the jet disintegrated and sank beneath the black waters. There were only random pieces of debris floating on the surface of the moonlit water to mark the destruction of the Gulfstream G500.

Alister

Schenectady, New York

Mother and I left the restaurant after eating another three desserts each, and walked to Riverside Park so we could sit by the river. As we walked along, she told me stories from when I was a little boy and some of the antics Bernie, Shelley and I got up to. We laughed together and I was grateful to spend this time with her, with no emergencies hanging over our heads. Once we got to the park, we sat on a bench and watched the lazy flow of the river.

"Earlier you seemed surprised when I told you that Malonne Farhana was the shifter living in Florida, do you want to talk about it?" I asked.

"Well, Malonne was my foster mother when I was growing up. She was kind towards me while I lived in Marsupia; once I left, I felt like she was happy to get rid of me. I felt like I'd been a burden to her. We're not what you would call close." Her smile was pained and my heart went out to her. I held her hand in mine and waited for her to continue.

"Over the years, I tried to bridge the gap, but she was always polite in her refusal to visit me in Theria. Your father and I would visit my foster parents once every few years, but it became increasingly difficult as the decades passed. When you hatched from your egg, I once again asked her to visit but she made another excuse.

"Your father had enough and traveled with Fritz and Frieda to Marsupia so he could tell Lord Elandorr and Lady Malonne how much their coldness hurt me. I wasn't there but from what Frieda told me, your father was furious on my behalf. They told him it wasn't like I was their actual daughter and I expected too much from them." A tear trailed down my mother's face and I could tell how much this memory still pained her. "Rather than do something he would regret, your father returned to Theria and that's the last time I heard from either of them. The last I knew, they still ruled Marsupia as wise and benevolent rulers; even if they were terrible foster parents." She laughed bitterly.

"I am so sorry for your pain. You are a wonderful mother and nothing at all like Malonne or Elandorr," I said as I gave her a hug.

She sobbed into my chest and I wondered how this powerful dragon could be reduced to tears by these painful memories.

"Believe it or not, I haven't thought about any of this for years," she said wistfully.

"Well, you were in a coma for thirteen of those years," I said dryly, trying to channel my inner Shelley and use humor to lighten the mood.

After a few moments, Mother broke out laughing at my comment and her laughter continued until tears ran down her cheeks. Once she stopped laughing, she turned to me with a smile and kissed me on the cheek. "Alister, you are a wonderful son, thank you for making me laugh. Even though this is an old, old hurt, it can still cause me pain."

"So how do you think she came to be on Earth?" I asked.

"The only thing I can think of, she was in Theria when everyone fled through the gate. But that makes little sense because that would mean she was coming to see me."

"After we get this business with the traitor and Paterson taken care of, I think you should go to Florida to speak with her," I suggested.

She nodded thoughtfully but changed the subject. "What do you think about Wayne? Do you think he could be a traitor?"

"I see what you did there, but we'll get back to Malonne later." I smiled to take the sting out of my words. "You've been at this far longer than I have but I don't think so. However, I am concerned he overheard us talking about Aileene and the rest of our team at Lake Okeechobee."

"He seemed genuine to me, but since the only two shifters unaccounted for are Alex and Wayne one of them must be the traitor," Mother mused.

"What if it's neither of those two?" I asked.

"What do you mean?"

"What if Neil Paterson was the one to send the message to the others and it was his crew that killed the shifters?"

"I suppose that's possible but if he's the one, I imagine he would have produced at least one body as proof of an alien invasion," she surmised.

"Rather than speculate we should probably eliminate both Alex and Wayne before we look at other options." I shrugged. "As much as I hate to admit it, we must wait until one of them reveals themselves to be the traitor; then deal with them at that point." An idea popped into my head then, but I'd need to talk with Bernie before I suggested it to anyone. Bernie could use her unicorn talent to tell which of the two men were lying.

I sighed and broached another subject. "What can you tell me about Tagas and Kistha Patel? You said they are nagas but I'm not familiar with that shifter. What are they?"

"Nagas are snake shifters and can assume three unique forms, depending on their need. They can be mostly human but with snakes on their heads, sort of like a gorgon."

"Like Medusa from Greek mythology?" I asked.

"Well, sort of. Remember, they base Earth mythology on eyewitness accounts of our people throughout the ages. There is a tribe of gorgon living about a half day flight from the palace. Which makes sense that the Patels would be in Florida since that is roughly where the gorgon tribe lives in Theria," Mother mused. "Anyway, they can also transform into true serpents or their third form as a half human, half serpent."

"Which half is human?" I asked.

"Their torso is human, like a centaur, and their bottom half is serpent. Their venom is highly poisonous and they can produce it in any of their shifted forms. They prefer any of their natural shapes to a human one, so it makes it hard for them to integrate with humans."

"I'm glad we're able to rescue them then. Aileene told me earlier they would meet with them and then return to Orlando. I imagine they're on their way since that was a few hours ago."

Mother smiled at me again and put her arm around my shoulders. "It pleases me to see you and Aileene together. Even though An'Ceann made you for each other I've never heard of true-mates coming together so quickly before."

"Maybe that's because she tried to kill me the first time we met," I laughed.

"Maybe if I'd tried that with your father it wouldn't have taken us so long to fall in love," she chuckled. "Actually, Alister you're special in so many ways."

"You're my mother, you're supposed to think I'm special," I teased.

"That's true but you've got a level of control over your connection to other shifters I've never seen before and your link with Aileene is unusual in its strength. Your ability to use magic is also something rarely seen among our kind. Each of us can use magic in small ways but I don't know of anyone else who has a magic reservoir like you do," she finished proudly.

"Aileene does," I replied. "It's not as developed as mine yet, but the more she practices gathering magic when I open pinhole gates to Middle Earth, the larger it grows."

"My son, I don't think you know how amazing that really is. You seem to have taught yourself how to use your natural powers as a Royal Dragon as well as magical powers with extraordinarily little instruction."

"I couldn't have done any of this without Gustav's help. He showed Shelley, Bernie and me how to use magic while we lived on Middle Earth and without his training, I never could have healed you and Father from the poison Dimitri gave you."

We were quiet for a long time after that until Mother once again broke the silence.

"If I weren't your mother, I would love you anyway and follow you as my King. You have impressive power, but you also have great humility. It is so easy for us Royal Dragons to lose our way because of the gifts An'Ceann has given us. But if you remember they are gifts, and not anything we deserve, it can help you stay grounded and true to your beliefs."

"I also have Bernie and Shelley for that," I grinned, "but I thank you for reminding me."

Mother laughed, "Shelley hasn't changed at all, and I hope he doesn't. Believe it or not, Fritz is the one who has helped your father the most over the years."

"He has?" I said in surprise. "I suppose it's because he knows all the protocols to follow and reminds you both about them all the time?"

Mother laughed. "He does that for sure, but he has a wicked sense of humor and can make your father laugh like no one else can. Stavros and Gustav are steady as mountains, but Fritz and Albert have been the ones to make things lighter when the burden gets oppressive. We can always count on Albert to do something outlandish, but Fritz is the one to use his words to bring humor and defuse tension."

"That's amazing, I never would have guessed that about Fritz."

"It's part of his charm and wisdom as a diplomat. He never does what you expect him to do but he is always aware of what's needed in a situation."

"I suppose Bernie must take after her dad then. She's the one to keep us steady when Shelley and I get off topic." I smiled fondly as I thought about my friends. After a moment I sobered. "How have you and Father dealt with the fact that it's easier for your friends to get hurt or killed than you?"

"That's difficult, but as your father and I were reminded after our encounter with Dimitri, we can be harmed. Having friends more vulnerable than you can help you make wise decisions; because you must think about ways to protect those weaker than yourself. When our friends can be hurt or killed when we rush into things without considering their welfare, it can help us slow down and use wisdom rather than just brute force. Sometimes brute force is just what a situation calls for." Mother smiled and held out her hand to me as she stood. "We should go back to the hotel; we've got a long day ahead of us tomorrow."

I took her hand, stood and stretched. "You're right, I would like to talk to Aileene before I go to sleep…"

Aileene's panicked sending interrupted me and it took me a moment to understand what she was saying but when I did, my blood turned to ice in my veins.

Alister, there are men with guns surrounding the bus and shooting at us. We're under attack!

CHAPTER ELEVEN

Russian Hind-Gunship Attack Helicopter
Twenty-five miles west of Lake Okeechobee

"Sir, Garrett here, our ETA is fifteen minutes. Unfortunately, the ground troops have engaged the bus early."

"That idiot Hunt has outlived his usefulness. Between his propensity for blowing things up and inability to follow simple orders, he's become a liability. Once we've secured the aliens, eliminate Hunt and his team," Paterson commanded.

"Very good, sir. What are your orders concerning the alien invaders?" Garrett asked.

"I would prefer one alive to test and question but if you can only bring back corpses, I want every single piece to study. Do I make myself clear?" Paterson asked.

"Crystal," Garrett answered.

"Leave the line open, I want to hear everything that goes on," Paterson demanded.

"Roger that," Garret said and flipped the switch to communicate with the second gunship and his men in the passenger section of their helicopter. "Lock and load, people. We have our orders. We are to stop the alien incursion and if possible, bring in one prisoner. Beta Team has made one too many mistakes, we are to take them out with extreme prejudice—no survivors."

Alister

Schenectady, New York

My heart pounded in my chest as I stood frozen to the spot and furiously thought through my options.

"Talk to me Alister," Mother said worriedly.

I took a deep breath. "Aileene and the others are under attack and under heavy fire from automatic weapons. She threw a shield around the bus but is afraid she can't keep the shield intact for long. She's unable to shift into her dragon form because she fears the shield will drop when she does, and the attackers will kill the others. While every adult on the bus can fight, they're all vulnerable to bullets.

"There isn't any way to fly to them in time to save them and since I've never been where they are, I can't open a gate to their location," I finished in a rush. I could feel myself starting to panic and wanted to shift into my dragon because my mate and my friends were in danger. *An'Ceann, I need your help. I don't know what to do,* I shouted in thought-speak.

There wasn't a verbal answer, but I felt a sense of calm and peace settle over me and then felt Mother's arms wrapped around me in a tight embrace.

"Alister, I need you to stop reacting and start thinking. How can your abilities help others from this distance?" Mother gently asked me.

Aileene's panicked thoughts were broadcast to Mother and me and broke through the quiet moment. *Alister, whatever you're going to do, do it quickly. I can't hold the shield much longer.*

I sought the connection we always had between us and widened it as much as possible. In the past I'd been able to send power through my connections with other shifters and I wondered if I could send magic to Aileene the same way. There was only one way to find out, so I concentrated on my magic reservoir and pushed that power towards my mate. It felt like I'd removed a plug from a sink as the magic drained from me and transferred to Aileene.

Whatever you're doing, keep it up. I can feel the shield growing stronger, Aileene sent to me.

I can keep sending you magic but what I really need to do is to open a gate so we can get to you. But I've never been there before so I don't think I can do it, I apologized in my mind.

"Wait, how were you able to open a gate to your father and me?" Mother asked.

"I saw Dimitri's fortress in a dream," I said.

"Can't you use the connection you have to Aileene to do the same thing?" she asked.

"I can try," I said but changed to thought-speak to once again include Aileene in the conversation. *I'm going to open a gate by using our mate connection. I might drop the magic flow going to you but if this works, Mother and I will be there in moments.*

I can hold the shield for a few minutes again since you gave me so much magical power. I believe in you, see you soon.

I opened my senses and traced the mate connection back to Aileene. I could feel her love for me and her utter belief that I would succeed, but I could also feel her anger that she was under attack and powerless to do anything to take out the enemies. Once I firmly established the connection, I waved my hand to open a gate to my trapped mate.

The gate opened in the trees within sight of the bus. I could hear automatic gunfire and see the muzzle flashes from many guns. Mother and I rushed through the gate and I closed it behind us. I hardened the skin all over my body so the flying bullets wouldn't injure me and ran at the nearest person who was firing at the bus.

We're here, I called out and sliced the man with my clawed hand. He collapsed to the ground without a sound. Mother had followed my lead and had taken out another attacker. Before I could incapacitate anyone else, I heard helicopters coming our way. I seriously doubted that the newest arrivals were here to help and knew Mother and I would have to take them out.

There are helicopters coming towards us, Mother and I need to handle those. We've eliminated two of your attackers. Can you handle the rest while we take care of the helicopters? I broadcast to everyone on the bus.

Go, Aileene shouted in thought-speech. *We've got this, now that you've given us an opening.*

As I launched myself into the air and transformed into my dragon, I looked back to see Aileene leading the others off the bus. I turned back towards the oncoming helicopter and roared a challenge and shot fire from my mouth. These people who only wish to kill and destroy are about to find out why you don't want to make a dragon angry.

Aileene

Once Alister gave me the infusion of his magic, I felt my reservoir grow and fill to the brim with magical energy. I'm not exactly sure how he does what he does, but I am constantly amazed by my mate and can't wait to tell him how proud I am of him. But for now, it is up to me and the others on the bus to take care of the evil men who were trying to kill the shifters under my care.

Alister and the Queen are here and have killed two attackers, but there are helicopters heading in our direction. They will take care of those but it's up to us to eliminate those who are still firing on the bus. I've got enough energy to keep the shield up now, but I'm tired of defending. What can we do to take the fight to the fools who seek to harm us?

Can you split the shield to cover those in the bus and those of us who need to leave? Shelley asked.

I'm not sure, I don't have the same control that Alister does.

Okay, Shelley continued, *can you make a small hole in the shield so some of us can leave?*

How big do you need the hole to be?

I'm not sure, Kistha how large a hole do you need for your serpent to slip through?

Kistha, Tagas and their twelve year old daughter Amaira shifted into their serpents and slithered towards the door at the front of the bus. I smiled and followed the three Patels. Jason opened the door and I waved at the surprised soldier who stopped shooting long enough for me to make a small hole in the shield towards the bottom of the door. The three shifters slithered out. Before the man could fire his weapon again, one serpent leaped at the man and bit him in the leg. The venom worked instantly and he was paralyzed before he hit the ground. The Patels moved on in search of their next victim.

Aileene, open the shield by the door so Jason, Bernie, Mkali and I can exit the bus. Get on top of the bus so you can keep the shield raised to protect those inside and let us know if you see enemies headed our way, Shelley ordered.

I looked at my friends with pride. Bernie had her sword and Mkali had her bow and quiver full of arrows. Shelley and Jason would use their shifter forms to take out the rest of the soldiers.

Let's go, I shouted in thought-speak, *but if you get killed Alister will be angry with you.* With that, I dashed through the door and the others followed.

Shelley roared when he cleared the door and turned into an enraged grizzly bear. He ran towards the back of the bus. Jason also burst through the door as a towering sasquatch and jumped on top of the bus so he could attack the men on the other side. I hardened my skin, manifested my wings and followed Jason to the top. I arrived just as he roared and dove off the side towards two soldiers who were still trying to kill the kids on the bus. They turned towards him to fire but since he had landed between the two of them, they hesitated; that was all the time Jason needed.

He reached out with one arm and grabbed the frozen soldier on his right and did the same to the one on the left. He picked both men up like they weighed nothing and smashed them together. He then threw both bodies at the next group of soldiers before jumping back on top of the bus to find other enemies to attack.

I watched Mkali and Bernie clear the right side of the bus as they quickly finished the soldiers who were on the ground because of serpent bites. They worked their way around the front of the bus to confront any enemies hiding there. Jason didn't leave many men standing, but that was fine with me because I didn't want to see Bernie or Mkali get hurt.

It was easy to maintain the shield while also watching the battle which was quickly winding down. I sowed more confusion into the remaining soldiers and let loose with my flame at one who was taking aim to shoot Jason in the back. My fire was hot enough to melt rock so the man was quickly reduced to ash. I was glad I interfered. Mkali continued to rain arrows on the remaining soldiers, then Jason or Bernie got close enough to take them out. There was another roar from Shelley as he rounded the back of the bus, chasing a soldier right into Jason's waiting arms.

Movement near the trees caught my eye and I saw one last soldier hidden behind some bushes. He stepped in front of the bushes, grabbed something off his vest and prepared to throw it. Before he could, an arrow struck him in the arm and he dropped the thing in his hand. He scrambled wildly on the ground to find it. I shouted, "grenade" when I finally realized what it could be while pointing my finger at the man.

If the grenade exploded, our people would be harmed. Before I could react, Shelley transformed into his human form as he ran towards the man on the ground. Shelley picked him up, threw him on top of the grenade then transformed back into his bear and dropped onto the man's back. There was a muffled whump and the explosion threw aside Shelley like a rag doll. As Bernie screamed incoherently, Shelley tumbled across the ground and landed in an unmoving, bloody heap.

Alister

Once Aileene told me they had defeated the ground troops, I could concentrate on the problems coming toward us. The helicopters were still a few miles out so I sent a message to Mother that we should fly out to meet them rather than wait to let them come to us.

These are attack helicopters and they can carry anti-tank missiles on the wingtips. They also have Gatling guns mounted under the chin. These are deadly weapons to our friends on the ground but could also be dangerous for us. Will those missiles or bullets be able to harm us? I asked Mother.

I could sense her shrug through our mental connection as she answered. *I guess there's only one way to find out. Do you want the one on the right or the one on the left?*

I'll take the one on the right. I sent and scanned for any humans nearby. The only ones I could sense were the nine in each helicopter flying towards us. *We cannot let them get past us or they will fire their missiles at the bus, I don't think Aileene's shield can withstand that kind of punishment.*

Don't worry, Son, we've got this. With that statement, Mother let loose a jet of flame towards her helicopter and it veered off to avoid her deadly fire.

I couldn't afford to watch what she was doing any longer because the pilot of the helicopter I faced started firing his forward gun at me. I really wasn't sure what would happen, and Mother had instilled no confidence in me with her 'only one way to find out' comment. I needn't have worried because, while the bullets hit me, they ricocheted off my scales and couldn't penetrate them.

Flaring my wings, I stopped my forward flight and hovered in the air before the helicopter, hoping to get it to turn aside. I shot flame towards the helicopter and it turned away from me, but not before it released four missiles in my direction. Time seemed to slow as I saw what I could only assume were anti-tank missiles streak towards my position. Even though the bullets didn't harm me, I wasn't sure what would happen when I was hit by weapons designed to destroy tanks.

I couldn't let the missiles get past me, so I made the only choice I could and let them come. The pilot fired them so close together it might be possible for me to destroy them all at once using my fire. I would only get one chance at this, so I continued to hover in the air and sprayed my flame from right to left to destroy the incoming weapons.

I destroyed three of them with my fire, but the resulting explosion threw my aim off enough that I missed the fourth one. I had already been tossed aside from the original explosion so when the fourth missile struck my side, the only thing I could do was absorb the blow with my body. The missile exploded on impact and the resulting shock wave threw me backward and I started falling from the sky.

I righted myself quickly and knew I had to destroy my helicopter before the pilot fired another barrage of missiles. I didn't have time to worry about any injuries I might have sustained, I had to protect my people. Scanning the sky, I saw the helicopter swinging wide to make another run towards the bus. I roared a challenge and flew as fast as I could towards the deadly helicopter. Rather than try anything fancy, I dove under it and lashed out with my tail as I passed underneath and hit the tail rotor so hard it shattered.

Without the stabilizing effect of the tail rotor the helicopter spun wildly in the air. The pilot was trying to counter the effect of the spin, but I knew he wouldn't get the chance. Even though I was sure the humans in the doomed helicopter wouldn't hear me, I shouted thought-speak at them anyway, *You should never have tried to harm my people,* and shot a blast of fire at the helicopter, engulfing it in flame as it plunged to the ground far below.

Since I had destroyed my helicopter, I scanned the skies looking for Mother to see how she was faring. I heard a muffled explosion and saw fiery debris falling to the ground, so I knew she had defeated her adversary.

Are you injured? I mentally called out to my mother.

No. The cowards ran when they saw me and didn't fire. It took me a few moments to catch up to them. Are you injured?

I'm not sure, I sent, *I don't feel any pain at the moment but one missile exploded against my side. Let me check on the others.*

Aileene, I sent, *Mother and I have destroyed the helicopters and are on our way back to you.*

Shelley's down, but everyone else is fine. Aileene called back at once. *He dove onto a grenade to save everyone else.*

We'll be right there, I shouted mentally and wheeled back to where my friend could be dead or dying.

Neil Paterson

I stared at the phone in my hand trying to understand what happened. One moment Garrett was reporting that everything was a go on his end and the next he was screaming into the radio that they were under attack by a monster. After a few minutes of confusing shouting there was a roar, a crash and then the line went dead. I tried to reach the lead in the other helicopter and even tried to reach Hunt, the leader of the ground assault, but no one answered.

Angry that I couldn't reach my people I scrolled through messages and found the text from an unknown, and untraceable number which had led to me sending my soldiers to Florida.

I've lost contact with my people in Florida, I typed.

That's your problem, not mine, came the response a few minutes later.

"Do you know who I am?" I shouted at the phone in my hand. "How dare you talk to me that way. If I find out you've betrayed me, you're dead. Do you hear me? You're dead." I shrieked, spittle flying from my mouth.

I waited for the unknown person on the other end to respond, but I realized we were texting rather than speaking on the phone. There was laughter coming from the closet, so I stormed in there and stood in front of the portrait of my parents. As I watched, they turned their faces to me and smirked at my predicament.

"Don't you dare laugh at me," I shouted. "I've got this under control and when I have proof that aliens exist you won't be laughing; you'll be falling over yourselves to beg my forgiveness for doubting me. Now, shut up," I screamed to drown out the sound of their mocking laughter, and turned off the light to punish them. After taking a few calming breaths, I typed my response.

Watch the tone you take with me. You wanted me to capture the aliens on the bus so you must have a reason to fear them. I'm not sure what happened, but my people aren't responding. My phone dinged with an alert that I received an email. I ignored it because I also received another message from my unknown ally.

If they're not responding they're dead or captured. You failed me, you sniveling little worm. Those weren't aliens, but something much, much worse. I could almost feel sorry for the trouble coming your way if I thought you would survive long. I must take care of this problem myself. You're useless to me.

How dare you? You're dead, do you understand me? You're dead! I typed furiously.

I stared at the screen so long I thought the person on the other end would not respond, but then saw the three dots showing a message was being typed.

Goodbye, Mr. Paterson. You cannot trace this number and when I end this conversation, I will eat my dinner and await my opportunity to eliminate those you could not. Based on some information I've just received; your life is about to get much more complicated.

Transmission Ended

I'd never seen that message before but assumed the number wasn't valid any longer. I was tempted to throw my phone at the wall but wanted to check the email I'd just received. The email was from CaineWarrior1776@gmail.com and I gasped as I read the message.

Paterson,

You're receiving this message because I'm dead and knowing you, you're the one who had me killed. I planned for your double-cross and set up a deadman's switch on my computer. If I don't confirm the password every six days the attached file will be sent to every local and national news outlet and the FBI, Homeland Security and every other government agency with initials representing their name. That information was sent to those organizations six hours before you received this email.

May you spend the rest of your miserable life rotting in prison. If I'm not dead and I accidently sent this out. Oops.

Caine

Alister

Phoenix, Arizona

We walked out the doors of Sky Harbor Airport and into a blast furnace. As a dragon I'm immune to fire, but the blast of heat that hit me as we walked out of the air conditioned baggage claim area was staggering. As I stood searching for the limousine Alex promised to send to pick us up, I thought about the events over the past twelve hours. It was almost three in the morning when we arrived at the airport in Miami to catch a flight to Phoenix.

When Mother and I arrived at the bus I was shocked at the amount of carnage surrounding the parked vehicle. After locating Aileene, I rushed to where she and Bernie were tending to Shelley's wounds. He was moaning and groaning so loudly I had to stop and laugh in relief when I realized he would be fine.

"Show some respect, Stretch, I threw myself on a freaking grenade and it blew me up," Shelley whined.

I looked at Aileene and Bernie and they both smiled and nodded.

"He was very brave," Aileene said as she dusted off her hands and came over to give me a hug and kiss.

"He was," Bernie agreed but smacked Shelley on the arm. "But they could have killed him. They hurt him badly enough that he broke three ribs, some of his guts were hanging out and he was unconscious. Thankfully, I could heal the damage to his body, but now the big baby is just begging for attention." Bernie smoothed Shelley's hair on his forehead so she could lean in and kiss his brow.

Jason and a man I didn't know came around the front of the bus where they had moved bodies out of the way so we could drive off. "I've checked the bus and Expedition out and there isn't any damage. I suggest we leave before the authorities get here," Jason said.

"Hey Alister, could you help me up?" Shelley asked, "I get dizzy every time I try to stand."

I picked up my friend and had to swallow the lump in my throat when I thought about how close I had come to losing him.

"I'm bummed no one was filming the fight, my grenade dive was epic." Shelley grinned at me and then passed out in my arms. As I carried him to the bus, I used the *Sanos* spell on Shelley to add my healing energy to my wounded friend. As I watched, his face lost its waxy sheen and he looked more comfortable. He must have been gravely wounded if Bernie's healing hadn't been enough. As I was getting Shelley in his seat, Jason drove us away from the scene of the battle.

Before I could sit, Aileen approached me, eyes narrowed in irritation, and ripped open my shirt and started feeling the ribs on my right side. "Mother told me a missile exploded against your side. What were you thinking?" she demanded as she searched my side for broken bones.

"I was thinking that if that missile got past me, everyone on the bus would be dead and I couldn't let that happen," I said quietly but jerked away from her and hissed the instant her hand touched me.

"You're damaged," she exclaimed and looked like she was seconds from shifting.

I grabbed her hands in mine and kissed her fingers. "I'm not hurt, your hands are cold," I whispered but since everyone on the bus had shifter hearing they all started laughing with relief.

Aileene threw her arms around me and sobbed softly and I murmured soothing words to her as I stroked her auburn hair and maneuvered her to our seats.

"Where to, Sire?" Jason asked from the front of the bus.

"The nearest airport, please. It appears we've found our traitor. The shifter we met with in New York overheard Mother and me talking about Lake Okeechobee and must have set up the ambush. Once I get everyone to Arizona, where I know you'll be safe with Alex, I'll take care of the traitor in New York," I growled in anger.

On the way to the airport, everyone briefed me on the fight and how they had destroyed the enemy. I met the Patel family and told them how grateful I was for their help and for their quick response against the attackers. Often, we would see emergency vehicles, lights flashing, flying down the road towards the scene of the battle. They didn't pay any attention to us.

We stopped at a rest stop about halfway to Miami. Thankfully, there were showers there and no other travelers were around. Everyone who had torn, bloody clothing handed them to me. I piled them on the concrete, quickly turning them to ash with my fire. I sent messages to Miriam, Gustav, Frieda and Mom informing them what had happened and told them to lie low where they were, and I would have them join us in Phoenix in a few days. Shelley was back to normal and I could tell we healed him as I watched him tease Mkali and the Patel kids.

I had a few moments of quiet with Aileene and I told her how proud I was of her. Without her use of the *Spheara* spell, none of the others would be alive right now. She was so exhausted from her efforts she fell asleep on my shoulder the moment she sat beside me and Jason started driving to Miami. I tried to call Josef to update him on what we'd discovered but got an out of service message and figured they were still in flight to England.

Before we boarded the plane in Miami, I called Alex to let him know we were on our way to Phoenix. I told him I'd figured out who the traitor was, and I would head to New York to take care of him once everyone was safe. He told me not to worry, he would handle everything, and assured me he would keep trying to reach Josef until he answered and would fill him in on the details.

"Alex, thank you for all you're doing. I will sleep on this flight knowing I can count on you," I said.

"It is my pleasure, Sire," Alex answered and disconnected the call.

Once the plane reached the proper altitude, I could lay my seat all the way back so I could go to sleep. I was thankful we paid the extra money to travel First Class.

As we stood on the curb waiting for our ride, I noticed a limousine and a large van with heavily tinted windows coming toward us. Once they pulled up to the curb, the driver got out and opened the back door. Alex stepped out of the limousine and came over to Mother and me with open arms. Mother hugged him first and then Alex turned to me for a hug. He smiled at the others standing there but didn't make a move towards any of them. Two enormous men got out of the van and started loading luggage. Both wore black suits and dark sunglasses. These men and Alex's driver looked like they were ex-military or some type of bodyguard.

Oh great, the Men in Black came to pick us up, Shelley commented and I had to stifle a laugh. *Who do you want to go with you, Bernie or me?*

I considered his question and realized neither of them could come because we still had Tionchar business to go over with Alex. *Sorry, Shelley, but Mother and I have some matters to discuss with Alex. You need to go with the others.*

I'll accept; for now. But, we will talk about this later, Shelley sent.

"Queen Beatrice and Prince Alister, please ride with me in the limousine. The others will be comfortable in the van. We have plans to make and I'm sure you would rather keep these matters confidential," Alex said persuasively.

Do you have any objections, Alister? Mother sent and after a tiny shake of my head she answered Alex. "Very well, that will be fine."

"I'm sure you are all famished after your journey so if I may be so bold, may I make another suggestion?" he asked. Mother nodded so he continued, "I have food and drink prepared for your Majesties in my car, but I can have my men take the rest of your team to breakfast then they can rejoin us later. How does that sound?"

Mother looked at me for confirmation, so I broadcast the question to the others.

After receiving agreement from everyone, I nodded, and Mother once again confirmed with Alex.

"Very well. My men have loaded the luggage, so we need to get going. Airport Police are rather quick to give tickets if we stay in the loading zone too long," he said and held the door open for Mother and me.

See you later, I sent the group. *I'm a little envious that you'll be able to eat as much as you want. I doubt Alex has enough food to satisfy my appetite.*

What are you complaining about? Shelley asked. *You already had breakfast on the plane.*

I've had one breakfast, yes. But what about second breakfast? I sent.

I don't think he knows about second breakfast. Bernie chimed in.

Aileene giggled aloud as I got into the limousine and the driver shut the door.

Have fun, Aileene sent. *Just not too much fun without me.*

I won't. See you soon, I answered as we pulled away from the curb.

While the food Alex served us was delicious, there just wasn't enough of it, as I predicted. As I ate, it occurred to me that I hadn't spoken with Bernie about using her unicorn talent to see if Alex was telling the truth. Even though it's apparent that Wayne is the traitor, I would still ask her to interview Alex when we stopped.

Alex raised the partition between us and the driver as we pulled away from the curb so we could have a private conversation. He asked us to describe the events from the night before; both our conversation with Wayne and the attack on the bus. Since Aileene didn't want Alex to know she was a Royal Dragon I glossed over her part in creating a shield. Instead I gave the Patels more credit for killing the soldiers using their venom. Alex was especially interested in how Mother and I took down the attack helicopters and was positively gleeful when we gave him the details.

"Oh, I almost forgot. I finally got a text from Josef that they had landed safely and would lie low for two days before completing their mission," Alex said.

"Thank you for your diligence," Mother remarked.

"There's also something else you'll probably be interested in," Alex said as he turned on the television in the back of the car. "I recorded this earlier, but the same story has been playing all day, just different variations of the same facts."

On the screen a news anchor was looking at the camera, about to speak.

"We continue to follow the story that broke here first on CFN late last night. We received an email from a mysterious source accusing Neil Paterson, head of Paterson Munitions, of domestic terrorism through the organization Hominum Primus. Attached to the email were documents supporting these claims and video evidence. Even though these videos are too graphic to show on daytime television, we will show clips during our special report, *The Mind of a Madman*, at ten tonight but I must warn you, we advise viewer discretion.

"We have learned that Marcus Caine, who composed the email, was killed in the car bombing incident in Maine last week. Mr. Caine claimed that if we received this email with evidence attached, it would be because Paterson had him killed. The FBI and Homeland Security have formed a task force to investigate these allegations and take appropriate steps to bring the responsible parties to justice. Neil Paterson hasn't responded to interview requests and his whereabouts are unknown.

"In other news, the mysterious happenings near Lake Okeechobee, Florida are under investigation—" Alex turned off the television.

I'd been so engrossed in the news report, I didn't notice that we had pulled up outside a one-story brick building in the middle of nowhere.

"This is our stop," Alex said cheerfully as the driver opened the door and waited until we exited the vehicle and entered the building before driving away.

"Where are we?" I asked when we stepped into a room that looked a lot like a waiting room in a doctor's office. It was complete with uncomfortable looking chairs and outdated copies of magazines lying on the table. The most prominent thing in the room was a large television that took up most of the wall and on the TV was a live feed of the rest of our party eating breakfast.

"This is an out of the way place I use for my most sensitive negotiations. It's far enough away from the city we're not bothered but close enough that I can go home and get a good night's sleep when I've concluded my business," Alex said

"Why have you brought us here?" Mother asked in confusion.

"It's very simple, really, I want you to do something for me and I needed some leverage to persuade you," Alex put his phone up to his ear. "Do it," he said.

On the screen I watched one man who had been in the van pull out a large handgun, point it at Aileene's chest, and pull the trigger. Aileene looked momentarily surprised but then folded in on herself where the bullet struck her. She then fell backward off the bench she was sitting on.

I was in shock as I watched my mate fall out of frame and a dozen men rush into the room holding automatic weapons at the ready and leveled at my startled companions. I narrowed my eyes and turned towards Alex, ready to rip him apart when he held up his left hand. He was holding a box and his thumb was holding down a red button.

"If I take my finger off this button an alarm sounds and my men will open fire and kill everyone else in that room. Both of you sit down and if either of you tries to come any closer, you will watch each person in that room die, starting with the youngest," Alex said with a sneer.

"Looks like I was wrong about Wayne being the traitor," I muttered and Mother nodded her head.

CHAPTER TWELVE

"Why did you shoot Aileene?" I asked in dismay.

"To get your attention," Alex answered. "Now, sit down and put your arms on the chair." Alex used his right thumb to push an icon on his phone and metal clamps slid out of the chair and tightened on our arms. While Alex smiled smugly to himself, I contacted Aileene and included my mother in the conversation.

Are you okay?

Yes, it tickled a bit when he shot me but I'm fine. I've also got a shield around the others so they're safe. When can I take out these guys?

Not yet, I want to see if I can get Alex to monologue. I've got some questions only he can answer.

Okay, but I really, really have some aggression I need to work out, that idiot ruined my favorite top. I don't think I should wear it with a bullet hole in it. Hold on a second—There was a lengthy pause. Okay, I'm back. I wanted to let everyone else know I was fine and to cooperate with these guys who keep yelling at everyone to sit down.

On the screen, my people sat, pushed their plates away and put their hands on the table. Alex's goons kept their guns trained on each person. Thankfully, no one approached Aileene, who was still lying on the floor.

So, you were wrong about Wayne?

It looks that way, hold on. Alex is saying something, I'd better pay attention.

Sounds good, see if you can hurry. I landed on my arm and it's falling asleep, I can't move it because I'm supposed to be dead. Aileene sent, her thoughts laced with humor.

It was hard to keep a straight face so I bowed my head to hide my smile until I could get my expression under control.

"Aw, does the little prince feel sad because his friend is dead? You should thank me because I did you a favor. She had a thing for you Alister and eventually you would have had to break her heart. Now she doesn't have a heart for you to break," Alex laughed at his cruel joke.

"What do you want?" Mother asked. "These restraints won't hold us and when we get loose, you'll face the king's justice."

"I don't think I will. If I hold the people in that room," Alex pointed to the screen, "you'll do exactly as I say. As for what I want, it's simple. I want you to give me all the names and locations of the remaining members of Tionchar on Earth and then I want you two to go back to Theria."

"Why are you doing this?" I asked.

"Power," Alex said with a maniacal gleam in his eye. "You do not understand what it's like to be a lesser shifter. You were born into privilege, the top of the heap, a mighty Royal Dragon with the strength and power of your kind. I may only be a coyote but on Earth, I'm better than these insignificant humans in every way."

"I don't understand, as the head of Rex Industries, you have power, wealth, prestige and—"

"But it's not mine," Alex screamed. "None of this is mine. This all belongs to the Crown of Theria. The same Crown that left us here with no word for fourteen years. Oh, I kept things going the way the King ordered me to do for the first few years but when I thought I'd be trapped on Earth forever I went a bit crazy. Can you imagine what it's like to feel you're the only one of your kind left and you can't do anything about it? At first, I worked on using the tablet to contact other Tionchar members but that turned out to be impossible because of the protection protocols in place.

"It wasn't until I ran into a fox shifter five years ago in Italy named Isabella that we could make headway in linking our tablets. We could finally contact everyone else to invite them to a meeting. Isabella wanted to join with the others to open a gate back to Theria and I tried to convince her that our best chance of success was to combine our financial resources and carve out our own kingdom here on Earth."

"Where is Isabella now?" Mother asked.

Alex hung his head as he answered. "She had to die with the others because she betrayed me. I thought I'd convinced her that my way was the only way, but she tried to warn the others gathered that it was a trap, so she had to die. My men were already in place and when I turned my back on Isabella, they opened fire. My heart was broken because I thought she could be my mate, but her betrayal proved she wasn't worthy of my love."

Alex slipped into silent introspection, so I prodded him along, I didn't have all my answers yet and I was sure Aileene was getting impatient. "You have no honor; you killed your brothers and sisters of Tionchar for money."

"Honor? What do you know about honor you stuck up prince?" Alex seethed. "You and all your kind put such stock in honor but there's only one person I need to be honorable to; me. I make my own rules, I forge my path, I control my destiny. Oh, I heard your sob story about being trapped on Earth, but you didn't even know what you were. You could go about your life, ignorant of your true potential. You do not understand what it's like to know what you're capable of and being unable to do anything about it.

"Look at that moron, Paterson. I easily manipulated him into attacking that bus and now he's taking the fall for everything, even things I did."

"How did he know where the bus was?" I asked.

"That was easy. I've been able to keep track of everyone who had the second batch of phones. Sinclair almost ruined my plans when he gave out the first group of untraceable phones, but you made life easier for me when you needed more for Josef. I could give Paterson the coordinates from your driver's phone. I don't know how you saved everyone on that bus, but I don't really care since you came to me instead of me having to find you again.

"It was more difficult to get rid of Josef. I thought he suspected me when he came to ask about the mysterious message, but I threw him off the scent and sent him on his way. My mechanic added a helpful device to the plane that dumped all the fuel once they were too far across the water to get help. I'm sure Josef figured out I was responsible for his death before they crashed into the water, but since he's dead, it doesn't matter."

"Who are the men in that room?" I asked, my voice choked with sorrow for losing Josef and his team.

"They're part of my special security unit. They've been with me for years and take care of most of my, let's say, dirty work. As long as I pay them well, they don't care what I order them to do. Now, let's talk about what you will do next." He said, sounding like a second rate movie villain.

I rolled my eyes, "I can't believe you just said that."

"Said what?" Alex asked, confused.

"'Now, let's talk about what you will do next,'" I mocked. "You're ridiculous and I'm tired of listening to you, even if I got you monologuing and telling me your entire plan. I've heard enough," I seethed.

Alex was momentarily stunned by my words but then repeated, "Do it," into the phone in his hand. At once one man raised his rifle and shot Arjun Patel in the back. Since Aileene had shielded the shifters in the room, the bullet ricocheted off the shield and struck another one of Alex's soldiers.

You can get up now Aileene, the men in the room with you are the ones who killed the shifters in Maine.

We watched Aileene stand and shake out the arm that had fallen asleep. She smiled into the camera and her beautiful, blue eyes turned molten gold and she manifested scales across her face and neck.

Have fun, I sent mentally, and she grinned showing off her elongated dragon teeth.

"Alex, I didn't properly introduce Aileene to you before," I said as I stood from the chair, easily snapping the restraints. Mother did the same. "Aileene is my mate, and a Royal Dragon."

The last thing we heard before she destroyed the camera feed was Aileene's T-Rex impression, automatic gunfire, and the screams of terrified men.

Mother held Alex's arm in an iron grip while smoke poured from her nostrils. Her eyes were bright and appeared to have fire dancing within their depths.

"Are you okay?" I asked her.

"Other than wanting to bite the head off this heinous nathar; I'm fine." She lifted Alex with one hand, so his toes barely touched the floor. She shook him as she continued. "You will go back to Theria where you will stand trial for your crimes and our laws will decide your fate. I won't stoop to your level, no matter how much I want to. You would have murdered a child, a child," Mother roared in his face and Alex cringed away from her anger as he dangled from her hand.

I put my hand on her arm to calm her and she lowered him so he could stand on his feet again. "What's a nathar?" I asked.

Mother reddened, "It means slayer or murderer. I slip back into Elvish when I'm angry."

That is so cool, I can't wait for you to teach me Elvish, I sent and could feel her calm down. *Aileene, we'll join you in a few minutes. How is everyone over there?*

I'm afraid I've made a bit of a mess, but our people are fine. Aileene paused and I could sense her roiling emotions through our connection. *Alister, we've found the bodies of the shifters who Alex murdered in Maine.*

We'll be there soon, I sent and whipped my head towards Alex with narrowed eyes. He shrank back from my fury as I told my mother,

"Aileene and the others are fine, but they've found bodies at their location. I've got to make a call and then we'll go."

I opened my contacts and selected Batman.

"Good evening, Sire, how may I serve?" Wayne said from the other end.

"Alex Farrel is the traitor and we've captured him. I've got to open a few gates and I need you to disable the tracking software at your end."

"I'm glad to hear you've captured the traitor. Are your people okay?"

"The ones with me are fine but I've learned another group of ours went down on a plane in the middle of the Atlantic."

"I'm sorry, Sire. You need not worry about the tracking software. Since they have declared Paterson a person of interest in a domestic terror investigation, things are rather chaotic here. I've destroyed the tracking programs, disabled the satellite, and permanently erased years of research into the aliens Paterson and his group were tracking."

"Well done, Wayne. Can you join us in Phoenix? I need someone to look into Rex Industries to see what damage Alex may have done to our companies."

"I'll have my jet prepared and can be there in about six hours."

"Thank you. I'll send you the address," I finished the call.

Before I could open the gate to Aileene my phone buzzed with an incoming message. It was from Josef's phone. *Alex Farrel is the traitor.*

Then another message came in.

Plane going down in Atlantic roughly 47 degrees 02' N, 31 degrees 44' W. Sent complete report using Tionchar tablet.

Another message followed.

Shifters who can fly will rescue those who can't. Will contact you when able.

A last message appeared as soon I finished reading the previous one.

Safe in London. Exhausted. Will sleep then contact you again. Sorry for delay, battery dead, lost charger on plane.

"Josef and his team are fine, they're in London," I told Mother with relief. I opened a gate to Aileene but before we stepped through, I said to Alex, "You should probably make sure there aren't any shifters who can fly if you try to kill them by crashing their plane."

We spent the next three days in Arizona cleaning up Alex's messes and uncovering everything he'd done. The first thing we did after stepping through the gate, after making sure our people were okay, was to find the bodies of the fallen Alex had kept in cold storage. As I examined each face of these brave people who were murdered by someone who should have protected them, I wept. Mother and Aileene were the only ones with me and each of us grieved as we saw the evidence of their ultimate sacrifice.

"Why did he keep their bodies?" Aileene wondered.

"The unicorns who interrogate him will find out everything we want to know." Mother said softly as she kissed the foreheads of each shifter lying on the cold slab in the middle of the refrigerated room.

"We must take their bodies back to Theria so we can honor them," I said.

"I agree," Mother sighed, "but unfortunately since they are Tionchar members, we cannot honor them publicly. The three of us and your Father will be the only ones who can know the complete truth about their sacrifice."

I protested but my mother held up her hand and looked at me with such compassion in her eyes I sobbed again. "I know this doesn't seem fair, but this is what each one of these brave people agreed to when they took their oaths to follow the path of Tionchar. Their deaths were not in vain, and we will honor them. We have long memories and their bodies will join their fellow brothers and sisters who have fallen in the course of their duties."

She looked at both Aileene and me and placed a hand on each of our shoulders. "My loves, this is one of the troublesome things about ruling. You will face pain and loss during your reign, and you must keep that pain to yourselves, because if you don't it could affect the Kingdom and the people we are sworn to protect. Laugh when you want to weep, act strong when you feel weak, build when you want to destroy and above all, trust An'Ceann when it makes little sense."

She enfolded us in her arms as she continued. "But you don't have to face these things alone. An'Ceann has gifted you to one another so you can share the burdens only you two can carry. And your father and I will help you bear these for as long as we are able."

We stood there for a few minutes before I broke the silence. "I must send Father our position so he can meet us on Theria. As much as I hate to do it, we must leave the bodies here until we can meet. We'll post honor guards outside these doors and no one except the three of us can come in here."

"Or you could just open a gate to the palace from here and save yourself a few steps," An'Ceann said as he suddenly appeared in the room's corner in his lion form.

Mother bowed her head in honor and Aileene jumped on An'Ceann and hung around his neck like a small child. I joined Aileene and embraced him, while sobbing into his mane at the lives taken because of Alex's greed and lust for power.

"Come here, daughter," An'Ceann rumbled and I felt Mother join us. I'm not sure how long we held onto the lion and each other but once I was filled with an overwhelming sense of peace, it was time to step back.

"I've contacted Phillip for you, and he will be waiting to help you carry these bodies, so you can lay these shells to rest. Take heart, dear ones, they are ecstatic in my kingdom and wouldn't return if they were able," An'Ceann informed us.

I thought you said I wouldn't see you until my adventure was over, I sent.

The adventure with the traitor is over, he replied.

An'Ceann rubbed his cheek against each one of ours; then disappeared.

I concentrated on the secret chamber where my father told me about Tionchar and opened a gate. Father was waiting on the other side and Mother rushed into his open arms and wept against his chest. Father looked at me with tears in his eyes then he turned his gaze to the silent forms on the slab. Such pain crossed his face it moved me to embrace him. Aileene joined us and we wept together at the senseless loss of life.

We went about the grisly business of moving the bodies into the Tionchar command center in the palace and down to the sepulcher below the chamber. Once we laid each body in its own place my father cleared his throat and said, "I will take care of everything else. Thank you for bringing them home. Even though Alex Farrel betrayed them, they died as heroes."

We left the sepulcher and Aileene and I made our way back through the gate to give Father and Mother some time to whisper with one another. They walked hand-in-hand across the room and then Mother joined us on Earth.

"How are things progressing with the other kingdoms on Theria?" I asked.

"The diplomats are doing what they should to prepare for your world tour," Father said with a wan smile. "The way I'm feeling at this moment, I want to fly to each of the troublesome kingdoms and kick some serious butt."

"Fritz would be unhappy with you if you did that," Mother replied. "That would undo everything the diplomats have been working on."

"I didn't say I'd do it, I just said it's what I wanted to do," Father grumbled.

"There's one last thing I need to give you before I close the gate," I said as I left the refrigerated room and walked back to where Bernie and Shelley were holding a bound and gagged Alex Farrel. I nodded at my two friends and told them, "I'm sending him through a gate to Theria where my father will take charge of him."

Alex's eyes grew wide as I led him back into the refrigerator and handed him off to my father who was so angry smoke was pouring from his nostrils. He took charge of Alex and gripped his arm so hard there was no way Alex could ever escape.

"We'll be back in a couple weeks," Mother said and blew Father a kiss.

I closed the gate and we left that room of death.

The next three days were a flurry of activity. Jason made many trips to Sky Harbor Airport to pick up our people and bring them back to the immense house in Scottsdale we'd rented through Airbnb. Mom arrived first from Georgia and introduced us to Antexio and Ferene. They were pegasi mates and were excited about going home to Theria. She also brought sisters Gwenivar and Noelle, garden gnomes who took one look at the back garden, tsked under their breath and went outside to fix what they thought was wrong.

Mother returned to Orlando so she could talk with Malonne. Josef and his team had arrived by then so both Robert and Todd offered to go with her. Gustav and Miriam brought Mateo and Carmela Hernandez, wolf shifters, along with their children, Noah, Liam, Mia, Emma, Sofia, Elijah and Olivia from Port Aransas, Texas. The children were excited to be at the house and they had plenty of adults to watch over them. We could give Mateo and Carmela a mini-vacation and they were extremely grateful; wolf pups are very energetic. Frieda was the last to arrive with Jane, a mountain lion from New Orleans.

Josef, Wayne and I spent hours each day at the Rex Industries building in downtown Phoenix righting the wrongs caused by Alex Farrel. I had a permanent pinhole gate open so we could communicate to Theria in real time and my father could update us as he got information from Alex on what he'd done, and how to undo it. By the end of our three days, Josef had agreed to assume control of the companies again until his replacement could arrive from Theria.

Since Josef had run the company decades before when he was stationed on Earth, it wasn't too difficult for him to take over. Thankfully, it was standard practice that images of Tionchar members were erased when their time on Earth was over, so we didn't have to worry about people recognizing him as the former CEO and President.

After discussions with my father, we'd decided that any Tionchar member who wanted to stay in their current position on Earth could do so rather than return to Theria. Now that we'd reestablished communications, their mission could go forward. We would have to change some of Tionchar protocols to accommodate them, but we were willing to do that. Every Tionchar member opted to remain, and Phanes and Lilly came back from Theria.

Each day there were more reports about the mounting evidence against Neil Paterson and Hominum Primus. They placed Paterson at the top of the FBI Most Wanted List and all his assets were confiscated. He was still at large but authorities expected he would be apprehended soon. However, since he was still at large, I extended Tiffany's Hawaiian vacation to be on the safe side; she didn't object.

Before we left Arizona, I contacted Radiance, a phoenix shifter, who joined us in Scottsdale. The night before we were to leave for California to finish our vacation, we threw a huge going away party at the house for those who would return to Theria. After all the trials we'd faced since coming to Earth it felt good to relax and have fun. We stayed up too late, ate too much food and laughed—a lot. Since there weren't any neighbors around to see in the backyard, the younger children shifted into their natural forms and played together.

The back garden looked different from when we arrived. The trees and bushes were pruned and looked healthier. Gwenivar and Noelle proudly showed the fruit of their labors to anyone who was interested and offered to help anyone with their gardens once they were back on Theria. I wasn't sure if the owners would appreciate the change as much as the gnomes, but I didn't care and was willing to compensate them if they complained. We had a marvelous time.

The next morning, I opened a gate from the backyard to the palace in Theria. All the shifters we'd gathered across the US were excited as they stepped through the gate with their belongings and went home. Father was waiting with open arms and a sizeable crowd had gathered to cheer on those who returned. There were tears of happiness and I was overjoyed to see the families reunited.

You've done well, Alister, I'm proud of you, Father sent. *Where are you heading next?*

There's one last shifter in California. I'm sure it's Cyndi since she's the only one not accounted for. We'll play in California for a week until Hero Con and then return to Theria when we're finished.

Have fun. There'll be a lot for you to do when you return before you meet your people in the other kingdoms. Have you heard from your mother?

Yes, she has been having an enjoyable time with Malonne and they've been able to work on their relationship. They'll fly into Los Angeles before the Con and we'll go together.

Please tell your mother I love her and cannot wait for her to get home.

I will, I love you, too, Father and look forward to spending more time with you once things calm down.

He laughed through our mental connection. *Alister, you're the High King, things never calm down, but we'll work something out—don't worry.*

I closed the gate and we went inside to gather our belongings. When we went to the front, our bus was waiting in the circular driveway. Steve had flown Jason and Gustav to Florida where they collected our bus and drove it to Arizona. It was an outstanding thing they did since most of the things we had bought on Earth were on the bus. We were back to our original group, except for my mother, and we were leaving for California to have the fun I'd been hoping to have with my friends. As Jason drove us away from the house, I smiled with contentment; this would be great.

The drive to California took over six hours but since we were so excited about reaching our destination the miles flew by. About an hour into the drive, I moved to the front of the bus and grabbed the microphone so I could address everyone at once.

"Hey guys. Shelley just asked me about our plans for the next ten days, so I figured we'd talk about it," I started. "The first thing we need to do is contact the last missing shifter. I think it's Cyndi because many times when I track her, she's in the middle of the Pacific Ocean."

"I will stop calling you Stretch and start calling you Sherlock," Shelley called from the back and everyone laughed.

Is Sherlock a good thing? Aileene sent.

Yes, it's a compliment. Sherlock Holmes is one of the greatest detectives of all time.

That's good, she sent back.

"But once we connect with Cyndi, we've got some options. We were planning on spending time at Disneyland, Knott's Berry Farm and Universal Studios but we don't have to do any of that if you don't want to. The only proper plan we have is attending Hero Con in Los Angeles next week on Friday, Saturday and Sunday. The plan is to relax and have fun before we have to return to Theria for our diplomatic world tour."

"Have you been having that dream about the armies battling again?" Mom asked from her seat.

"Yes, it started again last night, but I'm still not feeling a sense of urgency. Father says things are calm and the diplomats are doing what they're supposed to. We still can't do anything in Theria for another month or more, so this is the perfect time to enjoy ourselves."

"I've got some things that might help us make our decisions," Shelley said as he came towards me and held out his hand for the microphone. Shelley had quite the presentation prepared for us as he talked about the various amusement parks and attractions in Southern California. He showed YouTube videos of Knott's, Disney and Universal Studios as well as information about the various beaches and Hero Con. When Aileene saw the Jurassic Park ride, I knew we were going to Universal Studios.

Everyone voted that we would find a place to stay in Newport Beach tonight, spend the whole day at the beach tomorrow and then head to Disneyland to spend two days there, then Knott's Berry Farm, then Universal Studios. We could always adjust our plans as we went along. This was a vacation. We pulled into the In N Out I'd directed

Jason to. His parking skills impressed me since the parking lot was rather small. We decided to eat while we were here.

I knew Cyndi was here somewhere so I looked at people sitting at the outside tables to spot her. People enjoying their meals filled most of the tables, but there was one that had a sole occupant; it was Cyndi. She had long, curly, sun kissed blonde hair and her skin was tanned a golden brown. Even from this distance I could see the laugh lines around her eyes and mouth that only come from someone who smiles a lot. She was wearing a pair of yoga pants patterned with scales and a sweatshirt that read, "Mermaid Hair, Don't Care." She also wore a pair of In N Out drink cup shoes.

Young girls at tables surrounding Cyndi kept looking at her while smiling and waving shyly. She would smile and wave back while she was plowing through the stack of double-double burgers on her tray.

Cyndi, it's Alister and we're here, I sent to her.

She whipped her head around looking to see where we were and the moment her eyes locked on mine, they widened in surprise. She let out a squeal of delight and jumped up from her seat. Unfortunately, when she did so she tripped over her own feet and accidently swept her burgers and drink from the table and they flew everywhere. She quickly caught herself before she hit the ground but kept moving forward and broke into a run towards me. When she was about three feet from me, she launched herself into the air and landed on me with her arms and legs outstretched and she wrapped them abound my body.

She talked so quickly about everything that she'd been doing the past fourteen years, it was hard to understand her words. I finally got a word in after a couple of minutes and could disentangle myself from her enthusiastic embrace, and I introduced her to the others. Everyone got the same effusive greeting and before long, each of us felt as if we were the most important person in Cyndi's life.

"I'm so glad you're here and at my favorite place to eat if you've never had a double-double you're in for a treat I can't wait to show you my house of course you'll stay with me so we can get to know each other and I can tell you everything that's been going on." Cyndi blurted in a rush as she grabbed Aileene's hand and dragged her into the restaurant.

As the rest of us followed, Shelley laughed and said, "I guess she's happy to see us. She'll be fun getting to know."

If anything, I think that was an understatement.

CHAPTER THIRTEEN

We sat in Cyndi's third floor living room in front of the wall of windows overlooking the ocean. There had been a magnificent sunset while we ate dinner on the enormous deck surrounding the house on the second floor. The cooks served fish, lobster and other foods harvested from the ocean. Cyndi told us she'd gathered everything herself, but her cooks prepared the meal. While we ate Cyndi asked about our adventures but promised to share her story after dinner.

To say her home was a mansion would be an understatement. There were enough rooms on the first floor, each of us could have our own. While we were eating, Mkali asked Cyndi how she could afford such an enormous home and what she did for a living.

"I'm a mermaid," Cyndi smiled mysteriously, "but I'll explain everything later."

Even though Cyndi spoke to each of us during dinner, she would often glance at Jason when he wasn't looking just as he would do the same when she wasn't looking; it was cute. The only strange thing during dinner was when Cyndi ate her lobster; she ate the entire thing shell, and all. It didn't bother me to hear her crunching as she chewed, but it was an interesting sight. After all, in my dragon form, I would crunch the bones of the animals I consumed.

"I've kept you waiting long enough I suppose," Cyndi started when we sat in the living room with dessert and coffee. "When we came to Earth all those years ago, I went to the ocean because, while I can survive on land, it's not best for me to do that long term. It was fortunate we came through a gate only an hour from the coast because I wanted to explore Earth's oceans. Time seems to pass at a different rate underwater because there's no suitable way to mark its passage. Night and day look the same to me underwater, it's one benefit of being a mermaid. I saw so many wonderful sights, I was lost in awe for a while. Along the way, I explored many undiscovered shipwrecks where I picked up a lot of pretty things. There were also amazing creatures that would do well on Theria but are natives of Earth; they're just considered legends here.

"I finally got homesick once I explored the ruins of Atlantis and saw evidence of Therian culture. Amazingly enough, some of the equipment I found was still functional, but I left it alone. One day someone should go back to retrieve it, but I think it's safe for now. Anyway, after Atlantis I made my way here to California and found I'd been exploring the oceans for almost ten years. Once on shore, I tasted my first In N Out burger and made this place my home.

"I've amassed quite a fortune from the pretty things I've picked up and moved to my underwater vault near here, where it won't be discovered. I had this house built and have made a pleasant life for myself."

"That's an amazing tale," Bernie said in wonder, "but earlier you told Mkali you also work as a mermaid; what do you mean?"

Cyndi smiled brightly and stood. "Come with me and I'll show you." We followed her along the hall on the third floor where she stopped in front of double doors. "I prefer not to lie so I wanted to create a job for myself where I could be who I am." She opened the doors and we stepped into a shrine to mermaids. There were photographs, paintings and statues of mermaids and each of them looked like Cyndi. There were also mermaid tails displayed in glass counters and posters advertising Cyndi the Mermaid along the walls.

"I have a mermaid business and perform at birthday parties, corporate events and even travel around the country to the various Cons where they have mermaid groups." Cyndi said laughing with delight. "I get to be who I am, and people pay me to do it, all while disbelieving there are such things as real mermaids."

She impressed me with her ingenuity and ability to survive alone. My heart went out to her because she had made a life for herself, even though she must have been lonely for others from Theria.

"I'll miss all this, but I'm lonely here and looking forward to going back home," Cyndi said wistfully.

Her words germinated a thought in my mind, but I didn't want to say anything before I sought wisdom for the direction I was considering.

We spent two fun-filled days with Cyndi, and she begged us to stay with her rather than checking into a hotel. She was so fun to be around; it wasn't hard to accept her offer. The first day we spent on her private beach where Aileene, Mom and I swam with her in the ocean in our natural forms. Dragons and drakes can swim well underwater and we can hold our breath for a long time. Everyone else enjoyed lying in the sun and playing in the waves. When Jason went to pick up my mother at the airport, Cyndi offered to go with him in the Expedition. We smiled at the growing attraction between those two.

On our second day of vacation, Cyndi took us to some of her favorite costume shops so we could order outfits to wear at Hero Con. There were so many options for us, and since money wasn't a concern, each of us would wear what we wanted.

After browsing through the pre-made costumes and through the catalogs of what they could make; the shopkeeper asked if we'd decided.

"I would like to dress as this Mother of Dragons person," Mother answered, pointing to a picture of Daenerys Targaryen from Game of Thrones.

"I would like to be Galadriel," Bernie blushed.

"Can I be Storm from X-Men?" Mkali asked.

"Cyndi, how would you feel if I dress like Ursula from *The Little Mermaid*?" Miriam said with a wink. Cyndi laughed and clapped her hands enthusiastically.

"I choose Captain Marvel," Frieda said with a grin.

"Alister, would it be okay if you and I dress as Arwen and Aragorn?" Aileene asked shyly.

"That would be perfect," I said and gently kissed her.

"I'm partial to Black Widow," Mom said as she pointed to the picture of the costume she wanted.

Gustav grinned, "I think I'll go as Frankenstein's Monster. Since I'm so tall, I won't need to wear special shoes to get me to the seven foot mark."

"I don't need a costume," Jason commented, "I've already got a sasquatch suit of my own."

We couldn't help laughing as we thought of Jason walking around in his natural form and everyone would think it was an elaborate costume.

"What about you Shelley?" I asked.

"Even though I'll be the tallest dwarf ever, I want to go as Gimli," he said with an enormous smile.

They fit us for our costumes and the shop owner promised they would all be ready in three days. As I paid the deposit for the costumes, I told the woman there would be a ten thousand dollar tip for her when they were completed because we were making her work so hard. She was so grateful, I thought she would cry.

Once we left the costume shop, Cyndi proved to be an excellent tour guide and took us to many of her favorite places. We ate at In N Out at least once each day, but none of us complained. It soon felt like Cyndi had always been part of our tight-knit group and we all liked her, but Jason enjoyed being around her the most.

"Are you going to come with us to Disneyland tomorrow?" Mom asked Cyndi before we retired after our day of shopping.

"I hadn't planned on intruding on your time," Cyndi answered.

"Nonsense," Mother piped up. "It's impossible for you to intrude, you're welcome to join us. You are letting us live in your home and you're now part of our little family."

"Then I'd love to come," Cyndi said and in her typical fashion almost tackled Mother in an enthusiastic hug.

We were some of the first people in line when Disneyland opened the next day. I'm not sure how Cyndi did it, but she has friends at Disney, and we got the VIP treatment. We did everything we wanted; ate a lot of food, rode every ride we wanted and even got to see some areas that are off limits to most guests. It was during another food break, this time at the Bengal Barbeque while enjoying some Banyan Beef Skewers, that I asked Mother about how her time went with Malonne.

She took the time to finish another four skewers before she answered me with a sigh. "Things went well between us, but she asked permission to stay on Earth and I granted her request."

Aileene put her hand over Mother's and gave it a squeeze. "Thank you my dear," Mother said and continued her story. "When I arrived at Malonne's house she gave me an enormous hug and was emotional as she asked me to forgive her for her attitude over the centuries. She explained that her perspective had changed since being trapped on Earth and she realized how wrong she'd been."

"How did she get trapped here?" Frieda wondered.

"She came to the palace to meet Alister to make sure he was safe. She'd been having dark and disturbing visions of death and destruction for about a year but had ignored the feeling that she was supposed to warn Phillip and me. It wasn't until she saw Alister's lifeless body in a vision that she finally came. She arrived moments after the messenger from Dimitri's fortress announced our deaths. She was so distraught and felt guilty that she had refused to give us the warning beforehand, she disguised herself and fled to Earth with everyone else.

"Since no one except Lord Elandorr knew she had come to the

palace, I'm not sure anyone knows she's gone from Marsupia even now. Things are so different in that kingdom and I've learned that one way they protect themselves is to cut off their emotions," Mother said sadly.

"So, they're sort of like Vulcans?" Shelley asked.

"I'll explain later," I said to Mother when she looked at me quizzically.

She nodded. "Anyway, Malonne wandered alone on Earth for a long time thinking about how her coldness over the years had hurt me. She also thought about how she had let her bitterness that she couldn't have biological children of her own overwhelm her. She found herself drawn to Florida where there was a school for children and adults with autism. As an elf, she could relate to these individuals uniquely and her very presence helped calm them and allowed them to cope with life in a more positive way.

"Malonne told me for the first time since I had moved to the palace in Theria, she felt like she was making a difference in someone's life and having a positive impact on the world. After she begged my forgiveness, she also asked for my permission to stay and continue to help those less fortunate." Mother smiled weakly, "I'm glad she's found her purpose, I just wish it hadn't taken her so long."

While I agreed with my mother, I didn't have any words of wisdom for her so all I could do was put my arm around her shoulder and hold her as she cried for the years lost with her foster mother. I was once again grateful for both sets of parents I had and how I'd always known they loved, wanted and cared for me. I squeezed Aileene's hand under the table as she wiped the tears from her own eyes.

When we arrived at the convention center where Hero Con was being held, Shelley led us to the will-call windows to get our VIP packets. I'm not sure how he'd arranged for us to get these precious tickets so close to Hero Con, but we were all excited as they led us to the special entrance reserved for VIP ticket holders. Even while we walked past the other attendees waiting in line, we heard comments about our amazing costumes and had many requests from people to take pictures with us. We were in such wonderful spirits we agreed, so it took us an extra thirty minutes before we finally got inside. Cyndi wasn't with us, but we would join her later at the Mermaid Lagoon where she was performing with other women dressed in mermaid costumes.

After our day at Disneyland, we'd spent a day at California Adventures, a day at Knott's Berry Farm and a day at Universal Studios. Even though we had an amazing time at each park, it exhausted us by the end of each day. I loved seeing Aileene's face when we rode the Jurassic Park ride at Universal Studios. She really loves her dinosaurs. We cut our day short at Universal so we could pick up our costumes and they looked so good I doubled the tip for the owner. She was grateful.

Once we were inside the convention center we were in for another surprise as a security detail met us. The woman in charge asked us to go with them into a secure area off the main entryway. We weren't nervous, but curious why we were walking along a back corridor. When I asked what was going on, the lead security guard just smiled and said, "You'll see." We stopped in front of a door, she knocked, and we waited until we were told to come in. Once we were all in the room, the guard went to an interior door and knocked twice and opened the door. After a moment Dwayne "The Rock" Johnson stepped into the room with his recognizable smile and trademark one eyebrow cocked.

"Oh, man, this is awesome," Shelley gushed and The Rock laughed.

Once the security team left the room, he spoke. "Hey, my friend Josef asked me if I would meet with you for a few minutes before my panel talk. I'm not supposed to know this, but I saw him shift into his gargoyle form one time and I've got a feeling the rest of you are like him; am I right?"

I'm not sure if he expected us to admit it or not but after Shelley shifted into his grizzly bear, The Rock didn't have any doubt that it was true.

"Man, that's awesome," he breathed, "would you mind if I made a movie about you some time?"

"That would be amazing," I said. "Josef is staying on Earth so you can get some information about our kind from him." It may not have been wise to show The Rock who we really were but when Bernie shifted to her unicorn and confirmed that he wouldn't share our secrets I felt much better.

We spent thirty minutes taking pictures and answering his questions about Theria. I told him I would allow him to visit some time when he was able. "But, probably not for the next year, I'll be busy taking care of some things where we come from."

We said our goodbyes and let the security guards back into the room. We followed one of them through the winding passageways behind the scenes at the convention center. He led us out of hidden areas of the convention center and into chaos.

We emerged from the passage and found ourselves in the primary convention area. There were already hundreds of people streaming through the hall on their way to the various panels and displays. Almost everyone dressed in some type of costume and people were stopping to take pictures with others in the crowd. There were superheroes, characters from animated films, characters from Star Wars and Star Trek and I even saw one guy dressed as Cousin Eddie from *Christmas Vacation*.

As we stood against the wall watching the Hero Con fans stream by, I smiled at the variety of people and costumes on display. I watched a group of six people dressed like characters from the movie *Galaxy Quest* roll a Beryllium Sphere down the middle of the hall.

This is even better than I thought it would be, Bernie gushed in thought-speech as she hugged Shelley's armor clad arm.

Where do we want to go first? Shelley asked.

Let's take a look at the Hero Con programs and decide, Miriam suggested.

It took us ten minutes and a lot of mental conversations before we made up our minds. Mother really wanted to attend a panel discussing the origin of mythological legend on Earth and Gustav chose to go with her.

I think—I'll take a look at the mermaid exhibit. Jason stammered mentally. Since he was in his natural form, he could only use thought-speak to communicate. *No need for anyone to go with me, unless you really want to go.*

"You're probably safe on your own." I laughed and everyone else teased him good-naturedly.

"We're just going to wander around and people watch," Mom said and walked off with Fiona and Miriam in tow.

"What do you guys want to do?" Aileene asked.

"We could split up," I suggested hopefully. I really wanted to spend some one-on-one time with Aileene.

"Oh no, we won't." Shelley deadpanned, "you've left us behind too many times on this adventure. Let us do our jobs as your Knights."

"That works for me," Aileene said and hugged my arm.

The Exhibit Hall filled the bottom floor of the convention center. Here, vendors of all kinds had booths set up to showcase their wares. The vendors were divided by costumes, replica weapons, comic books, artwork, miscellaneous and Author's Alley. There were also food options around the perimeter of the hall so we had a lot of choices when we got hungry.

We spent hours browsing the merchandise on display, and took pictures—a lot of pictures. Either we would see someone in a great costume and ask to take pictures with them or we would be stopped and people would want to take pictures with us. Part of the fun was getting into character for each photo.

We also bought a lot of things we wanted to take back to Theria with us. I was grateful for the pocket dimensions Aileene and I had on our necklaces because we never would have been able to carry everything we'd bought. At first Mkali was tentative when she saw something she wanted to buy, but after Shelley told her she earned income as Bernie's squire, she was able to find some things for herself.

When we were browsing through Author's Alley a book called, *The Legend of Beams* caught Aileene's attention. The cover of the book featured the eye of a dragon and Aileene laughed delightedly when she saw it. "Look, Alister, I think this book is about dragons."

"Do you like books about dragons?" asked the blonde woman standing behind the table. She was wearing a witch's hat crocheted from purple yarn.

"Oh, I adore dragons," Aileene smiled.

And she adores one dragon, in particular, Shelley sent to us. Bernie and Mkali snickered behind their hands and walked a few feet away to admire the crocheted creations displayed on another table.

"Are you the author?" I asked, ignoring Shelley's comments.

"My daughter, Ella and I collaborated on these books but they really are her works. She also crocheted the things your friends are looking at," the woman said warmly.

"These are beautiful," Bernie said as she held up a brightly colored hat.

"I'll let her know you said so. She just left with her papa to look at some of the other vendors. My name is Jennifer."

"Hello, Jennifer. My name is Aileene and this is my m—Alister." Aileene stumbled over her words.

"I'm Shelley and those two are Bernie and Mkali," Shelley answered and the girls waved.

"Warm welcome to you all. I love your costumes," Jennifer said.

"Thank you. I love your hat," Aileene answered Jennifer with a smile as she looked at *The Legend of Beams*. "I would like to buy this book and I see there is a second one, so I would like to buy it as well," Aileene said as she handed both books to Jennifer to ring up. She pointed to a poster of a smiling girl. "Is that a picture of Ella? She looks so young."

"It is, she is eleven," Jennifer said proudly.

"I'm sorry we didn't get a chance to meet her," I said. "I'm impressed she's accomplished so much for someone so young."

Jennifer beamed with pride as we handed her the things we chose to buy from her talented daughter.

We left the convention center and wearily followed the crowd towards the street. Jason told us he would bring the bus to us so we wouldn't have to walk all the way back to the parking lot where he had parked. As he jogged off, we moved out of the way and leaned against the wall outside the entrance to the convention center. We'd had an amazing day but were ready to head back to Cyndi's to get some rest.

It was fun watching people enjoying themselves so much as they left Hero Con. A group of superheroes walked by laughing and I smiled and waved. Behind them was another group of attendees dressed like members of the Cantina Band from *Star Wars Episode IV.* Their costumes were perfect, and they looked like typical aliens with gigantic heads and equally large black eyes.

At that moment, a man in a long tan trench coat pushed his way through the crowd and pointed a shotgun at the people in alien costumes. They stopped in shock and uncertainty when the man in front of them screamed, "I'll never let you invade this planet. You may have other people fooled but not me."

Even though the man was wearing a hat and dark glasses, I realized it was Neil Paterson and he had lost his mind. He continued to rant at the hapless attendees, and I knew that if we didn't do something, this would turn into a tragedy.

That's Paterson, I broadcast to my team, *we must stop him.*

I'm already on it Alister, Gustav sent.

Somehow Gustav had moved so quickly I didn't notice him do it even though he was dressed as Frankenstein's Monster. Paterson continued to rant and rave and rather than move away, people were recording the entire episode with their phones thinking this was some kind of stunt. When Gustav was parallel to where Paterson had the gun trained on the people in costumes, he made his move.

Time seemed to slow and I could see everything in perfect detail. Gustav put himself between Paterson and the guests dressed as aliens. His back was to Paterson so he could sweep the people out of the way with his arms. At the same second Gustav moved them, Paterson opened fire and hit Gustav in the back with the shotgun blast. Paterson continued to scream obscenities and threats against alien invaders as he pumped the shotgun and fired again into Gustav's body.

Gustav fell to the ground at the same time a police officer shot Paterson in the head. Paterson dropped and other guards and police officers rushed in to disarm him. Since police officers also surrounded Gustav, we couldn't get to his side. I reached out to him to connect, so I could pour healing energy into his body. But, instead of finding his life force, like I'd been able to do with every shifter I'd ever connected with, I only found emptiness. Gustav was dead.

It was hours later and we were sitting in a packed ballroom waiting to be interviewed by the police. They had ushered many of us inside the main hall shortly after the shooting. We had to walk by the covered bodies of our friend and the man who killed him. We were heartbroken and wept for our loss, but I was also simmering with rage. If it hadn't been for Aileene's connection with me and her calming presence, I'm afraid I might have transformed into my dragon and flown away from this tragic place.

I know it doesn't help, my love, but if Gustav hadn't done what he did, those people would have died instead, Aileene sent to me when my rage was again threatening to spill over.

Why him? Either of us could have stood in that place and be uninjured.

You didn't notice, but Paterson was watching us against the wall waiting for us to make a move. He didn't know Gustav was with us, so he didn't pay attention when he moved towards him.

You mean he knew who we were and that we'd be here? How?

Aileene must have included the others in our conversation without me realizing it because Shelley answered in a small voice. *It's my fault.*

What do you mean? I sent.

I wanted to surprise everyone with VIP passes to Hero Con, so I talked to Alex Farrel about getting them for us back when he visited with us in Maine. He got them for us and I had him add one for himself so he could join us. Gustav got Alex's pass instead.

He never met Gustav. He didn't know what he looked like so he couldn't give his description to Paterson. I sent as realization dawned on me.

It's my fault Gustav is dead. Shelley sobbed and covered his face with his hands.

My rage melted away as I thought about Shelley's words and the guilt he was carrying. I stood, walked over to my best friend and lifted him by his arm. I embraced him and he cried freely.

"It's not your fault Paterson killed Gustav. None of us knew that Alex was a traitor. You were trying to be kind and give us all a gift. Paterson is the only one responsible for Gustav's death." I pushed Shelley away and made sure he was looking me in the eyes. "Gustav stood between those innocents and Paterson. He died a hero's death, doing exactly what he knew was right; he protected the weak. We can grieve our loss, but we mustn't belittle his sacrifice by holding onto guilt that isn't ours." I let go of Shelley and Bernie took my place as she and Shelley slid to the ground to console one another in their grief.

"Pardon me for interrupting. My name is Detective Moon and I'm with LAPD," said a man in a black suit and a badge hanging from the breast pocket of his jacket. He held a notebook and looked at his notes before asking his questions. "I understand that you're friends with the deceased. The only identification he has on him is his lanyard with the first name, Gustav. What was his full name?"

Mother stepped forward and answered his question. "His name is Gustav Schliebe, he lived in Bangor, Maine and until recently was an elementary school teacher."

"Were you close with Mr. Schliebe?" Detective Moon asked then held up his hand to forestall Mother's objection to the question. "I only ask because I need to know if there are any next of kin we need to notify."

"No, we were the only family he had. However, he has a fiancé, but she is out of the country. We will inform her of this tragedy."

"Who was the shooter?" I asked.

"I'm afraid I can't officially tell you that," Moon said but looked around to make sure he wasn't being observed. "But since your friend saved lives today, I'll tell you. The assailant was Neil Paterson and your friend was a hero. Do you need help making arrangements for his body?"

"No, thank you," Mother answered. "We've already contacted a local mortuary and once you release his body, they can collect it." I had contacted Josef when I was able, and asked him to arrange something for us. He flew a crew from Phoenix to escort Gustav's body back to a mortuary where it would be cremated.

Moon nodded, "I'll see what I can do to speed up the process. Again, I'm sorry for your loss," he said and walked away.

Cyndi was waiting for us by the bus when we finally left the convention center to return to her house. Each of us was alone with our own thoughts as we felt the gaping hole in our hearts where Gustav used to be. I thought back to the conversation we had in the car a couple weeks before and how much he meant to me. Gustav was such a part of my life, I wasn't sure what it would be like without him in it.

None of us thought we were hungry but once Cyndi set out food on the counter in her kitchen, we dug in. We'd had nothing to eat since breakfast, so we were ravenous. As I looked around the kitchen at everyone still in their costumes I laughed. When Aileene asked me what I was laughing at, I only laughed harder. In a moment, Shelley must have realized the same thing I had because he started laughing with me. Soon, everyone in the kitchen was howling with laughter and tears were rolling down our faces. Even though we were saddened by Gustav's death, we could also find something to laugh at. We'd be okay.

My emotional roller coaster hit a low later that night when I went into Gustav's room to pack his belongings. It was hard enough packing his clothes but when I opened the black jewelry box on the dresser and saw it held a ring I started crying again. Seeing the ring he had bought for Seraset filled me with a sense of deep sadness for the things he'd left undone. Curling up on the bed, I wept and must have cried myself to sleep.

I opened my eyes and found I was standing next to Gustav on the edge of a cliff. I recognized this place from the time I had saved my parents lives and almost killed myself in the process.

"It wasn't your time to leave," Gustav said to me as he stared at the mountain, "but it is my time."

"We're heartbroken that you're dead," I said.

"I know. It's harder for you than it is for me," Gustav remarked. "While you will feel a sense of loss at my death, I can only see everything I've gained. I loved my time on Theria and on Earth and all the relationships I made, but now I get to go where I truly belong. I can't explain it any better than this. Everything I've done before has prepared me for this moment and now I feel like I'm absolutely free and alive for the first time."

Gustav laughed with joy. He turned to me with a light in his eyes and said brightly, "I will not tell you not to weep, but I will tell you not to weep for me; I'm better than I've ever been. Weep for yourself, weep for your loss, weep to let the pain and anger out so you don't hold it in. I've loved you like a son," Gustav said and hugged me.

"Is there anything you want me to tell Seraset or the others?" I asked through tears.

"Yes, tell them to be happy, live life in service to An'Ceann and I'll be waiting for them," he said and stepped off the cliff. Instead of falling, he rushed towards the mountain. Even though he was miles away I could see him clearly and the crowd of people waiting to greet him once he crossed over.

"Do you know why I allowed you to see this?" An'Ceann asked from beside me.

"No," I answered softly.

"As King, you have to lead your people in good times and bad; in times of joy and sorrow. As King you will feel things as deeply if not more so than your people and you will need to lead by example. You have great power, Alister, and with great power comes great responsibility."

I thought about his words and then turned my head to look at him. "Did you just quote *Spider-man* to me?"

An'Ceann chuckled, "I prefer to think that *Spider-man* quoted me."

I laughed as the dream faded and I found I was smiling as I awoke on Gustav's bed.

We stepped through the gate and returned to Theria almost a month after we left. We'd experienced great triumphs and great tragedies during our trip.

"Welcome home," Father said with his arms wide. Mother rushed into his embrace and Miriam, Frieda and Mom did the same with their spouses. Aileene and I held hands as we walked towards Seraset with two boxes. One box held Gustav's ashes while the other box held the ring he had bought for her.

"We are so sorry for your loss," Aileene said to Seraset as she handed her the ring box.

"Gustav asked me to deliver a message to you. Be happy, live life in service to An'Ceann and he'll be waiting for you," I said as I handed her the box with his ashes. Seraset smiled at me as she unabashedly wept.

While everyone else got reacquainted, Shelley and I walked back through the gate into Cyndi's living room to move our belongings through the gate into Theria. I picked up a chest and grunted because it was so heavy.

"What do you have in here?" I asked.

"Let's see," Shelley said as he looked at a label on the side of the chest. "Those are movies A-F. And this chest," he said with a smile as he picked up an identical one, "contains TV shows A-F."

I started towards the gate. "Are you telling me all these chests are full of movies and TV shows?"

"Yep, and the ones downstairs are full of video games," Shelley answered cheerfully.

"When do you think we'll have time to watch all these?" I wondered.

"Your parents are over five hundred years old; I figure we'll have plenty of time." Shelley replied.

"What will we do if the Blu-Ray player or TV breaks down?" I asked as we stepped through the gate and placed them on the Therian grass.

"Not to worry, I've thought of that too, I've got a hundred TVs, Blu-Ray players and game consoles being delivered over the next few weeks."

"And Cyndi is okay with you turning her home into a Best Buy?" I asked as I picked up another chest.

"Since you said she could stay on Earth with Jason, she was so happy I could have asked her for anything and she would have agreed. Besides, I only had to tell her I would get you to do her a favor and she was good with the idea."

"What did you tell her I'd do?" I asked suspiciously.

"I told her I'd get you to officiate their wedding when they wanted to get married," he smiled smugly.

"But I would have done that anyway," I said as I deposited the second chest beside the first one.

"I knew that, but Cyndi didn't. We were walking on the beach when I told her that and she was so excited she tripped. I've never seen anyone trip over a wave before, but she did. It was hilarious, she fell down, got right back up again while wiping sand off and acted like nothing happened."

"You must feel good about yourself, don't you?" I asked as I picked up another chest.

"Yep," Shelley said but then flew across the room to land on the couch against the wall.

"The next time you try to pull one over on me, make sure I'm not in the room when you explain what you've done," Cyndi fumed.

"Shelley, I'll keep moving these chests for you while you think about this. Not only are mermaids incredibly powerful in water, they're also exceptionally strong on land," I laughed.

"Now you tell me," Shelley said as he sailed across the room in another direction to land on another couch.

"One last thing you should know," I chuckled as I saw Cyndi place Shelley in a hammerlock. "When she's done with you, it's my turn. Cyndi, would you mind tossing him through the gate into Theria? There's more room there to wrestle."

"It would be my pleasure," Cyndi said as she tossed Shelley through the gate and followed by jumping on his back.

Even though I had a lot to do to reunite the kingdoms of Theria over the next few months, it was good to be home and enjoy the simple things in life; like watching Shelley get his butt kicked by a girl. I hummed to myself as I continued moving the chests from Earth to Theria.

EPILOGUE

I stood high on a cliff, overlooking the valley far below teeming with six armies. There were shifters of every description and each kingdom was represented by their battle flag. Eutheria, a golden drake on a field of red, the Metatheria, a snarling golden jaguar on a field of black, the Sirenea, a red Long dragon on a field of yellow, the Carnivoria, a brown lion on an orange background, the Marsupia, a Mallorn tree with silver bark and golden leaves on a blue background and the Cetacea, a green mermaid on a purple background.

I watched in horror as the armies converged and the decimation commenced. As the last shifter fell, I saw myself in dragon form flying with Aileene towards the field of carnage. The bodies of Shelley, Bernie, Mkali and the rest of my friends lay amongst the other shifters on the battlefield. I fell to my knees and wept as I heard keening wails coming from Aileene and me in our dragon forms.

A gentle paw rested on my shoulder and I knew An'Ceann was standing behind me. He spoke to me, his voice hoarse with emotion. "All your people across the planet need you. You must circumvent this rebellion and unite them under one banner. They need the High King."

The End
To Be continued in *Rebellion,* Dragonborn Book Four

AFTERWORD

Thank you for reading *Reunite* and especially for reading all the way to the end. I hope you enjoyed the book enough to write a review on Amazon. Independent authors need reviews to get noticed.

It's fun to write about Alister, Bernie, Shelley and now Aileene, and to see how they are developing as characters. One of the hardest things to do is to put characters you care about in heartbreaking situations. However, just like life, my characters need conflict so they can grow.

Currently we are experiencing some uncertainty and difficulty ourselves as we deal with the COVID-19 pandemic. There are many things to fear but there are also things we can celebrate at the same time. My hope is years from now we'll look back at March-April 2020 as a time of strength, resolve and growth as humans. Even during chaos and uncertainty we can be kind and loving to our neighbors.

I hope you can relate to one of the characters in my books (hopefully not one of the villains) and use the things you like about that character to strengthen you. There are a few characters in this book based on real people I know. Cyndi the mermaid is based on my sister. Yes, she is that clumsy. Ella C. Lopez and her mother Jennifer Lopez are the collaborative authors of *The Legend of Beams I & II*. Ella is currently eleven years old. I am inspired by her creativity and encourage you to check out her Etsy Store at www.etsy.com/shop/ella-tionscreations. Her mom, Jennifer, is the character who sells the books and knitted hats to Aileene in *Reunite*.

The next book in the series is *Rebellion, Dragonborn Book Four* and I really look forward to sharing that story with you as well. I plan to publish *Rebellion* this year, but I don't have a target release date yet.

I plan to add five fans as characters in my next book. Here's what I want from you. Send me your name, age and what type of shifter or mythological creature you want to be, and I will choose five fans at random and add them to *Rebellion*. I would also love to know your favorite scenes in my books and hear about parents reading these books to their kids.

My contact information is on my website. Visit www.bretthumphreyauthor.com for cool stuff and updates on what's next in this series, and beyond. While you're there, I invite you to join my text notification service and sign up for my email distribution list for announcements, random stuff and weekly dragon jokes. Just follow the **Stay in Touch** link on the menu. I look forward to hearing from you.

I hope Alister and his friends inspire you to make a positive impact in the life of someone you connect with every day.

Brett Humphrey

April 2020

Protect the Weak!

SHIFTER GLOSSARY AND PRONUNCIATION GUIDE

Aileene: (Eye-Lean)

An'Ceann: (Awn-Sheen)

Anemoi: Creature with the ability to control the winds. Is able to fly and turn invisible at will.

Áthas: (Ath-az)

Banshee: A female creature with the ability to foretell death and freeze people with her voice. Known for power over weather.

Barghest: Creature resembling a black dog with sharp teeth and long claws. Has the ability to pass through solid objects, often thought to be a ghost.

Brownie: Type of fairy with special abilities and magic related to houses, comfort, cooking and cleaning

Centaur: Creature with the body of a horse and torso of a human. Excellent archers and considered very wise.

Cockatrice: A dragon-like creature with the head of a rooster. Has the ability to turn others to stone.

Dies Spell: Passage of Time (Dee-Ess)

Dochas: (Doe-Chas)

Dóchas: (Doe-Chaz)

Dryad: A creature with great affinity and power over growing things, especially trees. A Dryad lives within a tree and can command creatures near her tree.

Dyosonus: (Die-oh-nye-us)

Fire Drake: Type of lesser dragon. Can fly and produce fire. Much smaller than a Royal Dragon.

Garden Gnome: Small creature with an affinity of gardens and growing things. Although small in stature, they can accomplish a lot of work in a short period of time.

Gargoyle: Creature resembling a very large, two legged bat. Can fly and its skin is as hard as granite.

Glacies Tempestas Spell: Ice Storm (Glaceez-Tempes-tas)

Gorgon: Creature similar to a Naga. Usually seen as a human female with snakes for hair. Has the ability to turn others to stone.

Grebalar: (Greb-alar)

Griffin: Creature with the body of a lion and the wings and head of an eagle. Fierce fighters and highly territorial.

Hillaes: (Hill-y-ess)

Kelpie: Creature resembling a horse usually found near rivers and lakes. Known for its ability to control fresh water creatures and environments.

King Guimart: (Guy-mart)

Kingdom of Carnivoria: (Car-ni-vor-eeya)

Kingdom of Cetacea: (Set-a-see-a)

Kingdom of Eutheria: (Eww-there-eeya)

Kingdom of Marsupia: (Mar-soup-eeya)

Kingdom of Metatheria: (Met-a-there-eeya)

Kingdom of Sirenea: (Siren-eeya)

Kingdom of Theria: (There-eeya)

Kitsune: Fox-like creature from Japan skilled in magic. As Kitsune ages, they grow extra tails and their abilities expand with each one.

Kobold: Creature resembling a two legged dragon without wings. Highly skilled at building things, and creating inventions.

Malonne Farhana: (Mal-won Far-hanna)

Mermaid: Creature with the torso of a human but instead of legs has a tail like a dolphin. Known for their strength in and out of the water. Can survive on both land and water.

Milleadh: (Mill-head)

Mkali: (Mmm-kalee)

Naga: Creature with three serpentine forms. The torso of a human with the body of a snake, the form of a human with snakes for hair and a completely serpentine form. Highly poisonous in all three forms.

Ogre: Creature known for its great strength and almost impervious skin. Fiercely loyal.

Patefio Spell: Open (Pate-fee-o)

Pegasus: Creature resembling a winged horse.

Queen Tiffonia: (Tiff-o-neeya)

Relevium Spell: Pain Relief (Relief-ee-um)

Royal Dragon: Majestic Dragon, can fly, has four legs and massive wings. Able to produce multiple types of flames. Can only be injured by another Royal Dragon, some poisons and weapons made from body parts of deceased Royal Dragons.

Saeclum Spell: Mapping (Sack-loom)

Sanos Spell: Healing (Sane-os)

Sasquatch: Creature resembling a very tall, hairy human. Known for their ferocity, great strength and affinity for nature.

Síocháin: (Show-chain)

Somnum Spell: Sleep (Som-numb)

Sphinx: Creature with the body of a lion, wings of an eagle and head of a human. Known for their wisdom, faithfulness and love of riddles.

Spriosh: (Spree-osh)

Tionchar: (Tee-on-char)

Turbine Ignis Spell: Fire Storm (Tur-bean Ig-nise)

Unicorn: Looks like a horse with a large, sharp horn growing from its forehead. The horn can be used for healing as well as truth-telling.

Wyvern: Type of lesser dragon, with two back legs and two wings. Can fly and its long tail can be used like a spear.